D1246513

DAMAGED

TRIPLE CANOPY

RILEY EDWARDS

DAMAGED
TRIPLE CANOPY
BOOK 1

RILEY EDWARDS

Cover design: Lori Jackson Designs

Cover Photographer: Golden Czermak | Furious Fotog

Cover Model: Chase Ketron

Written by: Riley Edwards

Published by: Riley Edwards/Rebels Romance

Edited by: Rebecca Hodgkins

Proofreader: Julie Deaton, Rebecca Kendall

DAMAGED

To my family - my team – my tribe.
This is for you.

PROLOGUE

Four years earlier – Hadley

"Girls, come here," my dad, Jasper Walker, called out to Adalynn and me as soon as we walked in the front door.

My eyes did a quick scan of my parents' house, noting all the usual suspects were in attendance. Cousins, aunts, uncles, my siblings—everyone smiling and laughing. Well, everyone except my eldest sister, Delaney. I hadn't seen her smile in a while, and whatever was bugging her, she wasn't sharing.

With my twin sister Adalynn by my side, I made my way to my dad and stumbled when my eyes locked with the guy next to him.

No, not a guy, a man.

All man.

Tall, broad, a little older than me, hot as all get-out. But it was his gray eyes that held me captive. The color of storm clouds—the description was apt, there was sadness brewing behind his gaze.

"Brady, these are my youngest daughters. Hadley and Adalynn," my dad introduced, pointing to each of us. "Girls, this is Brady Hewitt, the newest member of the team."

"Nice to meet you." Addy offered her hand and I watched as Brady's much larger one engulfed my sister's.

"Nice to meet you, Adalynn."

Their hands released and Addy kicked my foot, pulling me from my stupor.

"Hadley, good to meet you as well."

Brady's deep, rough voice washed over me as he extended his hand. The very moment I placed mine in his and his fingers curled around my palm, I vowed that one day I would take the cloudiness away.

"Nice to meet you, Brady."

ONE COULD SAY my family didn't have the best luck. It had started with my FBI profiler cousin, Nick. He found himself a woman who had been almost killed by a serial killer. I was a kid at the time and was mostly shielded from the details even after Nick had moved Meadow from Virginia to Georgia.

Then my cousin, the police officer Ethan, met Honor. By then, I'd graduated high school and was very aware of Honor's troubles, which had resulted in her being kidnapped and almost killed.

And of course, there was my DEA agent brother, Jason. Who, after years of mourning his wife's death, had finally found a woman, Mercy, also a DEA agent. She brought him back to life only to have a case they were working on cause her and Delaney to be taken, beaten, and almost killed.

Are you seeing a theme yet?

My family wasn't unlucky, but my male cousins, which should be noted, weren't cousins by blood but by a bond my father had forged with Carter Lenox, Nolan Clark, and Levi McCoy—collectively known as my uncles. And they were, in every sense of the word. I'd grown up with these men, my father's battle-brothers. Anyway, my cousins had a type and they'd all found strong women who'd overcome a great deal but still needed to be protected. This was because every single male in my family had a gene—an overprotective instinct—that was annoying most of the time when they got in your business. But in truth, it had allowed me to grow up surrounded by love. So much love, it could be suffocating. But the alternative was not having it so I didn't bitch—too much.

That brings us to now.

My cousin, Jackson, had of course followed in the footsteps of those who'd gone before him, and fell in love with a beautiful, bona fide supermodel, Tuesday. She was Mercy's best friend. Unfortunately, Tuesday had herself a stalker. Everyone—meaning my dad, my uncles, Ethan, Brady, and Jackson—had been keeping her safe while searching for the stalker.

Today, she almost died.

Almost died.

Hours later, my heart was still pounding and my stomach knotted up just thinking about it. Brady had gotten to her first, then Jackson and his fire company had arrived and taken over.

And if that wasn't bad enough, Brady had almost died, too.

He'd rushed into the house without thought for his own safety to rescue a woman he barely knew.

That didn't just make my heart pound—it made me queasy.

He could've died. Tuesday and Jackson, too.

My family was all at Jackson's condo. This is what we did—we rallied. Tuesday had been treated for smoke inhalation and released so everyone was at Jackson's to make sure she was okay.

I wasn't ready to go to Jackson's. I wasn't ready to face my family or Tuesday. Luckily for me, I'd forgotten my cell phone in my dad's office. I'd been at Triple Canopy when I got the call about the fire and in my panic, I stupidly tossed my phone on his desk and ran.

Now I was standing there staring at my dad's desk, unable to move.

Fear and relief mixed, making me dizzy.

I was pissed and happy and I didn't understand how I could be both of those at once.

"Hadley?" I turned and saw Brady standing in the doorway. "You okay?"

"No," I croaked.

That was all it took for Brady to close the distance and pull me in his arms.

He smelled like a campfire and the sob I'd been holding back finally broke free.

"Shh, they're okay."

"You," I sobbed.

Brady's body went solid before he relaxed. "I'm good, babe."

I sagged in his arms and he held on tight.

It wouldn't be until much later, days later when I thought about that day for the millionth time that it would dawn on me—he'd called me Hadley. No hesitation. No guessing. He knew I was me and not my twin.

ALMOST A YEAR LATER – *Hadley*

I came to a screeching halt in front of my parents' house and jumped out of my car.

Shots fired at Mom and Dad's.

That was all Addy had told me when she called.

But it was worse. Way worse. I knew it by the hard look on Brady's face.

"What's wrong?"

"Get to Quinn, babe. I have to go."

I grabbed his bicep as he passed me. "What's happening?"

"Some bitch nabbed Delaney. Got to get on the hunt, Hadley. Take care of Quinn."

Right. Take care of Quinn. Lock down my fear and see to one sister while the other was missing.

"Please be careful," I begged.

Brady's eyes softened, but the storm clouds were still present.

"Always am, honey."

And with that, he was gone.

Once again putting his ass on the line for my family.

It wasn't the first time nor would it be the last. But the next time would be the worst.

———

Almost another year later – Brady

"No!" Jasper let out a blood-curdling roar and I froze.

Right there in the ambulance bay of County ER, I felt my heart stop.

I watched in absolute horror as Jasper's legs gave out. Neither Levi nor Lenox were fast enough to catch him before he went to his knees. Nothing, but nothing, took Jasper to the ground—unless it was family.

Jesus fuck.

My eyes took in the scene. Brice Lancaster,

Quinn Walker's man and still in his turn-out gear, was on his ass, back against the wall, knees up, pure terror on his face.

Fucking Christ.

Nolan Clark and his son, Jackson, both stood looking shell-shocked until Jackson broke away and knelt in front of Brice.

"Brother?"

"Two GSWs to the chest. We...um...fuck." Tears welled in Brice's eyes. "We lost her right before we pulled in. We started CPR, then she was wheeled up to the OR."

Jackson shot to his feet and Brice closed his eyes.

Quinn Walker took two to the chest.

Christ.

I felt her before I heard it.

A heart-shattering sob.

I turned and there she was, Hadley Walker.

Even in her grief, she was the most beautiful woman I'd ever seen.

She turned to rush out of the sliding glass doors. I easily caught up to her and folded her into my arms.

"Brady," she wailed.

"I got you, baby."

My arms wrapped tighter around her.

"Which one?"

Fuck, she didn't know. Didn't know which family member had been injured. Just knew if her dad was on his knees, it was bad.

"Quinn."

Hadley's body convulsed in my arms and I'd have given anything to take away her pain. Anything to make sure Hadley Walker never shed another tear.

It would be a long time before Hadley stopped crying. A long time with her standing in my arms before she whispered, "How bad?"

"Bad, baby."

She nodded against my tear-soaked tee and nuzzled closer.

Jesus fuck.

It was too soon.

She needed more time.

But with each day, it was harder not to claim what was mine.

Hadley tilted her head up and I caught her gaze. Pain, fear, worry. But there was something else behind those beautiful glossy eyes. And I knew what that something was. I knew it because I felt the same. Every time I looked at her, I knew when the time was right, she'd be mine.

But with her sister clinging to life, today would not be the day I told her.

"It's always you," she whispered.

"Always me?"

Hadley didn't answer but she did repeat herself and when she did, I let her words settle over me.

"It's always you."

I knew in my soul Hadley Walker was my forever love. She made me wish I was strong enough to face my demons, be better, be the man she needed.

I could love her from afar but she'd never be mine, I was too damaged.

1

———

"I dare you."

Even with the crowd in Carter and Delaney's backyard, I knew she was there before she spoke. I always knew when she was close. It seemed I'd developed a sixth sense when it came to Hadley Walker.

Which was unfortunate.

Seriously unfortunate, when I needed to keep my distance.

Jasper called her Hurricane Hadley. He was not wrong. The woman blew in, and without warning, caused maximum damage. It wasn't that I didn't like her. Just the opposite—I adored her. What I didn't like was her constant bombarding. She was nosy as hell and picked and picked and fucking picked more until I caved and told her what she wanted to know.

That shit had to end.

"What are you, ten?" I snapped as she sat at the picnic table.

This was my new strategy and it fucked me that, at thirty-one years old—seven years older than her—I'd stooped to this level. It was an all-time low for me. I was being an asshole and I was doing it on purpose. But nothing else worked and Hadley had gotten too close.

"What are you, a hundred-and-ten with a stick up your ass that prevents you from having fun?" she shot back.

There it was—all that sass and attitude that turned me right the hell on. Some men liked soft and easy, I liked attitude and sass. Both of which Hadley had in abundance. I didn't have to look over at her to know her jade eyes were dancing.

"Like a big ol' butt plug." She laughed. "A fun stopper. A joy killer. An entertainment obstruction. There might be a colon cleanse for that."

"Christ. You *are* ten."

"And you're a stick in the mud. Lighten up. Life's too damn short to always be so unhappy."

And with that, she slid off the picnic table. My jaw clenched and sour hit my gut.

Good Goddamn, this woman.

"What's your dare?" I sighed and finally craned my neck to look at her.

Mistake.

I should've kept my eyes glued to the birthday festivities playing out in Carter and Delaney's backyard. Watching Hudson chase Emma around was safer than looking at Hadley. Hell, a low-altitude jump with a faulty chute was safer than being in close proximity to her.

Then Hadley smiled. Not her usual beautiful, carefree grin that never failed to make my body tight, but a wicked, playful smile that turned my mistake into a major fuck-up. Her father would kick my ass if he knew the dirty thoughts I had running through my head.

We were at her niece Emma's birthday party. There were kids all around, Hadley's whole family in attendance, and all I could think about was stripping her out of her sundress, laying her out on the picnic table, and finally taking what I wanted. What she'd been offering for months. What I knew I could never have.

Goddamn, the woman was hell on a man's control. Hence the reason why I avoided her until I needed a fix, then gave in. I seemed to give in a lot. Though I'd never touched her like that. No, I preferred to torture myself—and being in Hadley's company, knowing I'd never have her, was pure anguish.

A small pail hit the bench next to me and I glanced down at it, then my gaze went back to her.

"Water balloons?"

"Oh, yeah. How good is your aim, soldier boy?"

My aim? It's legendary—the best that the Army ever trained.

"It's all right," I answered.

Hadley rolled her eyes. My answer was stupid but so was her question, considering I'd taken her to the range many times. This was done at her request under the guise that she wanted to learn to shoot. She didn't need to learn, her father had taught all his children at a young age about gun safety, which included taking them to the range. But because I was a junkie jonesing for my fix, I agreed every time Hadley asked me to take her out.

I was playing a dangerous game. One that could leave me jobless at best, my ass kicked more than likely, and depending on Jasper's mood, full of bullet holes. Yet, I kept going back for more. Hadley was like a breath of fresh air and I couldn't get enough. I had enough problems without adding her to the very long list.

"What's your plan?" I asked, resigning myself to playing along.

Hadley glanced around the backyard. Her eyes squinted and her brows pinched as she plotted her water balloon assault.

Christ, when was the last time I'd done something as silly as throw water balloons at my friends? I couldn't even cast my mind that far back.

My life quarantined into sections. There was Before Nicole, After Nicole, Army, Special Forces, and Triple Canopy. Segmented into partitions, times, and places I refused to allow myself to go. Before Nicole was one of the sectors I vehemently rejected. Therefore, I wouldn't remember a time when life was fun, carefree, or *silly*.

"Jason and Carter first, they're the closest," Hadley told me, pulling me from my musing. "Once they're hit, Nick, Ethan, and Jackson will move in and we'll nail them."

"You take Jason and Carter," I amended, less than enthusiastic about throwing water balloons. "I'll take the others."

"Brady?"

"Yeah?"

Those damn eyes locked onto mine, and I saw it.

Sadness.

I fucking hated, despised, loathed when she looked at me like that. The wordless pleading gutted me.

"Never mind," she murmured.

I was impatient by nature, but as with all things Hadley, my impatience was exacerbated as were my finely honed observational skills. I knew when the woman was close, not because I was clairvoyant, but because when she was in proximity, *everything* intensified. All cognitive thought narrowed to just her.

"Spit it out, Hadley. What's on your mind?"

"You don't have to humor me. I just thought it would be fun."

She turned to leave. On impulse, I reached out to grab her hand. Though when I did and I felt her soft fingers curl around mine, I was taken aback. The curl was immediate like it was natural, intuitive, automatic. I wanted to drop her hand and put much-needed distance between us but I was caught in a web of awareness.

A dangerous web spun by a girl who was too young, too innocent, too sweet for the likes of me.

I'd snuff her beauty and steal the good she had in her.

But before I could turn away, water hit me in the face.

Hadley shot forward and her body collided with mine as she tried and failed to avoid getting doused. We were sopping wet, holding on to each other. Teenage laughter rang out but I ignored Carson's loud giggles, as well as her father, Ethan's, encouragement. Like always, I tuned in to Hadley. Her scent, her breasts pressing against my chest, her soaking-wet hair that still looked silky even though it was plastered to her head, her body shaking against mine with laughter, the way her hands gripped my sides. I seriously needed to get the fuck away from a very wet, very beautiful, very sexy Hadley Walker.

"It's on!" Hadley shouted, and thank fuck she pushed off of me, reached inside her pail, and started rapid firing balloons.

Her aim sucked.

She missed Carson more than she hit her. But her face was lit, her smile so big and beautiful, I couldn't stop myself from grabbing a balloon and launching it at Ethan.

My aim was true.

I hit my next three targets and soon the backyard

birthday party was mayhem. Carter rushed forward and scooped up his daughter Emma as she toddled around and just as quickly, he reached for his nephew, Hudson, as Ethan ran to his daughter's side and took the hose.

Squirt guns, buckets filled with water, and more balloons came out. Six grown men engaged in a hostile water fight.

Six—seven if you included the teenage girl— against Hadley and me. The women stood off to the side, cheered their men on, and laughed themselves stupid. Usually, this would cause my chest to burn with jealousy and I'd abruptly excuse myself and leave the party I hadn't wanted to attend in the first place. But with Jasper, Clark, Lenox, or Levi's urging, I always went. My bosses refused to allow me to be the loner I enjoyed being. They pulled me into the fray, into their family.

"Watch your three o'clock, Nick's coming in hot," Hadley announced.

Coming in hot.

Cute as fuck.

It was then I let go and had fun.

It didn't take long for Hadley and me to lose what Delaney had deemed the Water War of the Century. We were soaked to the bone, all of our ammo was gone, and we stood hand-in-hand while the others pelted us by any means they could find.

Of course, I could've charged one of the guys and gotten us more balloons, but I'd take a pelting anytime if it meant I got to stand next to Hadley and hear her excitement, see her smile, smell her flowery perfume, breathe in her innocence.

I was royally fucked.

2

"Can't tonight, Addy," I told my sister as I balanced my cell between my ear and shoulder.

"Mom's making twice-baked potatoes," she returned.

If anything could get me to hightail my butt to my parents' house for dinner, it was twice-baked potatoes.

"Wish I could but it's the first Monday of the month. The Writers' Club meets and I can't leave the library until they're done." I reminded her of something she knew because I stayed late two times a week for after-hours clubs. "Mom knows this, too, so you can tell her I'm seriously disappointed she's making my favorite dinner on a night I can't come."

There was a stretch of silence both coming from

the phone and the empty library as I made my way out the doors to the outside return bin.

"Out with it, sister," I sighed.

One of the many awesome things about being a twin was I knew my sister. Not like regular singletons knew their siblings. Adalynn and I took it to a whole new level. Normally, it was totally cool to be able to look at someone and just know their thoughts. Other times when you wanted to keep something to yourself, not so much.

Addy knew me better than anyone. And I, her.

"Brady."

One word.

She knew. Of course, she did—everyone knew I was in love with a man who wanted not a single thing to do with me. And they knew because I didn't try to hide it. My family was nosy as hell, and they had ways of finding shit out, so why bother?

But it was only Addy who knew the truth. I wasn't in love; I was head over heels and I had been for a long time.

"Nothing's changed," I told her.

"But, I saw you two at Emma's party. He looked different."

Indeed he did. I could count on one hand the number of smiles I'd seen and never had I heard him laugh. But yesterday at my niece's first birthday party he'd gifted me with both. And coming from Brady Hewitt they were gifts, precious gifts that I wanted more of.

However, Brady had a whole host of reasons why he'd never give me anything. His first excuse was because he worked for my father. Though, technically he no longer did. My dad and the uncles had all retired and turned Triple Canopy over to their sons and nephews, Carter, Nick, Jason, and Drake.

In my opinion, his excuses were ridiculous. He respected my dad—and there was a lot to admire, my dad was the best—so he wouldn't go after me, but I still found the excuse invalid. He was too old for me —I was twenty-four and he was thirty-one. Again, totally invalid. I was an adult, even though Brady seemed to miss that.

Two cars pulled into the library parking lot and pulled me from my thoughts.

"Hey, Addy, I gotta go. Cars are pulling in and I have to grab the books out of the collection bin."

"Don't think you're off the hook," she mumbled.

"With you? Never. I'll call you later if I have any energy left."

"You'd have more energy if you laid off the soda, drank more water, and started exercising." My mind wandered as she gave me the same lecture I'd heard a million times. "...you can't live off sugar and caffeine."

Knowing I wasn't going to change my unhealthy habits, and not having time to hear about metabolic-something-or-other, and really not caring about sleep patterns, I rudely rushed out, "Love ya, sis, gotta go, have fun at Mom and Dad's, hugs and kisses to all. Bye."

I hung up and smiled at Mr. Jennings as I pushed my cart past him.

"Good evening, Miss Walker," the older man greeted me.

"Hello, Mr. Jennings. The door's unlocked."

"Thank you, sweet girl, I know I'm a little early."

"No bother. Go on in."

I made my way across the lot to the box and was happy to see there were just enough returns to keep me occupied with check-ins while the Writers' Club had their meeting and I wouldn't have to stay any later.

I was pushing the cart back into the library just as Anne, a lifestyle blogger and author of three books on parenting, walked in.

"Hey, Anne, how are your hoodlums?"

This was not derogatory, it was ironic, because

Anne's four children were the most well-behaved children I'd ever met.

"I left them sitting at the table doing their homework."

"Of course you did." I smiled.

Within ten minutes, the rest of the authors had arrived and they were sitting at their normal spot talking about word counts and revisions as I checked in my cart of returned books.

I much preferred to hear their conversation to the knitting club's. Not that the group wasn't pleasant, but after an hour of listening to knit, knit, purl or knit a stitch, slip a stitch, the repetition was burned into my brain and I'd dreamed about cable cast-offs and rib stitches.

I was ten books in when I came across it and an angry growl slipped out.

"Everything okay?" Simon, one of the authors, asked.

"Yeah, yeah. Sorry." I waved off his concern but inside I was seething.

This was the fourth book in the last month that had been returned defaced.

I scanned the bar code, and like the others, it hadn't been checked out. Unfortunately, this happened sometimes. People walked out with books without properly checking them out. Sometimes they were returned, other times they were just gone. It was hell on our budget when we needed to replace stolen copies. Luckily, it didn't happen frequently but it happened.

This was different.

This bit my ass.

This infuriated me beyond belief.

Some asshole had taken Ernest Hemingway's *The Garden of Eden* and scribbled on the pages. I thumbed through the book and found more blacked-out passages. There were also notes in red pen in the margins.

Vile. Disgusting. Evil. Lesbian.

My blood boiled and I flipped back to the title page.

Godless heathens be warned.

What the hell did that mean? Be warned? Hell to the no.

I set the book aside and finished the stack of check-ins as the Writers' Club finished. The hour had passed by in a blur, my mind unable to stop thinking about why someone would think it was okay to destroy a book. Why someone thought they had the right to be judgmental in any way one could judge. It was wrong, it was vile, it was disgusting and evil. And frankly, it said a lot about the person who called up God's name and used it in judgment.

After I delivered a round of half-hearted good-byes to the authors, I noticed Simon hadn't left. This wasn't unusual—he often stayed behind to walk me to my car, especially in the winter months when it was dark by the time their meeting was over. But sometimes he stayed in the spring and summer even though it was still light out. He was a nice guy. Geeky. But nice.

"What's wrong, Hadley?" he asked as he stopped in front of the circulation desk. "And before you tell me nothing, you've been huffing and sighing for the last thirty minutes. Not to mention your face is bright red."

As I mentioned, Simon was a nice guy. He also wrote erotic romance under a female pen name. Not that he'd told me this, but I'd overheard the club discussing one of his novels. Which, being the nosy person I was, meant I'd gone home, looked him up, and bought one of his books. It was good, so good I was sucked into the plot. Therefore when I read the first scorching hot sex scene, it conjured up about a million new fantasies about Brady and I forgot the nice guy, geek guy, Simon, had written those words. And when it finally hit me, I turned my tablet off and couldn't finish the book. The next time I saw him, I blushed red and hid in my office the whole meeting.

That was a year ago, and thankfully I could now face him without remembering he either had an active imagination or an extremely adventurous sex life, one in which he tied his partner to the bed and did insanely hot things to her. Either way, I didn't want to know.

But he'd understand why I was angry about a book being ruined.

"Someone vandalized Hemingway's *The Garden of Eden.*"

I handed him the book and started to close down the computer. Approximately two-point-five seconds later, I heard him make a disgruntled sound.

"Fucking asshole." Then he muttered, "Excuse my language."

"No need. I agree. That's the fourth book in a month," I told him.

"Seriously?"

"The first was *Lolita*, and as much as I disagree with censorship or books being ruined, that book has always been controversial and always will be. But *The Handmaid's Tale?* I don't get. I didn't see the book but I heard every page had "vulgar" written across it. *Thirteen Reasons Why* had "going to hell" written on the pages. Now this one."

"What does, "be warned," mean?" he asked.

"No clue and I don't care."

"Hadley. You should care," he gently warned.

"No, I shouldn't. Whoever wrote that, their opinion is meaningless to me. The only thing I care about is stopping this person from removing any more books from this library."

"Had—"

"Nope. No more talk about judgmental pricks," I told him and grabbed my purse from under the desk. "I have a new book I'm dying to get home and start. Speaking of, how's the new work in progress coming?"

"Look at you, trying to sound all authory," he teased.

"Is authory a word?" I laughed.

"Artistic license. It's a beautiful thing, I can make up any word I want to, and as long as it makes sense to my readers, I'm golden."

I set the alarm while Simon waited for me at the door, then he followed me out of the library and again waited while I locked up.

"You don't have to wait around, Simon. I appreciate it when it's dark but it's summer."

"Freaks and criminals don't just lurk at night, Hadley."

Jeez, how many times had I heard that from my dad, uncles, brother, and male cousins? Enough to carry pepper spray and a stun gun in my purse. We started toward my car.

"I might find that offensive if I hadn't grown up with a bunch of overprotective apes around me. So, I'm choosing to believe you're being gentlemanly and not apeish."

"Is apeish a word?"

"Nope. But as long as you understand what I mean, I can make shit up, too."

"Right." He chuckled and stopped at my car. "See you next month."

"Yeah, see you."

Simon waited until I was in my car before he got into his.

I was out of the parking lot and down the street when I realized I left my cell on the desk. I contemplated leaving it behind. But if Addy tried to call and I didn't answer she'd drive to my house. Normally I'd welcome this but I hadn't lied to Simon. I had a new book waiting for me at home and I couldn't wait to start it. I also had some work to do around my money-pit of a house.

Everyone thought I was crazy when I purchased my condo, and there had been a few times since I'd started renovating it I worried I'd made a mistake. But I was determined to finish it. That meant every night I did a few hours' worth of work. The downstairs bathroom was almost done and it looked fabulous.

I drove around the block to get back to the library, which took for-freaking-ever with all the traffic. Fifteen minutes later, I pulled into the lot, scanned it to make sure it was empty, then hurried back into the building to get my cell.

With my phone in hand, I locked back up, walked to my car, opened the door, and my stomach flipped. Then all the hair on the back of my neck stood on end and tingled. My gaze left the copy of *Sex is a Funny Word* on my seat and I looked around the parking lot again.

Then I decided I was being one of those stupid women who hung out in an isolated area when there was obviously a crazy person around. So even though I didn't want to, I picked up the book, tossed it in my back seat, got in, locked my doors, and reversed out of my parking spot faster than I needed to.

I was no less irate when I got home. I was more infuriated when I opened the book, and in the same slanted, perfect handwriting I read, "Teaching children about sexual intercourse is a sin. You're going to hell."

With a heavy sigh, I set the book on my kitchen table. The board of trustees for the library was already hemming and hawing over some of the books we had in circulation. They looked at the American Library Association's list of challenged books as a list that meant banned. This was something I'd fought against and would continue to fight.

Censorship was a slippery slope.

One I wouldn't support.

Now I had four books that at some point had been on the ALA's list. Four books that the board would not replace. Which meant I would purchase copies and donate them to the library. Wasn't the first time I had to do that and it wouldn't be the last.

What I didn't do was start my new book. I didn't work on my bathroom. Instead, I stewed. Not just about the asshole trashing books, or the creepy fact someone had been in the parking lot watching me and broke into my car.

No. My mind went to Brady.

Always back to Brady—and his beautiful, albeit sad, eyes.

It was good Jasper Walker had raised me. Even

better, I had three uncles who helped make me the woman I was. I was used to hardheaded men. But more than that, Emily Walker was my mother. And she was the master of taming wild and stubborn. She'd shown me the way. And if I stumbled, she'd be there to give me advice.

Brady Hewitt wasn't going to know what hit him.

I was done playing games.

3

I was five minutes from my apartment when my radio cut out, to tell me I had an incoming call. It was annoying as fuck, and every time it happened, I vowed to unpair my cell from my truck.

Today's interruption was from Hadley.

My jaw tightened, reminding me I had a splitting headache. I hit the decline button and two seconds later, it rang again.

This wasn't annoying, it was alarming. Hadley called, not every day, but with regularity. The calls consisted of her inviting me places. Some I accepted —like taking her shooting, going rock climbing at the indoor rock wall, and once I'd gone paddleboarding with her off Tybee. I didn't accept the invites that involved food, drinking, or watching a movie.

But she'd never called multiple times.

"You okay?" I answered.

"Thanks for sending me to voice mail," she hissed.

"What's wrong?"

"What's wrong? I'll tell you what's wrong. I have a flat tire. And before you ask, yes, I know how to change a flat. And, yes, I've tried. But I couldn't get one of the stupid, freaking lug bolts loose, and I stripped it. And before you say it, yes, I know that was stupid, and I know it's a damn problem. My dad is in Atlanta with my mom. I called my loving, sweet brother, and he told me he was busy and to call you since you'd left work. But since I didn't want to bother you, I called Ethan and he's on shift. Jackson is, too. Addy's with a patient. Since Jason told me Nick and Drake were both with him finishing paperwork, that leaves you. Can you please come pick me up?" She rushed all of that out without taking a breath.

Of course I was the last resort.

That made me feel like a dick.

"Sure. Where are you?"

"Really?"

Christ. I wasn't a dick, I was a total douche.

"Yes, Hadley, really. I'm not gonna leave you stranded."

"Thanks. I'm at the library. I called a tow truck."

The relief in her voice made my gut roil. Did she really think I'd tell her I wouldn't help?

"Wait in the library. I'll be there in five."

"Already ahead of you. And thanks, Brady. I appreciate it."

Sweet Jesus, her soft, sweet voice did crazy things to me—mentally and physically.

"Be there soon."

Hadley disconnected and I changed lanes.

What the hell was I doing? She had a million cousins I could've suggested she call. She had friends and she had other siblings besides Addy and Jason. But like the weakling I was, I was going to pick her up. Not because I was a gentleman who'd never leave a woman stranded, but because it had been over a week since I'd seen her and I was jonesing for my Hadley fix.

The craving had become unbearable.

Every night, I lay in bed and wondered what it would be like if she was mine. What would it feel like to have her pressed against me? To kiss her, to get her naked, to make her writhe, to hear her moan my name.

Fuck. I reached down to adjust my dick, knowing that could never happen. And what kind of sick asshole did it make me that the thought of her was the only thing that could get me off? How many times had I stroked myself thinking about her mouth wrapped around my cock? Too fucking many.

How long had it been since I had a woman in my bed? Way too long. Maybe that was my problem, I was sex-deprived. But the thought of touching another woman made my stomach churn and my dick revolt.

By the time I pulled into the library parking lot, my dick was fully hard and throbbing. I pulled into an empty spot next to her car and Hadley wasted no time bouncing out the door.

"Jesus," I muttered in the empty cab as my dick twitched.

Hadley Walker didn't have just one fashion style like some women. She had many. Some days, I saw her and she looked fresh-faced and young—cut-off shorts, cute tank top, hair in a ponytail, no makeup. Sometimes she wore stylish jeans, Chucks on her feet, wearing a tee featuring a heavy metal band from way before her time, looking like a rock groupie. And other days she wore athletic gear, ready for outdoor activity. It didn't matter what she wore—she always looked good, she was comfortable with who she was, her body, how she looked. She had confidence and rocked whatever look she was going for.

But right then, she was strutting her fine ass toward my truck in a tight skirt, heels, and a sheer blouse. Her hair was down and it had a sexy wave to it, and on top of all of that, she was wearing makeup. Enough that even from a distance her jade eyes were highlighted to the extreme.

She was the epitome of sexy librarian.

A wet dream fantasy come to life.

And when she smiled, my cock jerked and I clenched my jaw. If I'd been fifteen years younger, there was no doubt the vision of her would've made me instantly come in my pants.

She opened the passenger side door of my truck, tossed her purse in, and looked up at me.

"Thanks so much for getting me."

I mentally chastised myself for not getting out and opening the door for her. But with my dick hard enough to pound nails, that wasn't an option.

I cleared my dirty throat before I answered, "No problem."

Hadley tilted her head slightly at my tight response.

"I hope I didn't put you out too much."

"You didn't. When's the tow truck gonna be here?"

She squinted her eyes, and sweet Christ, getting a good look at her sophisticated makeup that enhanced her natural beauty instead of creating it, I fought the urge to haul her ass into my lap and take her glossy lips in a kiss that would once and for all show her the fire she was playing with. The inferno that burned inside of me. The flames she kept fanning but didn't comprehend.

"Thirty minutes. But I don't have to wait. I called the garage my dad uses. They'll take care of me." She paused, and for a moment she looked unsure, something I'd never seen coming from Hadley before. "Um...I'm really sorry—"

"Nothing to be sorry for, babe," I sighed, realizing I was acting like a total asshole. "Get in."

She hesitated a moment, then hefted herself up. Since I was already behaving like an ass, I continued my bad behavior when my gaze dropped to her bare thigh. An involuntary growl left my mouth as her skirt rode up. I tore my eyes from her legs and when they hit her face, the pink tinging her cheeks had me swallowing a groan.

Good goddamn, I was going to hell. Life hated me, fucking *hated* me, putting her in my truck in the sexy librarian getup. All that thick black hair, those green eyes, that damn skirt that looked hot pulled tight while almost exposing her panties. But it would look infinitely better bunched around her waist with those panties around her ankles, her heels still on and hooked over my shoulders, with my mouth between her legs.

Yeah, life fucking hated me.

God must, too—not only putting Hadley in my path but installing her in my life.

She was inescapable.

She'd intruded on my thoughts, my dreams, and had taken over my body.

"Brady?" she whispered.

"Don't. Not right now, Hadley. Don't say a word."

"Okay."

"Okay?"

"Yeah, okay. I don't ever want to make you uncomfortable."

I was uncomfortable, all right. My cock throbbed, my chest ached, and I wasn't a big fan of my heart pounding.

I didn't allow myself to get uncomfortable. I controlled every part of my life so nothing intruded. I liked boring, I liked bland, I liked tasteless.

When you crafted every experience to mean nothing, you didn't risk losing things or people that meant something to you. And when you'd lost everything, you protected yourself against losing more.

The biggest reason I had to stay away from Hadley—she wouldn't mean more, she'd mean *everything*. And that kind of loss was one I'd never recover from.

"Do you have everything?" I asked.

Her forehead furrowed then her eyes widened. "Shit. I left my phone on the desk."

Hadley threw open the door, hopped down, and I was treated to the backside of her as she made her way back to the building.

Coming or going, the woman had it going on.

I closed my eyes, gripped the steering wheel, and willed my cock to soften.

Nicole.

That single thought deflated my erection but made my soul hurt.

I didn't watch Hadley make her way back to my truck. I didn't turn my head when she climbed in and I said not a word as I drove her home.

Her condo was decent, it was the neighborhood that was iffy. I knew her father had tried to talk her out of moving into the area, but Hadley being

Hadley had dug in and moved into the neighborhood anyway. She'd explained it was not her forever home. It was an investment.

I agreed with Jasper. The complex was nice, but that was all the condo had going for it. Though I had to admit, Hadley had gotten a screaming deal, and once she updated the inside, she could flip it and make a nice profit.

I pulled into her spot under a covered carport and glanced around. Decent cars, trucks, and SUVs were parked in the lot. The landscaping was well-kept, mature trees offered shade, neat flowerbeds were abundant. Lampposts scattered every fifty feet or so provided good lighting.

"Looks better than when you helped move me in, doesn't it?" Hadley broke the silence. "I love all the flowers. It's not as pretty as Mom's yard, but at least it's something."

She wasn't wrong—it was not as pretty as Emily's yard. That was because Emily tended to her home like she tended to everything else in her life, with nothing but love. I'd been to the Walker home many times and never had I gone over there and seen a single weed in her garden. She liked surrounding herself and the ones she loved with beauty. She enjoyed her home, her yard, and her family.

What would it have been like growing up with Emily Walker as a mother instead of Helen Hewitt? I didn't have a response to that because the answer was incomprehensible.

"Hey," Hadley chirped. "As long as you're here, you wanna see the bathroom I updated? But I need to warn you, most of the downstairs floor is still plywood." Her nose scrunched. "The new laminate is taking so much longer than I thought it would."

"Why?"

"Why what?"

"Why's the floor taking so long?"

"Well, I didn't take into consideration having to remove all the baseboards, which was a huge pain in the ass because the builder caulked them to the drywall. Anyway, huge mess trying to get them off without tearing off the drywall paper. Which I did in like five places, so now I'll need to skim the wall and repaint, but whatever. But I also didn't think about the waste I'd have cutting the planks to make the joints staggered, so that's necessitated another trip to Lowe's to buy more." She shrugged. "You live and learn. It's my first time, so I expected some hiccups. I naïvely thought it would only take a week to do the downstairs. I'm on week two and I'm barely halfway done."

"And you're doing this by yourself?"

"What's that mean?" she snapped.

"It means exactly what I asked. You're laying all that flooring with no help?"

"Why would I need help putting down a laminate floor?"

Good Lord, the woman's argumentative.

"I don't know, Hadley. Maybe so it doesn't take you three months to do something that could take a week if you enlisted the help of the fifty-two million family members you got."

Her eyes narrowed, her shoulders pushed back, and irritation flashed.

"I'm not asking one of my *fifty-two million* relatives to come over and help me do something I'm capable of doing on my own. I like to save those favors when I come up against something I can't do."

"Really? And how many times have you called them in to help?"

"I haven't."

"Right." I shut down my truck and made a decision I knew I was going to regret. "Let's go check out your pad."

"If you point out—"

"Come on, Tim the Tool Man Taylor, let's go see what you've done."

"Are you making fun of me?"

"Not even a little bit."

I was actually impressed and I hadn't even seen the work. But the mere fact she'd done it on her own was impressive enough. And knowing Hadley the way I did, her determination, I was sure everything looked great.

It wouldn't be for hours later that I'd realize how deeply I'd come to regret going into her home.

A decision I wished greatly I could take back.

4

_____

So, this wasn't part of my new plan to get Brady's attention. I actually did have a flat tire and I had stupidly stripped the lug bolts while trying to change the stupid thing. And I had called numerous people before I'd called him for help.

This was not how I wanted to start my new strategy. Hell, I hadn't even had time to come up with something foolproof. My first thought was a full-scale seduction, but he'd sniff that out a mile away and shut me down before I got my hand down his pants.

Now, at this point, you might be wondering what type of woman sticks her hands down a man's pants in an effort to seduce him—and I'd tell you, a desperate one. A woman who knew she'd found everything she was looking for in a man, yet he refused to budge. How did I know he was the perfect man? Well, let's see, there was the time he rushed into a burning house to save Tuesday Clark's life. Then there was the time he took Liberty, Drake, and Carter's back when a crazy guy broke into Triple Canopy wanting to kill my cousin Liberty and Carter.

But even before his last act of bravery, I knew it because of the way he treated the women in my family. The way he spoke to my mom and aunts with respect and tenderness. The way he respected my dad and the uncles openly and reverently. Like he was grateful they'd taken him in and given him a job. He was a man—*all* man—and showed his appreciation and loyalty. He was protective, he could be annoyingly bossy, and had I not been raised by Jasper Walker, I might have found this annoying in a different way. But to me, protection meant care. It meant I was of value. You didn't protect worthless things.

And finally, I knew because since he'd come to work for Triple Canopy, he'd become my person. You know, the one you turn to when trauma strikes. I didn't know how this came to be, just that it happened and it felt natural for him to be that person. It had started after Delaney was kidnapped by a crazy bitch named Dana who'd also shot at my other sister, Quinn.

That was nearing three years ago. And since then, he'd stood by me during the absolute worst time in my life when Quinn almost died. No, he didn't stand by me, because I wasn't *standing*. I'd crumbled and he'd picked me up and held me until I was strong again. And when my badass GI-Jane cousin, Liberty McCoy, had been taken as a POW, he'd gotten me through that, too.

So I knew he cared about me. I knew he had a lot to give and I knew he wanted to give that to me. However, something held him back. And I knew it was the same thing that put the sadness in his eyes.

I was not one of those women who saw a man as a project and wanted to fix him. I had my condo for that. But I couldn't deny I wanted to help Brady with whatever was wrong. I wanted to help him find a way to let go of it, help him dig it out. I owed him that.

And that was why I was willing to try anything, including shoving my hand down his pants and using sex to get what I wanted. Not to mention, I just plain wanted to get Brady into bed because he was hot, and sweet when he wanted to be. But I knew that wouldn't work because he didn't ever let me get that close to him unless I was suffering some great trauma.

Which led me to now—Brady in my house looking at the new laminate flooring I was putting down—and not having a firm plan in place about how to get him to let me in.

He wandered around the living room which was devoid of furniture. I'd pulled out the ugly-assed brown carpet the day after I'd moved in and discovered it wasn't just ugly, it was so dirty I didn't want furniture touching it, much less my feet. So I hadn't gotten around to buying any new furniture and I still couldn't walk through the downstairs barefoot due to the renovations. But, I was no longer worried about getting a fungus that might lead to me losing a toe.

I did have a kick-ass new bedroom set and a kitchen table I found on sale because one of the legs had a scratch and it was missing one of the eight chairs that went with the set. I didn't care about the scratch or the chair so I got the table for a steal.

There were two other rooms upstairs. One was empty and would remain that way. The other had my childhood twin bed and a dresser.

"So, the color's not really my jam, but it's neutral,

and from what I read, neutral makes a house easier to sell."

"Not your jam?" Brady looked at me and smiled.

His face was lit with amusement. Something I didn't see coming from him very often, as in so infrequently, it was always a shock when I saw it.

A man like Brady needed to smile more. He needed to have fun.

"Anyway, as you can see, the dining room is done. I haven't started the kitchen yet. That's next after I finish the floor in here."

His gaze slid to the kitchen and his brows pulled together.

"I saw that," I blurted.

"Babe. That kitchen. I forgot how bad it was." He smiled again and I didn't care he was teasing me about the state of my house. I felt like I'd won a prize.

I also took no offense because the kitchen was horrible.

"What? You're not down with the peeling paint look?"

In an effort to spruce up the cabinets, the previous owner had painted the oak cabinets white. They did it without priming them first so now the paint was peeling off and bubbling.

"I'm more concerned that your countertops are

yellow and the flooring in there is...what color is that exactly?"

I had no idea what the original color was, only that the linoleum was now the color of dirty bath water. And no amount of bleach helped.

His gaze came back to mine. Seeing his face—the mock horror, the playfulness—I couldn't fight the laughter so I didn't try. I let it loose and watched as his face changed. The playfulness vanished. Something heavy took its place and my chest squeezed like it always did when I saw the sadness creep in.

"Worry not, friend, the kitchen's next," I said, ignoring his mood. "The countertops will be the first thing to go. Hopefully, I can salvage the cabinets and just strip the paint off and refinish them." When Brady didn't respond I blathered on. "New cabinets would cost a whack and I want to buy new appliances and re-do the master bathroom, therefore cabinets are not in the budget. Otherwise, I'd have to stay here longer than I intended."

He still said nothing, but his eyes hadn't left mine and something funny started to stir in my belly.

"Brady?"

Nothing. He was just staring at me like he was in a trance.

"Everything all right?" I asked and his torso jerked. What the hell was that about?

"Yeah," he lied.

There was nothing all right with the way he was looking at me. It was an odd mixture of pain and, well, more pain.

Pain I hated seeing with such loathing I wanted to make it stop. But he wouldn't let me close enough to do that and I was beginning to wonder if he ever would. He'd given me bits and pieces of him, but only when I needed him. The rest of the time he held back. Physically and emotionally, he'd drawn a line. Any time my toe inched over that line, he shoved me back where he wanted me—on the other side.

Maybe it was a fool thing to do. Maybe I was setting myself up for more heartbreak than I could handle. Maybe Brady would destroy me.

Yet, I wasn't willing to give up.

I knew you got good when you fought for it. I'd witnessed it. I'd watched Carter and Delaney struggle for years before they pulled their heads out of their asses and went for it. I'd watched Quinn go after what she wanted and land the man she loved. Liberty had fought her demons and won, and in doing so hooked up with Drake. I knew it was possible. I knew love could conquer.

But I wasn't so sure Brady wanted his pain conquered. And that killed.

It hurt like a punch to the gut. The kind that winded you, stole your breath, and left you gasping for oxygen.

I also knew he was gearing up to run out on me and I wasn't ready for that.

"Wanna see the bathroom?" I inquired as breezily as I could, hoping I didn't sound desperate.

"Yeah, let's see it."

And his mask of indifference snapped back into place. This annoyed me greatly. I wanted to claw it off but I couldn't. I wanted to ask him why he constantly shut down on me but I wouldn't. Not because I didn't want to know but because I'd skirted the question before he flat-out refused to answer.

So instead of doing what I wanted to do, I semi-stomped across the living room, through the dining area, through the kitchen, and rounded the corner, flipping on the bathroom light as I stepped in, and turned around.

Brady was on my heels and I hadn't realized he'd followed so closely. This meant when I abruptly stopped and turned I slammed into him. I started to stumble back when his hands shot out and caught me by my biceps and hauled me upright.

The movement brought me face-to-face with an extremely good-looking Brady.

Up close and personal, I had the pleasure of witnessing his gray eyes focus intently on me. They heated and darkened until that intensity grew to searing. I felt rather than saw his chest expand as he inhaled. And finally, I felt his fingers curl tighter and he dipped his head. His lips moved to a hair's breadth away, so close they brushed mine. Without thought, my tongue traced his bottom lip. And because he tasted so damn good, I went back for seconds.

That was the moment my life changed.

It was forever altered in a way I'd never recover from.

I talked a big game. I'd been told a time or a billion that one day my bravado and half-cocked schemes would get me in trouble. This had never been a deterrent that was because I was deter-mined—though others would call it careless—to get what I wanted. This was not selfish, it wasn't ugly, and it wasn't because I was spoiled. I worked for it; whatever I was determined to get, I was willing to do whatever I had to do to accomplish my goal. But the truth was, I hadn't been ready for Brady Hewitt.

I'd been with only two men. So, no, I wasn't *actually* going to ever shove my hand down his pants in an effort to make him notice me, because I wouldn't have had the first clue what to do. However, until right then, at that moment when Brady's tongue pushed mine back into my mouth and *he* swept his in, I didn't know just how clueless I was.

I also realized I'd never been kissed. At least not the way Brady did it. And when his hand glided up my arm, over my shoulder, and his fingers dug into the back of my neck holding me to him so he could take what he wanted, something deep inside flared to life.

Brady deepened the kiss and a whimper slid up my throat. The effect of that noise was astounding. He one-upped my moan and growled down my throat. The hand not controlling my neck jerked my skirt up and my clit pulsed.

My stomach dropped when his hand went between my legs and his fingers traced the edge of my panties before he pushed them aside then pushed in. As in—inside of me. Belatedly, I remembered now was my chance to explore, to finally touch him, and I didn't delay shoving my hands up the back of his t-shirt. My palms met hot skin over hard muscles. His fingers pumped in and out of me and my nails dug into his back. My legs were already trembling, but when his thumb circled my clit, they shook. Brady must've felt it because his grip on the back of my neck tightened and he deepened our kiss. A feral growl slipped from him and washed over me then coursed through me. Straight through my skin, my muscles, and settled in my bones.

All of it was so hot, felt so good, it started to happen. Only it was different—bigger, stronger than anything I'd given to myself. Even the buildup was better. It wasn't slow to develop. It didn't grow and blossom—it hit. And when it did, my climax exploded in a kaleidoscope of colors so bright, so vivid, it dawned on me I'd been living a dull life.

My body arrested, my lungs burned, and pleasure like I'd never felt pulsed through me. The top of my head to the tips of my toes tingled. And a full-body moan tore from my mouth.

Then Brady's hand disappeared and I came up off my feet. Before I could comprehend what was happening, my ass was on the vanity and I vaguely thought it was a good thing I'd sprung for the bigger size or my ass would've been in the sink. That thought fled when Brady stepped between my thighs, forcing my legs to open.

My skirt was mostly bunched around my waist but the material stretched tighter as I spread my legs more until finally the seam gave way and I heard it rip. The sound was so erotic, so raw, so damn sexy, my still-quaking body shivered.

I groped Brady's back but it wasn't enough. I needed more. I needed everything. My hands moved to his front over his abs and I took a moment to enjoy the feeling of them jump and tighten as my palms glided over the ridges and valleys.

Me.

I did that to him.

I made his stomach muscles jump.

I wanted more of that. More of his growls, more grunts, more groans.

My hands moved lower. Feeling empowered by all Brady had given me, I unbuttoned and unzipped his jeans in record time in a one-woman race I was determined to win, then I struggled to shove them down.

Throughout all of this, he kissed me.

Bar none—it was the best kiss of my life. I didn't even know a kiss like that was possible. Demanding, wet, deliciously deep.

I was alive.

Finally.

Everywhere, everything alive and I wanted more.

One of his hands left my hip. There was movement, then Brady helped me shove his pants down.

I wanted to shout for joy. But that would mean disconnecting my lips from his and I was pretty sure I wanted to live the rest of my life fused to Brady's mouth, tasting him, inhaling his scent, touching his hard body.

Hell yeah, I wanted this forever.

I needed him closer so I wrapped my legs around his hips, locked my ankles, and drew him in. So close, his cotton-covered cock was pressed to my center. I didn't want that material between us. I didn't want anything between us. I needed skin on skin and in my impatience to get it, I scratched at the waistband of his boxers and I heard him hiss.

Damn, that was hot, too.

I would've had a mind to how my pussy convulsed hearing that sound, but before I could process that, Brady yanked my blouse open. Buttons scattered across the bathroom.

That wasn't just hot, that was fucking off-the-charts-hot-as-fuck.

The only bad part was he tore his mouth from mine. But that bad only lasted a nano-second because when his gaze came to mine the heat blazing in his eyes made up for it. Unfortunately, I lost his hungered stare when his head dipped down. A second later, all thoughts of losing his eyes vanished when I felt his lips on my breast, then I lost the ability to think at all when he pulled the cups of my bra down and his mouth latched onto my nipple.

Sweet mother of God.

My back arched, silently begging for more. Brady sucked harder and his hand cupped my other breast, his fingers found my nipple, and he rolled and tugged that one while his mouth played with the other.

I was so turned on I burned with it. My hands didn't know what to do, my thighs trembled from squeezing so hard, my breath was coming out in fast pants, my heart was pounding, and I still needed more. And the only way I knew how to communicate that was to lift my hips in an invitation. At the same time, my hands went into Brady's hair. I grabbed two handfuls and held him to me while I kept rubbing myself against his hard length.

Stupid fucking boxers.

They needed to go.

I felt Brady shift, forcing me to loosen my legs. As his boxers slid off, I lost his cock and an impatient growl slid up my throat. His mouth left my nipple and that forced a whimper to escape.

"Jesus fuck," he groaned, then in the third hottest move I'd ever experienced, he reached between us, and the sound of my panties tearing filled the room.

"Oh my God," I whispered and his eyes locked onto mine.

I felt the head of his cock slide through my excitement and I heard the air hiss through his clenched teeth. I watched as his jaw flexed and his eyes flared.

More wetness gathered between my legs. I dug my heels into his ass and Brady drove home.

"Fuck." Brady tipped his head back, giving me a prime view of his muscular throat. But I wanted to see more.

My hand reached for the hem of his shirt while my other stayed on the counter for balance.

Once again he proved he didn't need verbal direction. He reached around, grabbed a handful of material, ripped it off his torso, and tossed it aside.

I'd seen him shirtless before at a pool party but that was different. I could steal glances and I had. I could appreciate his broad chest and six-pack abs, and I'd done that, too. But I couldn't touch. Now I could, so I didn't delay. My hand went to his chest and I felt his heart pounding under my palm. Then I decided to roam. There was a lot to touch, a lot to look at, all of it sexy. I traced his tattoo under his right pec, down his stomach, circled his belly button with my thumb. I heard his groan and my gaze shifted up and found he was watching me. Our eyes locked and I froze.

No mask. Open desire. Gray eyes boring into mine, and a stare that was so unsettling, so intense, I wanted to look away. I could fall in love with that look, I was already halfway there so it wouldn't be far to fall.

But even with Brady connected to me, driving his dick inside, openly hungry, eyes locked on mine, I was still afraid he wouldn't catch me.

However, I was Hadley Walker therefore I stupidly fell anyway.

5

Good goddamn.

Hadley Walker was too much.

No, not too much, she was everything.

Crazy beautiful, every inch of her. From her shiny hair, her jade eyes, her ass, her tits, the tiny freckles that dotted her chest, the birthmark on her stomach, her lips, her mouth. There was so much to look at, so much to touch, but it was her eyes that held me captivated.

I couldn't look away.

Her heels were digging into the small of my back, her hips moving with my drives, taking me deep. Her tight, wet pussy rippled around my cock. All of that so unbelievably hot I was close to losing it and I needed her with me—needed it in such a way I'd die if I didn't get it.

She was an unhealthy obsession I had no chance of exhuming. Now that I had my cock buried inside her wet heat, she felt so fucking right that knowledge burned. So *right*, so *good*, so goddamned beautiful, but she'd never be mine.

Fuck, yeah, that burned.

"Brady," she moaned. Her back arched, her head followed, and I lost her eyes.

My gaze dropped to her tits bouncing with my thrusts even with her bra shoved down under them, nipples pebbled, the vision hot as fuck. But I continued my perusal lower, wanting to see it, needing it, craving it. When my eyes landed on her pussy, then my cock as I pulled out, seeing it glisten with her excitement, that was all it had taken for the last of my control to snap.

My thumb went to her clit and I watched that, too, me circling the tiny bud, adding pressure and fucking into her harder. I listened to her moans, felt her pussy tighten, and gave her more. In return, I gave myself more.

Goddamn perfect. All of her. Tentative yet bold. Sweet and sexy. She hadn't had the first clue what to do when I'd taken her mouth, but it hadn't taken her but a second to follow my lead. I fucking loved that. Loved that when my hand went between her legs, her body froze, but as soon as my fingers traced her sex and dipped in, she melted. Then with very little effort she melted a different way and climaxed around my fingers. Sexy. Sweet. Perfect.

"Ohmygod," she groaned. Those spiked heels painfully jabbed my back and her pussy seized my cock.

"Fuck," I grunted, and powered through her orgasm, fighting the urge to blow, making it good for Hadley as her pussy tightened, pulsed, and quivered.

Unbearably fantastic. The feel of her extraordinary. The sound of her exceptional. The smell of her amazing. Crazy fucking beautiful all of her.

But that wasn't what had me falling over the edge. It was her sweetness. The way her soft eyes searched me out whenever we were in the same room. The way she was as attuned to me as I was to her. An unspoken connection that would never be talked about.

"Brady," she panted.

Hearing my name in her sex-rough voice did it.

"Hold on tight, honey, gonna fuck you harder."

I reached down, hooked my arm over her leg, and

held her thigh to my ribs. My other hand left her clit, dove into her thick hair, and fisted a handful. I gave her no choice but to right her head and look at me. I needed to watch her as she took me. Needed to know it was me giving it to her.

My need had driven me to make a fatal error. I knew it the moment our eyes connected. Hazy, soft, satisfied. But they were filled with something other than desire. Something I didn't deserve but I couldn't deny with my cock planted in her. Seeing it made my soul come alive.

My climax rushed to the surface. I slammed deep, my cock throbbed as long jets of come pulsed.

"So fucking good," I grunted as my orgasm flowed through me.

A moan slipped past her lips, her pussy clutched tighter, milking the last of my come, and I froze.

Phenomenal.

The pleasure hadn't even waned when guilt encroached. When it waxed, a sick feeling took over.

What the fuck had I done?

My answer was obvious, considering my still-hard cock was planted inside her. I'd mauled her. Finger-fucked her. Ripped her shirt, torn her panties, and fucked her on the vanity in her renovated bathroom. Through all of that, I'd been rough. Hadley didn't need rough, she needed gentle. Something I knew I didn't have in me and certainly didn't have any fucking control over when I was near all that was Hadley.

She turned me into a savage. Need-driven and powerless to manage my addiction.

"Brady?"

Fuck.

I let go of her thigh, my hand in her hair loosened, and I watched in horror as the haze in her eyes started to clear and the tentative look crept back in.

I was a supreme asshole.

I lowered my gaze because I couldn't stand to see the look in her eyes, knowing what was going to come next would turn tentative into wounded. But I was going to do it anyway.

Only, looking down as I pulled out of her was no better. Seeing my cock slide out with our combined juices leaking out of her, my gut tightened.

My bare cock.

Bare.

Christ.

I tipped my gaze up and I was right—tentative had turned wounded and I hadn't even fucked her over yet. Or I had, she just didn't know it.

"Fucked up, Hadley. Took you without a condom and blew inside of you."

Her face closed down, her mouth got tight, and she muttered, "I'm on the pill."

I should've been elated that she was protected from my seed taking root. Protected from me and my fucked-up life. But I wasn't. I was pissed as fuck. Everything inside of me rebelled over all the reasons *why* she was on birth control. The mere thought of her taking another man inside of her beautiful body made me homicidal. She'd never actually be mine but that didn't mean I hadn't claimed her all the same.

Totally irrational. Unhealthy. Obsessive.

But there it was.

Not that I'd tell her that.

"Good."

I forced myself to take another step back, which meant Hadley had no choice but to unwrap her legs. The sight of her made both my cock twitch and my stomach roil.

Ravaged. There was no other word. Blouse hanging open, tits trussed up, skirt bunched around her waist, panties destroyed, heels still on, and my come leaking from her pussy. All of that sexy to such an extreme I wanted to fuck her again. At the same time, I wanted to fall to my knees and weep at what I'd done to her.

"Fuck, Hadley, I'm so sorry."

"Don't," she bit out. She closed her eyes but not her legs and I couldn't stop staring.

There was something so raw, so beautiful, so barbaric, seeing my woman laid out before me knowing that I'd put her in that state. That *she'd* lost control, that *she'd* been fully with me every step and gotten off, laid herself bare for me, let me see all of her. Dangerous thoughts—she wasn't *my* woman. She was just a woman who meant everything to me.

Before I could do anything else stupid like scoop her up and take her to a bed so I could fuck her again, I yanked my pants up, zipped them, and tagged my shirt off the floor.

"Here." I offered her my shirt and her eyes squinted.

She made no move to take it as she slid off the vanity. The sound of her heels hitting the tile echoed in the small room. My hand went to steady her as she swayed. But when her eyes narrowed more, I dropped my hand.

As fast as she could, she righted her torn skirt and her bra, leaving her blouse hanging open. I glanced down at the tile and shards of remorse cut deep as I took in the buttons.

Fuck.

My attention went back to her as she grabbed her panties off the counter. Heels clicked as she walked to the small trash can and tossed them in.

Fuck.

Without a word, she pushed past me and out the door.

Double fuck.

I drew in a breath that did nothing to calm the ache in my chest. There was no fixing what I'd done. No turning back.

I'd lost Hadley.

That wasn't just fucked, that was agony.

By the time I made it into her kitchen, she had her ass against the cabinets and her destroyed shirt held closed—which I was grateful for but I didn't think she'd done that for me—and her posture was stiff.

She saw what was coming, therefore she'd braced.

But I hadn't. When Hadley got in there first, her words felt like bullets tearing through my flesh.

"I suppose this is where you tell me that was a mistake. That you're sorry, you didn't mean for it to happen, you never wanted to hurt me, and it will never happen again." She sucked in a deep breath that kept me pinned in place and when she exhaled, she continued. "Next thing, I suppose, though I've never been in this situation so I can't say for certain, but I'd assume this is where I beg you to stay, tell you that you didn't hurt me, I don't think it was a mistake so I don't regret it, and I want it to happen again."

Direct. Fucking. Hit.

"Hadley—"

"No, Brady. I'm not gonna beg you for anything. You wanna go, go. You wanna continue to be a coward, be one. You wanna deny what just happened wasn't great, go right ahead. But you're not dragging me there. I don't regret it. I enjoyed it—immensely. I reckon you know you're good so it won't come as a surprise to know I've never had better. But that's not why I don't think it was a mistake. You denying we have something between us isn't why I think you're a coward. No, you refusing to reach out and take what I've been offering is what makes you one.

"You feel the connection. I know you do. I see it when you look at me. That's on you. So, you wanna bail, run away, pretend you weren't into what just happened? There's the fucking door, don't let it hit you on the ass on the way out. I know what I want, I know to never settle for anything, but most especially not when it comes to the man in my life. And I want a man who's all-man, who's not afraid to fight by my side to make something beautiful. Luckily, I was raised by men who showed me the way, taught me what a real man looks like, so I know. But I was also raised by strong women who taught me to take care of myself."

Christ, her verbal arsenal was deadly.

"Trust me, honey, if I was the man in your life, you'd be settling."

"Right." One word laced with sarcasm and disdain.

"You have no idea what I got buried inside of me. Ugly shit that would only stain all your pretty."

"You're right, I don't know because you won't tell me and that's on you, too. Because I'd bear that stain for you. I'd help you carry it until you could find a way to let it go."

"I shouldn't have done that—"

"Done what, Brady? Kissed me? Fucked me? Yanked my clothes off, which was the hottest experience of my life? Or maybe you shouldn't be doing what you're doing right now, blowing smoke up my ass because you feel bad you liked it just as much as I did and you want more of it just like I do."

She was scoring hits, ones I deserved so I'd take them. But I felt my temper rising with each truth she told.

"Yeah, honey, I liked fucking you. I liked that you were so into it you didn't bitch when I ripped your clothes off. Fucking loved that you got off on my fingers but you liked my cock more. Seriously loved hearing the sounds you made while your tits bounced and you didn't complain that I hadn't bothered to take off your bra. And I liked watching your face when you got off and your tight pussy sucked me dry. All a' that's hot as fuck. All a' that I'd take more of. I'd take it, I'd wreck you, and I'd leave you every time looking like you're looking right now—hurt and angry. Only, that hurt would grow and I'd leave you ruined. And that anger would grow into resentment. You think I'm a coward? Straight up, Hadley, I want you. But I am man enough to tell you the God's honest truth—I am not the man for you. I'm fucked-up in a way I won't ever get unfucked. You might not believe this now, but I respect you too much to put you through the shit I'd bring into your life."

I didn't miss the flash of desire in her eyes. I also

didn't miss them narrowing. And there was no missing that her patience had snapped. So I was ready when she pulled away from the cabinet and snapped her shoulders back. But I was not ready for her to put her hands on her hips, leaving her blouse to open and expose her cleavage.

"I don't get a say in any of this?"

"Nope. None."

"I was wrong, you're not the man I thought you were. Not only are you a coward, you're fucking blind, Brady."

Jesus, that fucking killed. My jaw clenched, my gut recoiled, and I knew it was time to leave. I deserved everything she was saying. I was a total dick, but hearing her tell me I wasn't the man she thought I was, shattered me because it was true. I wasn't. But I never wanted her to know the truth.

"You're right," I huffed. "More right than you understand. I am not the man you thought I was. Never will be."

"Whatever you say, Brady," she snapped snottily.

"Babe, there's no reason for us to be tearing each other apart and for this to get ugly. Straight up, that shouldn't have happened. I lost control and it was a dick thing to do."

Hadley's head tilted and her eyes roamed over

my face. Under normal circumstances, I'd shut this down. But I'd ripped her clothes off and fucked her in her bathroom without care or concern I was taking her hard. I also didn't think about the repercussions. I'd allowed all my pent-up need for her to come out and when it did, I couldn't control it.

I didn't regret it—not one single second of us coming together. What I regretted was the fallout, the irrevocable change.

I regretted the hurt I'd caused.

And I seriously regretted I'd never be the man she needed.

6

I'd learned a few things watching my sisters fall in love. I'd paid attention when it happened to my brother and cousins.

And what I'd learned was there were things worth fighting for. There were times when you didn't hold back. But there were also times to retreat and regroup.

What I didn't know was, which one of those things I needed to do now—fight or retreat. Did I keep him here or did I let him walk out the door? With Brady, I figured if I allowed him to leave, he'd avoid me and I wouldn't get another shot to get him alone.

My choice was made for me, because I only had right now.

"Do you lose control a lot?" I inquired.

"What?"

"You said you lost control. So I'm asking, does that happen to you a lot?"

"Hadley—"

"Answer me, Brady. Does it?"

"No," he clipped.

I released the breath I didn't realize I was holding. I wasn't sure what I would've said if he'd told me he lost control frequently but I knew it would've hurt.

"So why'd you lose control with me?"

Brady's mouth clamped shut and he closed down.

I was on the right track. Time to push.

"C'mon, tell me."

"Told you why."

"No, you told me you liked fucking me. You told me you wanted me. I'd suspect there have been a lot of women you've *wanted*." I had to stop and swallow the bitter taste saying those words brought. "So why'd you lose control with *me*?"

Brady stood straighter and crossed his arms over his chest and I made another decision—I wasn't going to hold back.

"The first time I saw you, I fell in love with you.

That was four years ago. I knew I was too young, I had to finish school, get a job, start my career, and get myself sorted. That didn't mean I was giving up on what I wanted, I just knew it wasn't the right time. I also knew you weren't ready, you needed time to settle in after getting out of the Army. And in those four years, I only fell more in love. So if you think after waiting all this time to finally get what you gave me tonight, that I'm going to let you tell me it was a mistake, you're wrong. If you think I'm not gonna fight for what I want, you don't know me. And if you think I'm gonna stand here and let you try to bullshit me and tell me that what we did meant nothing to you, you've seriously misjudged the type of woman I am."

"Hadley, honey," Brady murmured and his features gentled.

Not in a way that said he returned my feelings. In a way that said he was searching for an easy let-down. That hurt—but more, it pissed me off.

He was denying us something we both wanted.

Yeah, that hurt and pissed me off, so I said nothing.

"You gotta know you mean something to me. That's why what happened was a mistake. I can't offer you what you want."

No, he could offer it, he just didn't want to.

Total coward.

"Right," I whispered and my heart started to crack. "So what you're telling me is that the *something* I mean to you isn't enough. Because if it was, you'd see I'm laying it out for you. No bullshit, no games, just honesty. You'd see I'm standing here offering *you* what you want."

"One day you'll understand," he shot back.

God, seriously?

"Oh, yeah, Brady? And when will I understand exactly?"

"When you find a man who can offer you everything you deserve."

That single statement shredded me worse than hearing him say he regretted having sex with me. The finality of his words hurt like a bitch, further driving home he was totally going to deny us what we both wanted. He was going to run away from me and we'd never go back to what we were.

I wasn't a quitter but I also wasn't ever going to be the type of woman who begged a man to love her. I was at a crossroads. I didn't like either direction this was heading. But life was life and I had no choice but to roll with it.

So with that in mind, I backed down.

"You're wrong, Brady. I'll never understand, because when I find that man and he gives me all that I deserve, I'll give it back ten-fold. Which means I won't be thinking about you at all."

With that, I walked out of my kitchen, across my living room, up the stairs, and didn't stop until I hit my bed. I didn't bother changing out of my clothes. I just curled up, and it was then I let the sadness invade. But it wasn't until I heard the front door slam that I allowed the first tear to fall.

Apparently, I hadn't paid enough attention to my sisters and cousins—love hurt.

It hurt so damn bad I didn't want to feel it anymore.

7

"That the report from Dylan?" Jasper asked as he walked into my office.

At the sound of his voice, I lifted my head but couldn't look the man in the eyes. It'd been a week since I'd done his daughter dirty. And in those seven days, I'd avoided him the best I could. I'd also spent a fair amount of time kicking my own ass for being such an idiot.

"Yeah. Dylan's report is thorough but I'm still not finding anything that will help find who set Liberty up."

Liberty McCoy, soon-to-be-Hayes, had been sold out and used as bait. Her Special Forces team had been sent out on what had been presented as a recon mission. But it was a ruse, a two-fold mission to force

Roman Kushnir—a man who supplied terrorists with anything they needed to carry out their bad deeds—and an infamous bomb-maker called Lore, out into the open.

The government needed a way to take Roman out so they cut off Lore's supply chain. They needed to do this without it looking like an assassination so that no one pissed off his Uncle Marko, the envoy and crime boss. If Roman was killed during a business deal, the government had hoped Marko would turn his sights on Lore thinking the bomb maker had killed his nephew. Marko would take out Lore to avenge his nephew and everyone walked away smelling like roses. All they needed was a way to lure Roman out, and everyone knew Roman wouldn't pass a golden opportunity to take out a McCoy. That was because Levi McCoy, Liberty's father, had been part of the team that had killed Roman's father.

A vicious web of revenge had been cast, ensnaring Liberty—she'd been taken and tortured by Roman. Thankfully, Liberty had been rescued and Lore, Roman, and Marko were dead. But we still hadn't found who was behind the ploy.

"It's been nine months," Jasper noted. "And we've got nothing."

There was nothing to say to that so I remained

silent. It had indeed been nine months since Liberty had been rescued, we still had nothing, and each day that passed, Drake Hayes, Liberty's fiancé, became less and less happy about his woman being sent out on missions. The first time her unit was sent out to South America, Drake had to be locked down. Thankfully, that trip only lasted seven days. The second time, he pulled his shit together enough he didn't need a babysitter but he'd been in a foul mood until Liberty returned from Afghanistan.

The issue wasn't that Drake didn't understand Liberty's job or why she was compelled to serve her country. The problem was Drake *understood* the danger—seeing as he was a former SEAL, he was also the man who'd rescued Liberty.

The sooner we got to the bottom of the situation the better. Not that it would erase all of Drake's fear when Liberty went out but it would ease some of it.

"You ready to tell me why you're avoiding me?" Jasper's inquiry wasn't a question as much as it was a demand.

Fuck.

The uncomfortable vibe in my office intensified the longer I remained silent. But there was no correct answer. There was Jasper losing his fucking mind and there was him losing his *motherfucking* mind. Neither one ended well for me.

Consequences.

I'd screwed up, now it was time for my punishment.

"Hadley," Jasper huffed and sat in one of the two chairs in front of my desk.

"Jasper—"

"I'm gonna preface this conversation by reminding you she's my daughter. It's not lost on me, she's in love with you. And it fucks me to say this but I am not blind. I look at her and see all the gifts my wife gave her. One of those gifts is her beauty, another is her determination. I know she's been pushing you. I do not wanna know shit about shit and I think you catch my meaning." Jasper let that last statement hang and I fought against squirming in my chair.

I was a grown-ass man talking to the father of the woman I banged and walked out on. A father who was not stupid, knew his daughter was gorgeous, knew she'd been playing me for damn near a year, and there wasn't a man alive who, after being tortured by all that beauty, wouldn't eventually give in and take what was being offered.

So with all of that, grown or not, I was squirming

like a teenager who'd been caught with his pants around his ankles. Because while my pants might've been up over my ass at that very moment, they'd been around my ankles while I fucked Hadley, and Jasper knew it.

Christ.

"Not wanting to know shit about shit, we're gonna tread carefully during this conversation. But you not looking me in the eye tells me everything I need to know."

There it was; unwanted confirmation Jasper knew I banged his daughter.

"Jasper—"

"The only question I have for you is, what's hanging you up?"

"Come again?"

"Brady, you get I'm not blind, right? You get I pay attention. I didn't miss Hadley falling in love with you so I didn't miss you doing the same. Four years ago, not only did I understand it, I appreciated it. She was too fucking young to take on a man like you. She needed to start building a life. Even two years ago, when I saw her making moves to position herself in your line of sight I was grateful when you held off. The last year she's been making her plays and you've been fielding them but none of us missed her stepping up her game. I see something happened a week ago—and again, she's my fucking daughter so we're on dangerous ground here—but I figure she made a play you couldn't refuse. So with all of that, I'll ask you again, what's hanging you up?"

It was safe to say I was freaked the fuck out. We weren't on shaky ground, Jasper had shoved me in a pile of quicksand and there wasn't a move I could make that didn't include me sinking deeper.

"There's a lot hanging me up," I carefully told him. "Some of the reasons you already stated. She's too young, she doesn't have the first clue what taking on a man like me means, and she's your daughter."

"If I didn't know my daughter, I'd agree. You got seven years on her but I know my girl, she's far from dumb." That quicksand was sucking me in so I remained quiet. Unfortunately, Jasper misread my silence and felt the need to continue. "And you misunderstood me. I know the man you are. You're the man who ran into a burning house to pull Tuesday Clark to safety—"

"I'm also the man who spent nine years in the Army, five of those in the unit. Being as you spent time there, you know what I've done. I'm also the man who found and beat the shit out of Rey Patel."

Jasper's frame locked, his eyes narrowed, and the

temperature in the room went sub-zero. The man didn't like the reminder I'd tracked and captured the motherfucker who nearly killed his daughter, Quinn. And after I found Rey, I didn't offer the asshole tea and cupcakes while I waited for the police. I'd unleashed hell on the fucker. By the time Jasper had brought Quinn's man, Brice, around to get his licks in, Rey was seriously fucked-up. And when we were done, I didn't hand Rey over to the cops. I dropped him off in a rival gang's territory—after I'd put the word out on the location where I'd be leaving him.

"You think I give a fuck about that?" Jasper seethed.

"You should. She should. The violence I'm—"

"You call it violence, I call it protection."

Any other time I would've agreed with Jasper. But we were talking about Hadley. Sweet, innocent, young Hadley.

"I'm thinking this conversation is moot," I told him honestly and his eyes squinted.

"Let me guess. A week ago, you made sure she saw the light."

Now I was out of that quicksand and edging onto seriously dangerous ground. Jasper didn't want to know and I'd never tell him what went down in Hadley's bathroom.

"Respect, Jasper—"

"You get we're talking about my daughter, right?" he cut me off and my body went solid. "*My* Hadley. You know me, Brady, you know I got no problems putting my foot up some dickhead's ass if they fuck with one of my girls. Seeing as I know you're smart, you understand what this is. No way in hell would I sit across from you and give you my blessing if I didn't know I could trust you can give my daughter what she needs. But more than that, I trust Hadley has the tools to give *you* what *you* need."

That felt unbelievably good, but at the same time, it carved my insides hollow. Jasper wasn't wrong, Hadley was everything I wanted, everything I needed. She was strong enough to stand by me and take on my shit. But that didn't mean I'd allow her to be buried under it.

There was a line between want and need and doing what was best for the woman you loved. I was trying my hardest to stay on the side of the righteous. That was, I'd been succeeding until I'd failed spectacularly.

"I still dream about Nicole," I blurted. "I dream about a lotta shit. You sure you want a man like that sleeping next to your daughter?"

"You trying to piss me off?" he growled.

At that juncture, I wasn't sure. Maybe I wanted to push Jasper until he unleashed his wrath on me. Maybe I needed him to kick my ass since I was incapable of doing it myself. Maybe I needed to feel the bite of pain as knuckles met flesh.

"I'm trying to get you to understand that we're talking about *Hadley*. Beautiful, sweet, funny, free-spirit Hadley with the pretty smile and gorgeous eyes that hold nothing but innocent mischief. And I cannot for the life of me figure out why you're not sitting across from me warning me off. I can only dim her light, steal everything good she has to offer. Your daughter needs a man who can hand her the world. Not only does she need it, Jasper, she fucking deserves it."

A wide smile broke through his features and I didn't see a damn thing worth smiling about.

Jasper stood but didn't take his shrewd eyes off me. "One day, you'll understand."

One day, you'll understand.

Fuck.

I won't be thinking about you at all.

My chest caught fire and turned to ash.

"Something to think about, Brady. At no time during this conversation have you denied you're in love with my daughter." The ground beneath my feet started to shake and dangerous turned into something else. "And you haven't denied it because you're not a liar."

Unable to look at Jasper, my gaze dropped to my desk. A man I respected, a man I aspired to be like, a man who took protection and loyalty to extremes. He also had the uncanny ability to read the people around him, therefore he saw straight into my soul.

He knew I loved Hadley.

"One last thing for you to think about. Maybe I want Hadley for you, not because I want a good man at her back. One I trust. One I know will protect her in the manner in which I'd protect her—that being by any means necessary. Maybe I want Hadley for *you* because I want a good woman at *your* back, too. One I know will light those shadows. One I know will do everything she can to heal the pain *you* have locked inside. There's not a man in this building who doesn't have demons. Not a man who doesn't have the same nightmares you have. The difference for some of us is, when those nightmares come, we have exactly what we need lying next to us to help beat them back."

With that, Jasper walked out of my office. I sank back into my chair unable to catch my breath.

Approval from Jasper Walker.

Jesus fuck.

A man who loved his children beyond reason. A man who wasn't stupid, who knew exactly what giving his blessing would bring.

Hadley in my life, in my bed, and under my protection.

Protection I'd once failed to provide.

Nicole's sweet smile came to mind and I slumped down further. I let the guilt fortify my resolve.

Why the hell would Jasper give his blessing to a failure?

8

I was seething mad as I made my way across the library to the circulation desk.

"Uh oh," Ellen, who was working the desk, whispered, "I see you read the memo."

"Yes. I read the memo."

A memo that the library board had emailed stating that not only would the library not be purchasing new copies of the four books that had been destroyed but they were refusing to take the anonymous donation that replaced the damaged copies.

"Child," Ellen drawled. "I see you're all fired up. But you put those books back in circulation, you know the next email you get won't be a memo. It will be a formal write-up."

Ellen Potts was an older woman who had retired from teaching but found she didn't like puttering around the house and her husband didn't like to travel, which was how she'd prefer to spend her retirement. Since that wasn't in her future, she worked at the library three days a week. This meant she was smart, observant, and had played by the rules for twenty-five years.

I didn't play by the rules—not all of them, anyway.

Especially not the rules that removed books from library shelves. Not rules that forced someone's personal opinion on others. There were plenty of books I personally didn't like, didn't agree with the message, or I plain thought sucked, but it was not my right to tell others what they could or couldn't enjoy.

"Censorship is wrong," I told her.

"I agree with you. But the library board has made its decision."

"It's wrong, Ellen. You know it. If we restricted access to every book someone had a problem with, we'd have no books."

"I agree."

I knew she did. I was preaching to the choir. The difference was Ellen had spent years in education, where she had to succumb to the demands of the board of ed or face the possibility of losing her job. She had told me plenty of stories about the criticism she'd faced when parents complained about her teaching style or they didn't like the topics the curriculum covered. She'd loved her job, loved her students, so she'd given in.

I loved my job. I loved being surrounded by the written word. I loved losing myself in the pages and being transported into the universe the author created. I loved learning. I loved the creativity, the art, the beauty.

I loved it so much I was willing to face termination to stand up for it. To protect it. To make every book available to anyone who wanted it and I refused to allow my opinions color what others had access to.

I would abide by the ALA's banned list because that rule couldn't be broken. But I wouldn't allow the county's library board to strong-arm me into removing challenged books.

"I won't be bullied," I rasped, unable to keep the anger out of my tone. "I was taught to fight against anyone who wanted to oppress others' rights."

"Hadley, my sweet girl, don't you think you're making a mountain out of a molehill?"

"No. Because I know that molehill can very easily turn into a mountain if I don't push back.

What's next? Travel guides to the Middle East? History books? The Bible? The Quran? Books about Buddhism? Mahatma Gandhi? Romance? Murder mysteries? The list is endless. This building affords anyone who wants it free entertainment, a free education. It opens minds, it changes lives, it heals, it inspires. If the threat of that being taken away isn't worth fighting for then I don't know what is. And as long as I'm working here, I will fight them on every book they try to remove."

Ellen stared at me a beat. Then her wrinkled face broke into a smile and she nodded.

"The world needs more Hadley Walkers in it. You fight, child, and I'll stand next to you."

Overcome with emotion, I cleared my throat then said, "Thank you, Ellen."

"Now, go get me those books you bought so I can catalog them, then you go home. It's my turn to stay for the Knitting Club meeting."

Thank goodness for that.

Besides not wanting to dream about making whatever their latest project was, I had a floor to finish and only three days to do it before my new furniture arrived.

"You're the best."

I went back to my office, closed my computer

down, grabbed my purse double-checking I had my cell, grabbed the books, and headed out for the night.

IT WAS LATE when the knock came—past the time it was socially acceptable to knock on someone's door. But with a battalion of relatives who didn't adhere to normal standards, it could be anyone from an uncle, a cousin, or a sibling.

I stopped banging a board into place and looked around the living room. I'd gotten a lot done, but then I should've because I'd been at it for hours. So many of them, my knees hurt and my back ached.

But the pain was well worth it because the new flooring looked awesome.

I made my way to the door, unlocked it, and when I opened it, my breath arrested for a beat. Then my breaths came in shallow pants.

Brady.

"What's wrong?" I asked as I took in the deep creases in his forehead.

"You didn't ask who was at the door."

"What?"

"Door, babe," Brady snapped, and I jolted when he pushed himself into my house.

It took a few beats for me to come unstuck. I closed the door and turned, not comprehending what Brady was doing there and at the same time becoming increasingly annoyed that it had been a week since I'd seen him. Plus, I was irritated that I was in a ratty pair of shorts, my hair was piled on top of my head, and I had on an over-sized, paint-stained tee. In other words, I looked like shit.

Not the appearance a woman wanted to present to the man who'd shot her down. It went double if it was the man you were madly in love with.

I'd hoped the next time Brady saw me I'd be tricked-out and he'd take one look at me and know he'd royally fucked up.

But there he was in my living room nearing on midnight and I was dressed like a homeless person and probably smelled like one, too.

Annoying.

Then I remembered Brady and I were no longer friends. He'd closed that door, which begged the question of why he was at my house. Fear crept in. He worked for my dad and uncles and I was not kept apprised as to the jobs Triple Canopy took, but I knew enough to understand not all of the jobs they took were safe.

"Why are you here? Is everyone okay?"

His chin dipped and his gaze took me in before it settled on my face. He grunted, "Yeah, everyone's fine." I lost his eyes because he was looking around the room. "You're almost done."

What the hell was going on?

"Looks good, babe."

Babe? Okay, seriously, what the hell was happening?

"Why are you here?" I tried one more time.

"We need to talk."

Since our last conversation had ended with my heart broken I wasn't feeling particularly altruistic about giving him another opportunity to pour salt in the gaping wound that had yet to scab over.

And after seven days of doing nothing but mourning the loss of a man that was never mine to love, I was beginning to think the pain would always be raw.

"At midnight?"

"Yeah, at midnight," he confirmed.

I hadn't realized just how right he'd been when he told me that my hurt would turn into anger until that very moment. Seeing Brady standing in my living room days after he'd walked out on me made raw pain turn to raw anger.

"I have nothing to say to you."

"That's okay. All I need for you to do is listen."

"I see, you think you can come in and—"

"The first time I saw you, you stole my breath."

My heart seized and my body froze.

"You were twenty, in college, and way too fucking young, but there it is—one look and I was gone."

Did he...?

"For the next four years, it physically hurt every time I was with you. I knew you were mine but I had to fight against claiming you. And with each passing month that battle's been harder and harder to win and you damn well know that's the truth. You've been playing me and doing it dirty. Teasing the hell out of me, not knowing the other truth—I was already in love with you but the timing wasn't right. Then last week happened and straight up, Hadley, that should've gone down differently. But fuck, baby, that kiss, it did me in. That was the last crack in what was left of my patience."

With great effort, I became unfrozen and took a step back. I couldn't hear this. I'd never recover from knowing he was in love with me but he was still going to keep himself from me. That was worse than thinking he didn't return my feelings.

Way worse.

Knowledge I couldn't live with.

"Please stop," I whispered.

"I've tried to deny it. I've tried to keep you at a distance. I've tried goddamn hard to wait until you were ready. But fucking hell, Hadley, I can't do this anymore."

I didn't know what *this* was. And I knew it was stupid but I couldn't stop hope from creeping in. My legs were shaking and I wished I had a couch because I really needed to sit down before I fell and landed on my ass.

"What does that mean?"

"It means I'm done waiting. Ready or not, I'm making my move."

He was making his move?

Why did that fill me with elation *and* fear?

"I'm not sure I understand."

"I know you don't, baby. And that look on your face tells me that you're not ready. But I already knew that because last week you stood in your kitchen and you bared your soul. Something you never should've done with a man like me."

That statement didn't fill me with joy and it didn't scare me. It annoyed me that he was talking to me like I was an idiot.

"What kind of man are you?"

"One that will exploit your every weakness to get what I want. I'll use your emotions against you and manipulate you until you're so into me, you feel me so deep, you won't be able to run from me when I finally pile all my shit on you. I'll make you love me so you can't imagine your life without me in it."

I stood in a meditative trance, thanking all that was holy I'd been raised by Jasper Walker—who was all man, a man who would manipulate, exploit, and tie a woman deep. I knew this because I knew he'd done just that with my mother. Further, I knew it was not done ugly as the words would suggest, but done with adoration.

Brady was wrong. I was ready. I was also ready a week ago when I laid myself bare. I'd done it consciously because I was Emily Walker's daughter and she'd taught me good things came to you when you opened yourself up.

But now I had a dilemma. I knew I was ready but I was unwilling to open myself up to more hurt. I was done playing games with Brady. Either he was in or he was out, but I wasn't using my heart as a checker piece trying to reach his side of the board to see if I got kinged or jumped and captured.

I'd lost this game once.

I was determined, not stupid.

9

"Babe?" I prompted.

Hadley was six feet from me, which was six feet too far. But she was working through her emotions so I stood rooted to give her the space she needed.

That was not to say, I wanted or needed the space, but she certainly did.

I hadn't lied. I would exploit every opening she gave me, and if she thought she was hiding her feelings, she was sadly mistaken. Every thought she had flashed in her eyes. The war raged in full swing—panic, fear, love, belief, need.

It would be easy to reach out and pull her to me. One kiss and her thoughts would scramble. But I couldn't abuse the love I knew she felt for me by taking her to bed to convince her she wanted me.

First, she needed to understand the choice was hers. But once she agreed she was mine, all bets were off.

"What changed?"

Everything.

Jasper.

But I wasn't going to tell her about my talk with her dad. Though that was the final push I needed after doing nothing but thinking about her all week.

I figured turnabout was fair play, and since she'd given me everything I needed last week I'd arm her with enough ammunition to even the odds. Knowing Hadley the way I did, she was a woman who would exploit, manipulate, and fight to win.

And that was a battle I was looking forward to.

"Four years is a long time, don't you think? Years of waiting, years of wanting, building a friendship with you even as I tried to keep you away because I knew one slip-up would end in catastrophe. One taste of you and I'd never let you go."

Hadley's green eyes narrowed and her arms folded across her chest.

"So this is about sex."

Her indignation made me smile—chocked full of attitude and spice. Hadley was never afraid to voice her opinion. One of the many things I'd fallen in love with.

"How straight do you want it, baby?"

"What does that mean?"

"How much truth are you ready to take?"

"All of it," she snapped.

Doubtful, but I'd give it to her.

"All right, honest to God, banging you in your bathroom was by far the best sex I've ever had. No joke. No lie. Hands-fucking-down hottest, too. Better than I imagined it would be. And, yes, I imagined it a lot, starting at a time I was pretty disgusted with myself that I was going home and jerking off thinking about a twenty-year-old. But there you have it—for four years you've owned my cock. Stopped having empty sex with meaningless pussy the day after I laid eyes on you. So is this about sex? Fuck, yeah, it is. But it's also not. It's about me getting a taste of what's been mine for *years* and wanting more. It's about me loving you all that time and I'm tired of hiding it. It's about an infinite number of things. But bottom line, it's about the fact that you claimed me four years ago, the same as I claimed you, and we're gonna take a shot and see if what we think we have, we've got."

"What do you think we have, Brady?" Hadley whispered, giving away everything she was feeling.

Luckily for me, the woman couldn't hide a damn thing. Not her desire and not the fact she liked everything I'd said.

"Forever."

"Forever?"

"I see you like the idea of that, baby. So what do you say? You ready to take this shot or do you need more time?"

"Was that a question or am I a foregone conclusion?"

"If by foregone conclusion you mean us being together is inevitable, then yes."

"Well, that *is* what foregone conclusion means, Brady," she said testily.

"You think maybe you're gonna answer me sometime in this century so I can kiss my woman after a week of living a nightmare?"

Goddamn, she was cute when she got pissed. Concerning, because there would come a time when she'd be genuinely mad at me, and seeing the way her left eye twitched and her perfectly shaped eyebrows lifted, not to mention the way her nose scrunched, was adorable as hell and only made me want to kiss her annoyance clean away.

"It's not my fault you've been living a nightmare."

Smartass.

"No, baby, it was mine. And I'm sorry about the way that night ended. But the question's on the table and I'm waiting for you to put me out of my misery."

"I'm scared."

Fucking hell.

I glanced around her living room. Still no furniture. The only option for closeness was her sitting on her kitchen counter with me standing between her legs. Or, she could sit on my lap on one of the wooden dining chairs. Neither offered comfort—something we'd need because I figured this next part of our conversation was going to require time.

I moved to the front door, threw the lock, tagged her hand, and dragged her around the room with me as I turned off the lights. Then I headed for the stairs.

"What are you doing?"

"Seeing as you don't own a couch and I'm tired of you standing six feet away from me while we have this talk, we're going to your room." Her hand spasmed in mine and I rushed to continue. "Nothing's gonna happen. I just want to hold you while we finish."

"And if I want something to happen?"

"Hadley," I warned.

"Sheesh, you don't have to growl."

We were in her room when I stopped, tugged her hand, and she fell forward and caught herself with a palm to my chest.

"You get I haven't fucked another woman in four years, yeah?" I watched as Hadley's eyes flared and heated. Yeah, she was getting it. "I didn't mince words so I don't know how I could be any clearer but I'll try again. For seven days, I've fisted my cock thinking about how tight and wet you were. I stroked myself to the memory of the sounds you made, the way you looked when you climaxed, the way your pussy felt wrapped around my cock. I've had you once yet I have every inch of you memorized. Thinking about any part of that night gets me hard. So for the love of Christ, please cut me some slack and let's get through the rest of this conversation so you can tell me what scares you and I can put your mind at ease."

I was holding her close so I didn't miss the way her body shook. I also didn't miss her leaning closer.

"Baby," I groaned. "Bed. Talk."

The little minx smirked. She liked that she'd rendered me near-speechless.

I knew Hadley was of a different mind when she made no move to the bed. Instead, she tilted her head back and caught my stare.

"I'm scared because now I know what it feels like to have my heart broken." My stomach dropped and a bad taste slid up my throat. "You said some things last week about you not being the man for me. That scares me."

I'd said a lot of shit last week that I never should've said. Some of it in an effort to push her away, some of it because I was pissed as hell at myself and had taken it out on her.

"I got some shit I gotta work through. I wasn't ready to face it and I said some stuff I didn't mean in order to not face it. It was jacked-up what I said and you're right; it was about me being a coward for not wanting to sort myself knowing it's gonna be painful. But I have a feeling having you next to me to ride that out will make it easier. Bottom line is, I took a lot of crap out on you and I shouldn't have. Everything you said to me was spot-on. You scored deep that night and that's part of what I thought through this week. I wouldn't be here now if I wasn't sure I could be the man you deserve."

"What do you need to sort out?"

Fucking shit, I didn't want to do this ever and I especially didn't want to do it now. But I'd said some fucked-up things and now I needed to face the reper-cussions.

"My dad's been in prison for twenty years. He's being paroled in a few months and that's brought up a bunch of shit I keep buried at all costs. I got the letter the day before I picked you up from the library. It was fresh, it was burning a hole in my chest. Then what happened between us happened and I lost it."

I watched Hadley's face screw up and braced for her disgust.

"Honey." Her hand moved up my chest to my neck then the pads of her fingertips dug in. "I'm sorry."

"Nothing to be sorry about. The bastard should stay in there and rot."

"That's not what I'm talking about. I'm sorry you've had to live with that. I can't imagine. What about your mom? Where's she?"

More ugly. More shit. More stains I couldn't wash away.

"Seven years after my dad went down, she successfully drank herself to death. And don't feel sorry about that. Both of them were drunks. Not alcoholics. Mean, nasty drunks. Both of them rotten to their core. She was never my mom, she was the woman whom I lived with until I didn't have to anymore. And the day I left I never looked back. Never spoke to her again. Didn't claim her ashes, didn't attend her funeral if there was one, didn't go back to see what happened to her things, nothing."

Hadley stood in a daze staring up at me. The foul taste that always accompanied memories of the bitch pooled in my mouth. Hate wasn't a strong enough word to properly describe how I felt about the people who'd brought me into the world. They were vile, inhumane pieces of shit. The dog shit on the bottom of your shoe that you can't scrape off.

Hadley let go of my neck and stepped away. But she didn't untwine her fingers from mine and she pulled me toward the bed.

"Take off your shoes. I'm gonna change."

"Hadley, baby—"

"Brady. Take off your shoes and get comfortable, honey. I'm gonna get out of these dirty clothes."

And suddenly I felt like prey. I was unclear how I felt not being the one to give orders. I also wasn't sure after our rocky start if this was the best way to proceed. My cock didn't have the same reservations. It was fully on board with Hadley being the boss, and to make its wishes clear, it jerked in my pants.

Fuck.

When Hadley came out of her bathroom, her dark hair was freed of the confines of the band that had secured it up into a messy pile, so now it hung loose, framing her pretty face. But my attention was on her robe. I had a sinking feeling she was wearing next to nothing or nothing at all under the shiny material. My cock seriously loved that idea but my brain was putting up a good fight, reminding me I needed to have a care.

"Hadley—"

"Brady."

Our eyes locked and a stare down ensued.

She broke it when she said, "You're not in bed."

"And you're scared. Something we need to get you past before we go any further. Me getting comfortable and getting into your bed is not a good idea."

"I'm not scared anymore."

Jesus fuck. She's trying to kill me.

"Remember when I told you, if this is what I think it is, then we have forever?" Hadley nodded and I went on. "Then there's no rush."

"Four years," she oddly replied.

"What?"

"Brady," she pleaded.

Not liking the tone in her voice and the way she'd begun to fidget, I gently ordered, "Come here, babe."

She slowly made her way to me, her face set to

unsure, and I liked that even less. Once she stopped in front of me, I raised my hands. One went to her neck and the other cupped her cheek and bent her head back so I had her eyes.

"Explain to me what's going on."

"I don't know. You're the one turning me down so you're the one who's gonna have to explain."

What the fuck? She thought I was rejecting her?

"I'm not turning you down. I'm *slowing* things down. I thought it was a good idea coming up here so we'd have a piece of furniture to use. Now I'm seeing my error. Me, you, a bed. Way too fucking tempting. You coming out in nothing but a robe—torture. We got time."

"But..." She trailed off.

"Say what's on your mind."

Hadley stared up at me, hunger clear as day in her eyes. She tilted her head and nuzzled my hand. Asking for something but not knowing how to ask.

This was not the Hadley I knew.

"Baby, you want something from me?"

She nodded.

"What do you want?"

"You in my bed."

My cock jolted, reminding me I was hard as fuck and with a near-naked Hadley pressed against me.

"Just me in your bed?" I pushed, and stroked the soft skin under her chin.

"You in my bed naked."

Swear to Christ, my cock wept at her invitation.

"How about this, baby?" It took an extreme amount of effort to keep my hands where they were, not taking what she was offering. But I'd already fucked up once and I was determined not to do it again. "Tomorrow night I'll take you out and we'll talk some more."

"What else do we need to talk about?"

"A lot, Hadley. I jacked you around and said some stupid shit. I need to make up for that. But more, I need to make sure you're where you need to be before we take this further."

The desire slid from her eyes and irritation moved in.

"Don't be an ass and patronize me. And don't go back to using my age as an excuse."

I beat back the grin that she'd definitely find patronizing and said, "This has nothing to do with your age. You were honest with me and told me you were scared. I put that fear in you. And you're afraid because I was a dick to you. We've been dancing around each other for a long time. That ends now. You think you know me, but, baby, you don't *know* me. And what you find when I let you in you might not like. So we're slowing this down. Taking our time and building it right."

"You're not staying the night," she surmised.

That was an absolute fuck no. I wasn't sleeping in a bed next to her. Not until I explained what she might face if my nightmare crept in, and I certainly wasn't going there now.

"No, I'm not staying the night."

Disappointment.

Fuck.

"Babe, I know this is asking a lot but I need you to trust me. There's nothing I want more than to crawl into that bed next to you and see what you have under that robe. As hot as last week was, it was too fast. I didn't get to explore all the places I wanted to. Next time, we'll do that," I finished, not meaning to say more. Then I remembered all the honesty Hadley had given me and I knew I owed her the same. "I'm not ready to spend the night. I told you I was fucked up. I've never hidden that from you, not even way back in the beginning. Part of what's fucked-up is that I dream, and when I do, sometimes I wake up rough. I don't trust myself to be lying next to you when I'm not in control of my actions and not knowing what I'm doing, only what I'm capable of.

Sucks to tell you this, because I figure waking up next to you would be spectacular. But I can't give you that, and I'm not sure when I'll be able to."

Recognition and relief shone in her eyes. As much as it pained me to admit a weakness, I knew I'd made the right decision telling her.

"Has something bad happened before?"

"What do you mean?"

"Have you had a nightmare and not been in control and hurt someone?"

"Fuck no. Never slept next to a woman."

"So you don't know if—"

"Not a chance I'm willing to take."

"Not tonight, but in the future."

"Hadley—"

"Stop, Brady. I get it." And with her face set to stubborn, she continued, "I know you *think* you know me but you don't know me. Something for you to learn is, I'm not a quitter and I don't back down, not from anything. *You* came over here tonight asking me if I was ready to give us a shot. So now I'm asking you—are you ready? Because part of that is you sleeping next to me, Brady. Not tonight, not tomorrow, but in the future. You want me to trust you, then you've gotta trust me and believe I'm strong enough to deal with whatever happens."

She was wrong, I didn't need to learn those things about her. Part of the reason I fell in love with her was because she wasn't a quitter. She was outspoken, she went after what she wanted, and she did it with a laser-focus.

"I can give you that," I acquiesced.

"Thank you," she murmured.

"Now can I kiss my woman and put her to bed so she can get some sleep so she's not dragging ass tomorrow night when I take her out?"

"Yeah."

Fucking *finally*.

My head dipped and I wasted no time taking my woman's mouth. This kiss was far less frantic than our first but no less intense. Her tongue glided against mine, her arms wound around me, her hands went under my shirt. They skimmed up my back, she hooked them over my shoulders and held on tight.

Finally.

Hadley Walker was officially mine.

10

My alarm blared from across the room, necessitating me rolling out of bed and walking to my dresser to turn it off. This was by design, I needed my alarm clock across the room and not on my nightstand where I could easily reach it and hit the snooze button. And it was needed because I was not a morning person. According to my mother, I'd never been one, not even as a baby, and in all the time since, I'd never become one. My twin, Adalynn, was a morning person. This annoyed me to no end when we were growing up sharing a room. Addy would pop up out of bed before the first beep of the alarm sounded and she'd start making noise. Sometimes she'd whistle and that was even more annoying than her chipper-first-thing-in-the-morning mood.

Being as I was a gainfully employed adult with responsibilities, I couldn't hit the snooze five times if I felt like it. Therefore, my alarm was across the room so I had to get my lazy ass out of bed to shut it off. And once I was up, I was up, albeit not in a good mood ready to face the day. But at least I was upright.

But right then I was fully awake. I'd gotten up early even though I didn't need to be at the library until ten.

Last night Brady kissed me, which had led to a full-on make-out session, one he ended before groping could commence. Which also led to him tucking me into bed, something that I would've found a little condescending if it hadn't included more lip touches and him skimming his hand down my cheek, staring into my eyes as he told me he couldn't wait for our date.

A date with Brady Hewitt.

Hell, yes.

Being as I was Hadley Walker—impatient, impulsive, and prone to hatching a scheme if it got me what I wanted—last night I'd laid in bed and thought about everything Brady had said to me.

A lot of it was really great. But a lot of it was bad.

His dad had been incarcerated for twenty years.

Obviously, he'd been convicted of a heinous crime, one Brady hadn't shared. His mother was dead and he wasn't torn up over the finality of that. He'd been emotionless in a way I couldn't read. Either he seriously despised the woman like he said he did and had made peace with his mom being gone or he was burying something big. That was bad, and I'd do my part to dig into the mystery and help him deal if he needed to. The worst was the nightmares, and only because those would keep him from me. I couldn't help him get to the bottom of his feelings about his family if he kept himself locked away.

On that thought, I went in search of my cell. There were some people, young and old alike, who had their phones in hand or nearby twenty-four-seven. I was not one of those people. I wished against all hope that the cell phone towers in Georgia would mysteriously go down, cutting off service so I wouldn't have to hear my family bitch when they texted and called and I missed those attempts at communication because half of the time I didn't know where my phone was and the other half I was busy and didn't want to be interrupted.

Ten minutes later, I found my phone under a stack of empty flooring boxes and sent a text to my Uncle Clark asking him if I could stop by his house to talk before he went into work. Unsurprisingly, I received a response immediately telling me to come by.

I rushed through my morning routine and high-tailed it to my aunt and uncle's house. I knew he didn't mind but I didn't want to take advantage and make him late.

My uncles and dad were in the process of retiring and turning Triple Canopy over to my brother, sister, and cousins. I figured this would take years before they completely stepped back, but now that my brother Jason had left the DEA, meaning Triple Canopy was now fully staffed, all of my uncles were spending less time there.

All except Uncle Levi. He wasn't going anywhere until the person who set my cousin Liberty up to get captured was caught. I knew this not because I was told outright, but I overheard enough at family get-togethers to know. Everyone was on board and looking. But as of the last time we were all together a few weeks ago for my niece Emma's first birthday, they hadn't found anything.

I knew this worried the guys and it set Drake on edge knowing his woman was still going out on deployments. I was proud of my cousin; she was as badass and tough as they came. She'd overcome being a POW, she'd beaten back her nightmares, and she'd landed a great guy who fully supported her serving even if it scared him out of his mind.

I pulled into my Uncle Clark's driveway and scratched 'talk to Liberty when she's home' onto my mental to-do list. My keys weren't even out of the ignition when I saw my uncle on his porch. God had given me many blessings. One of them was an awesome family—full of men who were overprotective because they cared deeply and showed it. And women who were strong, supportive, and never short on wisdom.

My childhood had been full of love, understanding, loyalty, and family.

By the sound of it, Brady's was not.

The mere thought of him not having all that I had hurt my heart. It also made my adoration and respect for him grow. He didn't have love, loyalty, and family yet he was still the man he was.

I was at the bottom of the steps when I greeted my uncle.

"Thanks for making time for me, Uncle Clark."

"Anything for my beautiful girl. Come in."

"Is Aunt Reagan home?"

I heard the door close and Clark stopped at my side. His gentle eyes took me in.

As in all of the things life had given me, most of them good, I adored everything about my uncles except for one thing—they were extremely observant. They could read a situation in two seconds and know you'd either done something or were getting ready to. Couple that with my father's razor-sharp attention and I got away with nothing as a teenager.

And now as an adult, I still didn't.

My uncle's keen powers of observation were hammered home when Clark muttered, "Brady."

"Brady," I confirmed.

"Your aunt's kickboxing with your mom and sister," Clark answered my earlier question as he led me into the living room.

"Right, Friday. How could I forget."

That wasn't a question. I knew why I couldn't remember even though they'd invited me a hundred times. Kickboxing wasn't my thing. I was athletic, but I preferred outdoor activity to kicking and punching into the air in a gym. Addy went because she was a health nut and fitness freak, though I think she had her eye on the instructor, if constantly mentioning he was smoking hot was anything to go by. However, my twin would never make the first move, so if Mr. Hot Guy wanted a date with my sister, he'd have to make all the plays and so far he hadn't.

We made it to the kitchen and I smiled when two mugs sat on the counter and Clark motioned toward one of them.

"Thanks."

The mug was halfway to my mouth when Clark said, "Talked to your dad yesterday and he told me he spoke to Brady. I take it he broke through."

"What?" I wheezed. "Dad talked to Brady?"

"Brady didn't make his move?" Uncle Clark's eyes narrowed and my heart pounded.

"He did, last night. But he didn't tell me he talked to Dad."

My uncle nodded but offered nothing more.

"What'd they talk about?"

"I think that's a conversation you need to have with Brady."

"Why's that?"

He didn't answer. Instead, he continued to study me. Experience told me I needed to gather all the patience I could muster because my uncle was the type of man who took his time before he spoke. He was thoughtful and didn't offer empty words.

"We'll come back to that after you explain why you needed to talk to me."

Damn.

I took a fortifying breath knowing I was going to bring up something unpleasant. But I needed to understand what I was dealing with.

"I need to ask you something personal. And I hope you know I'd never ask unless it was important."

I watched my uncle's torso swing back and his shoulders tense.

Shit. Maybe this was a mistake.

"If I got it in me to give it to you, you know I will. So ask."

He meant that—my uncle would give anyone in our family anything they needed. Even if he didn't have it in him, he'd find it.

"Brady's got nightmares," I murmured. "We haven't had a chance to talk about them, but last night he said something to me and I can't stop thinking about it. I know you...um..."

"You know I used to have nightmares," he finished for me.

"Yeah. That, and I know one time something happened with Aunt Reagan."

I watched the color bleach from his face and I felt like a selfish bitch for bringing up something so personal and painful.

"Never mind. I'm sorry, Uncle Clark. So sorry, I shouldn't've brought it up. It's none of my business."

It took effort on my uncle's part, but slowly some of the stiffness drained from his shoulders though his face was still a mask of agony.

Crap. I did that to him.

Stupid me.

"Uncle—"

"She heard me having a nightmare and came into my bedroom and tried to wake me up." He paused and viciously scrubbed his hands over his face. "Christ, I could've killed her," he murmured and pinned me with his gaze. "Don't ever, under any circumstance, no matter what Brady's saying or doing, try to wake him up. You get up and get away from him."

I nodded my agreement because it was good advice and it sounded like those instructions were torn from his chest.

"I was caught in the nightmare and when she touched me I lunged and took her to the floor. Pinned her down and scared the hell out of her. Not only that, Hadley, I had my hand around her throat. I was out of my mind. I was back in the middle of a war zone trying to fight my way to safety. It was not my beautiful Reagan under me, it was an enemy combatant and I was prepared to kill."

Holy shit. I knew something had happened, but I didn't know *that*.

"I'm sorry. I shouldn't—"

"Sweetheart, you came here knowing I'd give you that, and I did because it's important you understand that Brady is capable of doing dangerous things when he's in the middle of a nightmare. No way would he ever lay a hand on you or hurt you when he's cognizant. When he's not in control, that's a different story."

"That's what he said. He told me he won't sleep next to me because of what could happen."

At that, my uncle's features hardened but I figured it was for a different reason than his memories of what happened with my aunt. I was still *his girl* no matter my age and he didn't like hearing about a man sleeping next to me.

"That's smart," he mumbled, sounding extremely pleased.

"Uncle." My head automatically tilted to the side as my attitude surfaced. "It might be smart *for now* but you can't think I'm gonna be happy if my man has to sleep away from me because we can't find a way around it. And you know it has less to do with my not being able to wake up next to him and more to do with me knowing something is screwing with his head and he's being tortured in his sleep and that's what's taking him from me."

"He's gonna need time. Stress is a trigger, and with everything going on between you and him, that's gonna fuck with his head. They'll come more frequently which causes more stress and the cycle begins."

"Are you saying dealing with me is stressful?"

My uncle barked a laugh before he sobered and gave me a dose of his badass wisdom.

"Hopefully the conversation your dad had with him yesterday will help alleviate some of Brady's worry. It's not lost on any of us that he's been in love with you for years and you him. Neither of you hides that. You because you're Hadley Walker and you let it all hang out—good or bad you let her rip. Him, because his desire for you was so strong he couldn't hide it. If this was four years ago and he acted on that feeling, your dad woulda ripped him a new asshole. But he didn't, he played it right and waited. He took his time and proved to your dad he had it in him to give you what you needed. I know you think your dad's in your face and protective—and he is, for good reason. You're his daughter and he understands how precious you are. He has accomplished a lot in his life but you, your sisters, your brother, and your mother are at the top of that list, and you know it because your dad has shown you your whole life what you mean to him. As with Delaney and Quinn, he was not going to give a man his blessing without knowing he'd do anything to protect the beauty he created.

"Now with all of that being said, he's given Brady his blessing. The specifics of that conversation you'll have to wait for your man to tell you. I'm gonna leave you with this: I've had the honor of watching you grow into a vibrant, strong, loving woman. You also played it smart and gave yourself time to grow into that woman before you went after what you wanted. But, Hadley, sweetheart, you have to be prepared for all that comes with Brady. Not just his nightmares, he's got shit buried that's gonna have to be seen to. And it seriously fucks me to say this to my baby niece, and you gotta know I got bile churning in my gut, but you hafta know who you're dealing with. Brady is a man and I mean that in every way a man can be. You might think you're ready for that because you've been surrounded by men your whole life. But, darlin', there is a difference when those men are your father, your uncles, your brother, and your cousins and when that man is in your bed." My cheeks heated and my uncle didn't miss it and that was punctuated by his mumbled "fuck" before he went on. "Right. I see you went there with him already."

I wasn't going to confirm my uncle's speculation, mainly because I didn't need to but also because he was my uncle and I wasn't going to discuss my sex life with him.

"I'm beginning to understand the difference," I told him.

"Don't let him walk on you, darlin'." Clark put his hand up to halt me from interrupting. "That's not a dig on Brady. That's me telling you that men like us, we need strong. We need a woman who knows when to push and when to concede. And just to be clear, when it comes to your safety you concede—always. If you can find it in you to allow him to be the man he needs to be, he'll give you nothing but beauty, darlin'. Through and through he loves you. If we didn't believe that he never would've gotten you where he has."

I knew that last statement was correct. My dad and uncles would've had words with Brady that made it so he never would've turned his head to even look at me much less tell me he wanted to take a chance at a future with me.

"He says he wants forever with me."

Everything about my uncle softened, his mouth quirked up, and he gave me a blinding smile full of uncle-ly love.

"And that surprises you?"

"Well, we haven't even been out on a date."

Knowing eyes danced with humor and mild disgust.

"Again, my sweet niece, it makes me uncomfortable saying this, but I suspect Brady wouldn't have taken it where he took it with you if he didn't know he found exactly what he wanted for his future. He wouldn't court your dad committing homicide if all he wanted was a piece of tail and he didn't intend to keep you."

Well, I certainly wasn't going to tell my uncle that that was exactly what had happened with Brady, because I was positive my father wouldn't get the chance to murder him because Clark would beat my dad to it.

Moving right along...

"Back to my problem. I shouldn't push Brady into spending the night, and when we get there if I feel him start to have a nightmare, I need to leave him to it."

"Correct."

"That doesn't sound helpful."

"You getting yourself to safety is the only thing you can do to help Brady. But just to say, your dad and I will put some effort into him letting us help him."

"I'd appreciate that."

"Not just doing that for you, Hadley. Doing it because I care about Brady, too."

"I know, and that's why I appreciate you and my dad looking after him. He's never had that so it would be good if he gets it from two of the best men I know. If you can recruit Uncle Levi and Lenox that'd be icing."

A warmth I'd experienced millions of times stole over me when my uncle's eyes went softer and his face gentled.

"Anything you need, darlin'."

I believed that.

So I asked for one more thing. "I need you to have his back. My dad may've given him his blessing, but I see a battle in my future. My dad won't be objective and Brady's gonna need someone in his corner."

"Taking care of your man." I didn't miss the approval in my uncle's tone. "I'll take his back."

"Thanks, Uncle."

Clark made his way to me and pulled me close for a hug. But it wasn't until his lips were on the top of my head did he mutter, "You're a damn fine woman, just like your mama."

Yes, I've received many blessings—family being the greatest.

My uncle rocked.

11

"Locked and loaded," Luke called out.

"Shooter, sector three-bravo, by eye go to the one-two board then one o'clock."

A second later, Luke responded, "Contact."

"Go to glass."

I glanced down at Luke's prone body as he adjusted his McMillan TAC-50, fitting the buttstock in the crook of his shoulder, his left hand coming to rest on the stock holding it tight, and his cheek on the cheekpiece.

Once I saw he was in place my gaze drifted back downrange and I squinted. With the naked eye, at five hundred meters Luke's target looked like a barely-there white dot. I brought my spotting scope up and easily found the eight-inch round steel plate.

I was pushing Luke today. Over the months, we'd graduated targets both in distance and size. Luke had been an exceptional marksman and an outstanding spotter. But that had changed when an explosion had damaged his eyesight. His left eye was worse than his right, and being as Luke was left-handed, therefore, left eye dominant, he was relearning his skills as a right-handed shooter.

"Target has red dot in center. Blue dot left bottom," Luke confirmed the plate.

"That's your target. Check parallax and mil," I instructed and looked down at my handheld ballistic computer while Luke made the proper scope adjustments to ensure his reticle and target were on the same plane and called out his range distance.

"Hold over six-point-five." Knowing that Luke was prepping his firing sequence—exhaling slowly, taking out the slack in his trigger, I prepared to give him my wind call.

"Ready."

"Left point five."

I heard the snap of the bullet leaving the barrel and three beats later there it was—the faint sound of lead hitting steel.

"Good splat, brother."

Luke lifted his head, and while I couldn't see his

face I heard the smile in his words when he muttered, "Fuck, yeah."

"Had enough?" I asked and Luke sat up.

"Yeah, 'preciate your time."

"Good calls." I heard from behind me and I tensed.

Jason Walker.

It was not unusual for one of the guys to wander out to the range, but Jason Walker and Nick Clark normally stay up at the pistol range. Both being former law enforcement, they'd taken over tactical shooting and close quarter combat training. Leaving me to handle long-range shooting.

Correctly reading Jason's appearance, Luke grabbed his McMillan, and with a lift of his chin, excused himself.

Not being a big fan of interrogations, I calmly waited out of respect. Hadley was close to her brother, Jason, and I knew that he—like the rest of the family—was protective. Jasper had obviously shared that we'd had a conversation and Jason rightly assumed I'd jump at the chance to finally connect with his sister.

"Heard you talked to my dad," Jason started, confirming my assumptions.

I also didn't miss the disapproval.

"I did. I see you don't approve."

"You're older than I am," he noted.

This was true, I was six months older than he was. Since he'd pointed out the fact, I didn't feel his statement required a response so I bit back my smartass comment and remained quiet.

"If you're looking for a place to dip your—"

"Watch your fucking mouth," I snapped and battled my rising temper. "I get you're looking out for your sister. Obviously, you've got concerns—one of those being my age. Something I admit fucked with my head over the last four years. But seeing as I held off as long as I did should tell you I had a mind for her and waited. I was also prepared to wait longer, something your sister didn't want, by the way, but I was still holding out. Some things happened last week that made it impossible to deny what we feel for each other. I was struggling with what that meant for us. Your dad talked to me and I went to her last night. We've decided to give it a go. I'm not gonna stand here and give you a bunch of guarantees and assurances. Any promises I make are to Hadley. She knows where I'm at and that's gonna have to be good enough. Don't warn me off, don't threaten me, don't say shit that'll drive a wedge between us. You've known me awhile, and in that time I've not given you one goddamn reason to believe I wouldn't treat Hadley with the care and respect she deserves. That's all you're gonna get from me, Jason, and I hope you know the respect I have for your sister extends to your whole family. Which means I wouldn't do dick to fuck her over, by extension fucking all of you."

Jason didn't look pleased and that sucked. I liked the man, liked working with him, enjoyed the time I'd spent at Walker get-togethers over the years. But I was who I was and Jason had to know this ambush wouldn't sit well with me.

"She know about your dad?"

His question pissed me off. The underlying insinuation his family was better than mine enraged me.

"Say what you wanna say, Jason? Does she know that my father's an asshole and has spent twenty years locked up, yeah I told her. Does she know my mother's dead and how that came to be, again, yeah. Does she know all of the details, no. Will she? Absolutely. But last night while I was trying to convince her to forgive me after I hurt her feelings wasn't the best time to lay the rest of my fucked-up family history on her. But she knows enough to understand that I didn't have what she had growing up. But unlike you, she didn't hold that against me."

"What the fuck, Brady? You think I'm judging you?"

"Sure as hell—"

"Then that's your shit, your insecurities you need to deal with. I was asking because I wanted to be prepared to help you guide my sister when you tell her about Nicole."

Hearing Nicole's name never failed to ignite a burn so hot it threatened to incinerate me.

"I'm not ready."

"I get that and I get why. But, Brady, her birthday's next week. I've only been around for four of them but each has been painful to watch. If you think you're gonna do your normal shut down, hole up in your house, and drown your sorrows now that you've let my sister in, you're crazy. You know she's not gonna stand for that shit."

Motherfucker.

Jason was correct on all counts.

Bad timing.

I was not ready to tell Hadley about Nicole.

I was not ready to deal with my douchebag of a father being released from prison, even though he should rot in there for the rest of his life. Nicole didn't get a second chance at life. Nicole didn't get to *live*, period. Brett Hewitt was a murdering piece of shit who took Nicole from me and the thought of him walking free set off a chemical reaction—venom and poison collided in my veins and turned into a homicidal rage.

"I'll deal with Hadley."

Jason barked a laugh that was not full of humor. It told me how big of an idiot he thought I was.

"Right. I see you don't know my sister, which is surprising since you've watched her and cataloged her every move for years. So it's shocking that I have to tell you this but you don't ever *handle* Hadley. The girl is a bloodhound. She'll sniff you out then she'll push until you spill. So here's the new deal—while my sister puts you through the wringer, you need something, you find me. I spent a lot of years shouldering guilt after Kayla died. The same kind of guilt you carry and that kind being—not yours. You didn't kill Nicole, Brady. Your dad did."

Yeah, my *dad* killed Nicole. A man whose blood runs through my veins, a man whose filthy seed made me.

Jason was wrong, I didn't carry the same guilt he had. His first wife, Kayla, had died of cancer and there wasn't a damn thing he could've done to prevent her death. Nicole drowned. I could've saved her but I'd failed. It was just as much my fault she was dead.

"I know this is gonna piss you off but I have to admit I wasn't all fired-up about my baby sister taking on a man seven years older than her. A man who has a fuckton more experience than she does, and I mean that in every way I can mean it. You've seen more, you've done more, you've had more women in your bed than I'm comfortable with. But that's my shit. That's my right as her big brother to watch out for her. But I've also watched you so I know you love her. Still not happy, but then I wasn't happy when I finally had to face one of my best friends laying claim to Delaney. And I was seriously not happy when Quinn got her hooks in Brice. Yet, I kept my nose out of it. And it's a damn good thing I did because both of them chose well. I'll give you and Hadley the same courtesy."

Before I could reply to Jason's not-so-ringing-endorsement, he walked away leaving me looking out over the rifle range.

Seriously bad timing.

I wasn't ready to give Hadley Nicole. I wasn't ready to tell her what happened and how she died. I had less than a week before the worst day of the year hit and I crumbled. It'd been over twenty years and I still couldn't stop the crippling grief. Every year it happened and every year I told myself I'd be stronger next year. And every fucking year I failed.

If I could've held out another few weeks, Nicole's birthday would've passed and I would've had a full year to prepare.

Now I had five days.

Shit timing.

12

I was running late.

Brady had texted me earlier to tell me he'd be at my place at seven to pick me up for our date. And I would've been on time had one of the uppity library board members not come in at the exact wrong time —when one of the volunteers named Sue was telling me she'd shelved the books I'd bought that Ellen had barcoded and left.

This was poor timing. Gayle Gains didn't like me much on a good day. Her reasons were only known to her, though I could guess she pretty much hated me because I argued with her. Since she was the board president, she didn't think anyone, most especially someone forty years her junior, should ever disagree with anything she said.

Once Gayle heard Sue mention *books* and *the ones you bought* in the same sentence, she'd started asking questions. That turned into a lengthy debate over censorship, wherein I argued my corner for the billionth time, Gayle argued hers, and just like all the times before, we didn't agree. But things got really dicey when she demanded Sue collect the books and discard them—as in throw them in the trash because that's where Gayle deemed they belonged.

I was so enraged I had to take a personal time-out and locked myself in my office before I did something stupid like yell at a board member. After ten minutes of deep breathing and every meditation trick Addy had taught me to calm my temper and smart mouth, I realized I was too pissed to calm down. I waited another five minutes before I left my office, grabbed the books out of the trash—yes, the trash— and left the library forty-five minutes after I was officially off.

Worse than arguing with Gayle and getting home five minutes before Brady was due to pick me up was that there'd been patrons standing around the circulation desk. Not many, but a few and no doubt they heard our argument.

I wasn't concerned that citizens heard my opinion, but I was concerned about how unprofessional it was to bicker in the library. Even though it was done quietly and most respectfully—even if I did get in a few sarcastic comments.

I kicked off my shoes and walked barefoot across my kick-ass new flooring to my dining room and tossed the books on the table. Then I turned to look at all I'd accomplished the night before. I only had another five long runs to go and I'd be done. The color was growing on me even though I'd picked it for resale value, not style. My new denim-colored couches would—

The knock at the door cut off my thoughts and I glanced down at my watch.

Damn.

I was late and Brady was early.

I made my way back to the front door, threw it open, and smiled.

"Hey. Come in. I'll just be a minute."

I stepped to the side, Brady entered, and I felt it. I wasn't sure what it was I was feeling but it was something—it was a different vibe than all the other times I'd been around him. And when I looked up and took in his eyes, I stopped breathing.

Brady Hewitt was staring at me—openly. Not a sidelong glance, not a quick peek before someone caught him, not the way he looked at me when he caught me staring at him. Open. Hungry. Beautiful.

Wow.

"Sorry I'm running late," I told him.

"Babe, come here."

"I'm right here."

"No, baby, *here*." He opened his arms and I wasn't sure if it was the tone of his voice or if I was still in a daze from the way his eyes were drinking me in. Whatever it was, I went there, and when I got close he hooked me around the waist. His head dipped and he brushed his lips over mine. Feather-soft.

"Love the way you dress for work," he muttered against my mouth and I shuddered. "Sexy and classy. Beautiful."

Holy wow.

"Thank you," I lamely returned.

I felt his lips quirk before he gave me a hard, fast peck and lifted his head.

"You wanna change or are you wearing that?"

"Where are we going?"

"The Brewery."

Fabulous.

I loved The Brewery, but it was not a skirt, blouse, and heels type of restaurant. It was an anything-goes kind of restaurant with a cool taproom, a tasting room, and outdoor seating.

"I better change."

He didn't let me go when he asked, "Didn't think to ask, is that okay? We could go to The Grille."

The Grille was another awesome restaurant, classy but not swank. Definitely skirt, blouse, and heels, or alternately a dress and heels, but not casual. It was a place you went for a special occasion. Not that my first date with Brady wasn't the very definition of special occasion, but I preferred casual.

Besides, Brady looked great in a pair of jeans that fit just right—not metrosexual tight, not loose, and since I'd seen him wear them before I knew they hugged his ass in a way that looked like he spent hours a day doing whatever exercise one did to get their booty high and tight. I wouldn't know about such an exercise, but Addy would. He was also wearing a navy blue tee. The cotton stretched across his chest, highlighting his impressive pectorals but it didn't make him look like one of those bodybuilders who loved to show off how much they worked out. Same with the material around his biceps—stretched tight but simply because Brady was built and there was no hiding it.

He looked hot. So no, I didn't want to go to The Grille necessitating him to change.

"The Brewery's my favorite. I'll hurry." I paused and looked around my empty living room before I looked back at Brady. "I'd say make yourself at home, but..." I threw my arm out to indicate the state of the room. "Still no furniture."

Then suddenly my world tilted. My crap day washed away. My argument with Gayle no longer niggled the back of my mind. Nothing else mattered but Brady and the way he was smiling at me.

An old smile, one I'd seen a lot over the years, mixed with something new I couldn't read. I had to know what it meant so I asked, "Why are you smiling at me like that?"

"How am I smiling at you?"

"I don't know. Different. The same as always, but more."

Brady's grin widened and it hit me—the change. He was now looking at me like a man who knew he was going to get lucky. Which meant *I* would get lucky.

"Babe, how 'bout you go change outta that tight-ass skirt and put on a pair of shorts that will do nothing to stop my head from filling with fantasies, but will stop the very vivid memories of what you look like with one of your work skirts hitched up around your waist, so we can go grab some dinner."

So I was slightly wrong. The smile wasn't him thinking he was going to get some, it was him remembering he'd already gotten some.

That made me shiver.

Then I turned and walked away, mentally going over my clothing options.

I hit my room and wasted no time pulling out a cute pair of white sailor shorts embellished with black buttons. I found the black wrap shirt and wedge sandals—an outfit I purchased because it was awesome—that I'd never worn. I rushed to get changed and without further primping, I was ready to go.

It wasn't until I was back downstairs that excitement turned into nervousness. I knew Brady, I'd been in love with him for years albeit from afar. Now he knew how I felt, I knew how he felt, and we'd agreed to explore those feelings. I wanted that, but I didn't. Seeing him standing in my dining room waiting to take me out on our first date made the doubt creep in.

What if this was a mistake? What if I screwed up or he did and we lost the friendship we shared? What if he was right and I was being my normal, cocky self thinking I could take on the world, but really I was unprepared to handle a man like Brady?

"Babe?"

"Huh?" I blinked and Brady came into focus.

Oh, man, he was gorgeous. The sight of him set off a new wave of doubts—this time second-guessing why a man as good-looking as him would set his sights on a woman like me. I wasn't ugly, I got my fair share of men staring and/or asking me out. Mostly due to the dark hair I'd inherited from my parents and my green eyes that I loved because they were the same shade as my dad's. But I wasn't stunning like Delaney, who had my mom's black hair and blue eyes. I wasn't over-the-top beautiful like Quinn.

"What happened to the book?" Brady asked, and my eyes dropped to the copy of *Lolita* he was holding up.

"Nothing, why?"

Thankfully, it hadn't been damaged when I rescued it from the trash.

"Um. Hadley, honey, the book's been written in."

"What?" I screeched, and made my way to him. I snatched the book from his hand.

Son of a bitch.

There it was on the title page: *You're going to*

hell. I flipped to chapter one and in red marker, *PEDOPHILE* was written across the page.

How the hell did that happen?

The book had only been on the shelf for a few hours.

"Someone's been taking books from the library and defacing them before putting them in the return bin," I sighed. "But this book is a new copy of the damaged one I replaced."

"You replaced or the library replaced?"

"Me. The library board didn't want to spend our limited funds replacing a book they deemed distasteful."

"Distasteful?"

"Yes. The book is about an older man falling in love with a younger woman." Brady's eyes narrowed and I thought maybe that hit too close to home so I rushed to explain. "A *much* older man and an underage teenager. Some people think it's—"

"I know what the book's about. What I don't under-stand is why you spent your money buying a new book."

I felt my eyes getting squinty.

"Because the library wouldn't replace it."

"You said that."

"Right. So I don't know why you're asking."

"And these?" he asked, abandoning his other question.

"The same. Those are the titles that some asswipe damaged. I replaced them and they were put back on the shelves today. But then Gayle Gains came in and threw a fit and demanded they be thrown in the trash. Since I'm not down with any books being thrown in the garbage, especially brand new ones that I just purchased, I dug them out and brought them home."

"Who's Gayle Gains?"

"An uppity bitch."

"Hadley." His growl had my eyes getting squintier.

I didn't like it when my brother, father, or uncles used that tone with me and I liked it less when Brady used it.

"I think we should drop this conversation and go get something to eat."

"And I think you need to tell me who Gayle Gains is. After that, you can explain why this one," he picked up a copy of *Thirteen Reasons Why*, "says, we warned you—"

Brady didn't finish. Probably because I yanked the book out of his hand, flipped it open, and on the copyright page in bold red fucking marker, there it was.

We warned you and you didn't listen. You must be cleansed of your sins.

What the actual hell?

Cleansed of your sins?

That was cray-cray.

"I don't know what that means," I told him. "Who says, you need to be cleansed?"

"I'm more concerned about who the "you" part is. *Who* has been warned?"

"Got me. The library?"

I was so irritated that more books had been destroyed, and even more pissed that someone had the audacity to do it *in* the library with other people around, that I missed the change in Brady. But when I lifted my eyes and caught sight of his tense posture, set jaw, and glacial stare, I went on alert.

I knew that look.

I'd seen it many, many times before.

"Brady—"

"Have you told your dad about what's going on?"

"What? Why? No."

"Why? Some whackjob is making threats."

Shit.

"No, some whackjob is defacing books."

"We warned you and you didn't listen. You must be cleansed of your sins," he snapped and I wondered how he'd memorized exactly what was written.

"I think you're making this into a bigger deal than it is," I noted, and wished I could rewind the words.

That was because Brady's features went stone-cold which meant I shivered for a different reason as a chill raced down my spine.

"Brady—"

"You got cameras in the library?"

"Brady—"

"What about outside?"

"Listen—"

"Honest to God, Hadley, if you think after I've waited my whole miserable life to find you, then had to wait four fucking years longer before I could at long last make you mine, I'd fuck around with some asshole making threats, then you think wrong."

His whole life to find me?

God.

Damn.

I didn't know what to say to that.

"I get that. But I don't think *I'm* actually in danger. I think the books are, not me physically. Besides, the library board approves what's in the library, not me. So if anyone was in danger it would be one of them. I just work there. And to answer your question, no, there are no cameras inside or outside of the library."

"I don't fucking like this," he grunted.

"I'm getting that, Brady, but I'm not in any danger. And besides, after the holy hell fit Gayle pitched today, those books aren't going back on the shelves so it's over anyway. The asshole won and censored what I can carry."

Relief so stark washed over him. My heart squeezed, only the constriction grated.

"I hope you know, I don't need to run to Daddy every time something happens. I'm perfectly capable of handling any problem if it should arise. I don't like it when my brother butts in so I can tell now, I won't like it any more if you try to do it."

"Noted."

Experience told me that Brady's response was too easy, too flippant to be real.

I quietly studied Brady trying to figure out his play. Then his lips tipped up into a cocky grin.

Um. Wrong.

"What does "noted" mean?"

"In this instance, it means I'm starving, I wanna take my girl to The Brewery, and I wanna do it in this lifetime. So I'm not gonna have a lengthy discussion about how I know she's fully capable of taking care of herself and whatever problems come her way, she's just not gonna do it."

So I was right. His reply was dismissive at best, asshole-ish at worst. But whichever it was, he planned on butting in.

"I don't like that, Brady."

"I can see how you wouldn't, being as your brother's probably butted in a lot because he's rightfully protective. What you don't get now but you will, is that I'm not your brother."

"I know that," I snapped.

"I'm your man."

I clamped my mouth shut and Brady's grin went from cocky to smug.

"Warning, keep smiling at me like that and you won't be my man for long."

If I meant to say more it died in my throat when Brady's hand darted out, tagged me around the middle, and pulled me to him.

"Right. I'm not your brother, meaning I don't have brotherly concern for you. That doesn't mean I don't have care and concern. That doesn't mean I won't wade in and make sure you're safe. This is who I am, Hadley. You take the good with the bad. And I promise you, baby, I'll make the good so good, you'll overlook the bad because you'll know I'm stepping in to protect you because I love you, not because I'm a dick."

The area between my legs fluttered at the mention of the good he could give me. I definitely wanted more of that goodness. But I didn't want another man bossing me around, even if that was coated in love. Jasper Walker took protecting his family to an extreme. He taught my brother to do the same. I can't deny my sisters and I didn't benefit from their efforts, we certainly did, but that didn't mean sometimes it wasn't annoying as hell.

"Sex doesn't—"

"Not talking about sex, Hadley. Though that's part of the good we're both gonna get. I'm talking about you knowing you're loved so thoroughly, so deeply, you'll look back over your life and wonder if you've ever been loved before."

That was big. No, that was huge. He knew my family, so he knew how deeply my family loved each other.

"And you think you can love me like that?"

"I already do love you like that. Up until now, I haven't been able to show you. But I will. I'm not some controlling prick who wants you reporting on your whereabouts. I don't need you to tell me about some jerk at the grocery store cutting in front of you at the checkout line, or some disagreement you have with a co-worker. What I need to know about is some crazy person is defacing books and writing threats. Whether they're direct or indirect I still wanna know. And not so I can step in and take over, so I can have your back, making sure you're safe while you're being Hadley."

I loved all of that, except the last part.

"What does "being Hadley" mean?"

"Baby."

He smiled but said nothing further.

"What? That's not an explanation."

"You're you. A force of nature. You zero in on something and you don't stop. Not even when you should. Part of the reason I fell in love with you. When Hurricane Hadley wants to do something, nothing stops her. You're the calm, the storm, and the rainbow. When you roll in, I never know if I'm getting the gale-force winds that're gonna steal my breath or a calm breeze that never fails to warm. That's you. That's my Hadley. Determined. Brave. A fighter. The only thing I want is to make you safe while you're being you."

Seeing as he knew me, he was right, that was me.

I didn't look before I jumped. Not because I was naive or stupid, but because I knew whatever the outcome, I'd be all right. And if I wasn't, I'd fight to make it all right. That was just who I was and Brady knew it.

So I made my decision the way I made pretty much every decision in my life. I went with my heart.

"Okay."

"Okay?" His lips quirked and I didn't let that irritate me.

"Yep. Are you ready to go?"

"Need a kiss first."

"You already had one." I pointed out.

"That wasn't a kiss."

"No? Funny, I remember your lips touching mine."

"Babe, quit fucking around and kiss me."

"What if I don't kiss on the first date?"

Brady's smile turned audible when he started chuckling.

"What's funny?"

"How many dates have you been on in the last four years?"

I pinched my lips and narrowed my eyes.

Bastard knew I hadn't had any.

"How many dates have *you* had?"

"Seeing as I already told you I haven't fucked a woman since I've met you, that'd be none."

I wasn't sure what was bigger—telling me he was my man, already telling me he loved me deeply, knowing me the way he did, or Brady not having sex for four years because he met me and knew I was his. They were all huge, but Brady being all man, extremely good-looking, virile, meant he could have any woman he wanted. Yet for years he lived celibate —for me, for us. That was massive. That proved all the other things he'd told me were true. He was mine and he loved me.

"Fine. You can kiss me."

With another chuckle, Brady dipped his head and took my mouth. This time it wasn't a hard press of his lips. It was tongues sliding, tasting, claiming, and so good my toes curled in my sandals.

Brady Hewitt was really mine.

13

"Ohmygod," Hadley groaned, then shoved her face back into my neck.

Her teeth sank into my flesh, then she used her tongue to soothe the sting, not stopping until she made it to my ear and whispered, "Faster, honey."

I didn't obey her command, something she'd been demanding for a good long while.

I was taking my time giving her what I should've the first time—slow and gentle on a soft mattress. However, Hadley was of a different mind. Any other time I would've gladly granted her what she wanted, but not this time—our first time in a bed after a great date that included good food and better conversation.

"Best date I ever had, baby."

"Brady," she moaned as I continued to rock into her.

"Dream come true you sitting across from me smiling."

"Honey," she whimpered when I swiveled my hips and ground down on her clit.

Hadley's neck bent back, her back arched and came off the bed, her hooded eyes locked onto mine, and her thighs pressed tighter against my ribs.

Fuck, yeah.

"Need you to come for me, Hadley."

"Yes."

"Wrap your legs around me."

I reached back, hooked my arm under Hadley's knee, and tilted her ass so she could take me deeper.

Nirvana.

"Good Christ," I growled, and drove into her drenched pussy, fighting back the urge to blow.

Hadley whimpered incoherently, her pussy fluttered, and with a deafening shout, she exploded around my cock.

So fucking tight and hot I slammed into her chasing my own climax. When I was nearly there she righted her head and I caught sight of her lazy, green eyes half-mast and dreamy.

Beautiful.

"Dream come true."

"Yes," she whispered, and my mouth collided with hers just in time for me to grunt my orgasm against her lips. Her tongue came out, gliding over my bottom lip and I stilled, allowing the bliss only she gave to wash over me.

Heaven.

My storm, my calm, my everything.

I started gliding, letting the last tremors leave my body, sliding slowly in and out, committing moment to memory. The feel of her under me, her soft skin, the muted mews against my lips, the way my chest had expanded—so full of love for her I thought I'd explode.

The great thing about this moment, unlike the first time I had her, was that I didn't have to hide. I didn't have to hold back how I felt. I could say what I wanted to say and do it freely.

"I love you, Hadley."

I felt the air rush over my lips as she swiftly inhaled. But before she could say anything I kissed her.

Different than the other times we kissed. Slow and deep, I drank from her. Needing to taste everything she felt, not needing the words as long as I had this. Her open to me, legs still tight around my hips, my cock still planted deep, her hands on my shoulders, fingernails digging into my skin, her tongue in my mouth.

Linked together.

Regrettably, I had to break the kiss.

"As much as it pains me losing your hot, slick, wet pussy, you gotta let go. Condom."

Hadley's legs tightened and her hot, slick, wet pussy spasmed. I cataloged that for future use. My sweet, classy librarian liked dirty.

Excellent.

"Seriously, babe, before we have a mess, gotta get rid of this."

Her limbs loosened, her legs opened, I pulled out and paused to look down at her.

Exquisite.

So beautiful, she wasn't just my dream come true, my fantasy. She was my everything. Breath. Sustenance. For years, she'd been my reason for living when so many times I wanted to give up. Give in to my family's curse and drown in a bottle of booze.

"Brady?"

"Yeah?"

"I love you, too."

Fucking hell. I was wrong, I'd needed those words more than I thought.

I rolled off her, then the bed, and disposed of the condom as quickly as I could.

I hit the bed, slid in next to her, and tucked her to my side.

"Are you staying the night?"

Fuck. Shit.

"No, baby, but I'll stay until you fall asleep."

"Okay," she sighed but said no more.

Her easy acceptance made me feel like a total dick. I knew I needed to talk to someone about my nightmares. They didn't come frequently but they happened. And with Nicole's birthday and the anniversary of her death coming up, I was dreaming every night, waking up coated in sweat, the taste of bitterness and failure in my mouth.

I needed to try and I would.

After Nicole's birthday.

Just one more week, then I'd give Hadley the rest.

14

Two days after my first date with Brady that had ended in outstanding sex but also ended with me sleeping alone in bed, I watched him saunter into the library. This was unexpected but not unwelcomed.

I was in my office on the phone with a first-grade teacher at a local elementary school. The call was important, but seeing Brady through the windows of my office, I wanted to hang up and find out why he was there.

Then I saw Ellen smile and point toward my office and my heart rate spiked when Brady turned and caught sight of me.

He wasn't smiling, as a matter of fact, his brows were pinched and it looked like something was wrong.

"Steph, I hate to cut this short but there's someone here to see me. I have your class down for every Monday for the next six weeks. All I need is permission slips and you're good to go."

"Thanks, Hadley."

"Anytime. We love having the kids in the library. I'll curate a special display each week to go with your lesson plan," I said and watched Brady as he made his way to my open door.

"That would be great. The first Monday will be about responsibility. We'll go through all the 'character counts' pillars."

"Awesome. I know just the books to pull." Brady stopped in the doorway and his expression looked no less troubled. "We'll talk soon."

"Yeah. Thanks again."

I rushed through saying goodbye and hung up.

"What's wrong?"

"Have you been outside today?" Brady weirdly inquired.

"In general, yes. Since I got to the library and started working? No. Why?"

His eyes glittered and I pushed away from my desk to stand. "What's wrong?" I asked again.

"There are a bunch of books dumped in front of the green—"

"What do you mean dumped?"

"Babe, calm down."

Calm down? Was he nuts? I'd had enough of books being destroyed.

"What does dumped mean, Brady?" I could hear my voice getting tighter as I spoke.

"Shit, Hadley, they're just dumped on the ground. Looks like some pages are torn out. I think you need to call it in."

Why hadn't I thought of that?

"I'll call Ethan," I told him and glanced around my desk for my phone. "Shit. I think I left my cell in the car."

"Baby, you're killing me with the cell. That's part of why I'm here. I texted you to ask if you wanted to get lunch. I didn't hear back so I called. After the third call, I decided to ask in person."

Crap.

"Sorry. But just so you know, you could've called the library."

"Right. I could've, but it'd be helpful if you kept your cell close."

We were back to treading on dangerous ground. I'd heard that enough from my family over the years.

"Brady—"

"That's not me being a dick. That's just smart. In

today's world, anything could happen and it's plain smart to keep your cell phone charged and close."

On a good day, I didn't want to argue about cell phones. I knew he was right, as was my mom and sister the five-hundred times they berated me about not being able to get ahold of me. Logically I understood I was a single female who left work after dark, lived alone, and didn't have a landline at home. But I seriously hated the stupid thing. I didn't like to be available twenty-four-seven. I enjoyed unplugging and relaxing.

It was no secret I loved my family. But growing up our house was noisy. There were seven of us, four of the occupants were girls. Delaney and Quinn fought about everything, then made up and were best friends, then fought more the next day. I was a twin, which meant Addy and I had done everything together. I loved my sister more than anything, but growing up in a house full of love that was expressed loudly made me appreciate quiet. I knew Addy did, too. We'd talked about it when we were moving out of our parents' house. Everyone thought we'd move out and get a place together, but she was of the same mind—she wanted her own space, too. That didn't mean we weren't close or that we didn't love each other, but it was time for us to be individuals and not Addy and Hadley—The Twins.

"If I say you're right, can we avoid a lengthy discussion? Because I want to see the books, call Ethan, then go get lunch."

"Yeah, Hadley, we can avoid a lengthy discussion as long as you keep your cell near."

I rolled my eyes and stared at the ceiling a moment wondering if I was crazy getting involved with a man who my uncle had warned me was going to be protective and I had to know when to push back and when to concede. I figured since no one in my family let up on this topic, this was a prime example of when I needed to concede.

"Babe?" he prompted, and I rolled my eyes back to him.

"Fine," I snapped and he smiled.

It took a lot not to call him out on his smug grin, and he knew it did because he started chuckling.

"I see that was hard for you," he noted and I narrowed my eyes. "Appreciate you agreeing to that."

He sounded sincere, reinforcing my earlier conclusion. He wasn't being controlling—he cared about my safety.

"How many books are out there?" I whispered.

Brady didn't answer until he made it across my office and wrapped his arms around me.

"Brace, baby, there looks to be at least a dozen. But some might be salvageable."

Shit.

I slowly exhaled and shook my head.

"I don't get it. How could anyone destroy such beautiful works of art?"

"I don't know."

I rested my forehead on his chest and tried to calm down. But not even the delicious smell of his cologne worked. His arms tightened and I felt his lips touch the top of my head where he muttered, "Let's get this done."

"I hate this. And what's worse is, whatever books are out there ruined I won't be able to replace. Gayle will make sure of it."

Brady's body went solid and he asked, "Is it possible she's destroying the books?"

"I wish I could say yes, because I seriously don't like her, but she's on a week's vacation in Florida with her family and they left yesterday. Those books weren't out there this morning when I got to work."

"You need cameras outside."

"Yeah, that's never going to happen. There's no money for that and our budget's on the chopping block for the third year in a row. With the way things are looking I'm damn lucky to have a job."

Brady gave me a squeeze and slightly pulled away. I looked up at him, giving him what he'd non-verbally asked for.

"Your job in jeopardy?"

"Yes," I told him honestly. "And I'd appreciate it if you don't talk to anyone about that. I love my job. It would suck to lose it, but I know there's a job waiting for me at Triple Canopy so I know financially I'll be okay. I just wanted to prove I could make it on my own without my family's help."

"I get that." Brady held my stare and something that looked a lot like pride shone back. "You got my word I won't mention it."

"YOU NEED CAMERAS," my cousin Ethan declared, and for the second time in the last hour, I rolled my eyes, this time toward the cloudy sky since we were standing outside.

"I've heard that before. But as I explained to Brady, that's not in the budget."

Ethan's gaze slid from me to Brady and after a moment he asked, "Are you gonna—"

"No," I cut in before my cousin could finish his question. "No one is using Triple Canopy resources for the library. And especially not for this. You said yourself that vandalism isn't a serious crime. And even if you caught the person returning the damaged books, it would be near-impossible to prove they actually did the damage. And if we could prove they did because the damaged property is books there'd likely be no fine, no probation, and maybe restitution if we're lucky. So it's not worth involving Triple Canopy."

"Babe. I'm not worried about the vandalism and neither is Ethan and you know it. What's written inside those books is so jacked it's freaked me out. Especially the part about cleansing. That's the second time I've read that fuckin' word in one of these books, and, baby, I was freaked the first time I saw it. Now seeing it a second time, I'm *concerned*."

"He's right." Ethan sided with Brady.

"Are you agreeing with him as my cousin or as a cop?" I snarked.

"Both. Don't stand there and hand me crap, Hadley. Our family's in the business of protection. We've seen more than our fair share of fucked-up shit and Brady's absolutely correct. A pile of ruined books sucks but the shit that's written in them is concerning—most especially the parts about the unholy needing to be cleansed. That's crazy talk, Had. That goes beyond someone who's spiritual or religious and straight to Crazy Town."

So they were both right and I'd gone from pissed to creeped out.

Whoever was defacing the books was coming unglued. Fifteen books outside. Each book had words blacked out. Not just a few—it seemed that any word the author used that the person deemed inappropriate was crossed out. And in each book, there was a threat varying from the author needing to be cleansed to the library needing to stop carrying such books or everyone was going to hell.

"I'm taking this seriously," I assured them. "But I still don't want Triple Canopy resources being used. I'll talk to the county commissioners, maybe I can get emergency funding. I know you have to take the books but will you send me pictures? I need to file a claim with the board."

"Yeah. And I'll put the word out around the station, maybe have some cruisers drive by if they're in the area, and I'll check in with the other libraries to see if they're having issues, too."

Damn. I hadn't thought of that.

"I appreciate you, cousin."

"I know you do," he sighed. "Please, for the love of God, be careful. Don't go all Hadley Walker and do something crazy."

"I resent that."

"I'm sure you do but it doesn't make my warning any less necessary." Then Ethan sobered and a look I didn't like sheered through his features. "This is Detective Lenox talking to you. I don't like this, Hadley. I've been a cop long enough to listen to my gut, and my gut's telling me not to fuck around with this. Be smart. Be vigilant. Be careful. You see something, you say something. You find another book, you call me. I'll have these books printed but my guess is we'll find a lot of them so it will be useless but I'm still doing it. You talk to the commissioners and see if they'll put cameras in the parking lot. They should've already been installed seeing as the library closes after dark and you have kids and the elderly walking out. What you do not do is go at this alone."

"Ethan," I started gently. "Don't you think we're overreacting a little? I mean, someone's just—"

"Learned the hard way to pay attention to the red flags," he returned and said no more.

Not wanting to witness the pain in my cousin's eyes I looked at my feet instead. It was a long time ago, but he had learned the hard way—his wife

Honor almost died because her crazy stepfather had kidnapped her. No one saw the threat, including Honor. But Ethan *had* seen the warning signs but no one thought the man would go that far.

"I'll be vigilant and I'll be careful," I promised.

"Good."

When no one spoke, I lifted my gaze and found Ethan smiling.

"Glad you finally pulled your thumb out." That came from Ethan and wasn't directed at me. He was staring at Brady. "Now she's yours and you've bought yourself the task of keeping her in line."

Before I could tell my cousin that no one kept me in line—*ever*, Brady got in there.

"You're damn right she's mine. But if you think anyone's keeping a Walker in line you're mistaken. The task I bought is keeping my woman safe, and that I'll do."

God, I loved that Brady knew that.

"But, babe," Brady continued before I could voice my appreciation. "No bullshit, you don't do anything but keep an eye out. That's it. No super sleuthing, no setting up stakeouts in the parking lot, no lurking around the library trying to catch someone in the act. You're a librarian, not a cop. You do your job and leave the rest to us."

I didn't like that.

"If I happen to be walking through my place of employment and see someone—"

"You immediately go into your office and call me. After that, you keep yourself there and I'll call Ethan on my way to you."

"You're annoying," I told him.

"You think that because I will not be running into a burning building to save my woman before she dies a fiery death. I will not find my woman shot and bleeding out. I will not hightail my ass to a cemetery to find a crazy bitch pointing a gun at my woman's head and threatening to take her away from me. You wanna know why that is, Hadley? Because you're not gonna do a damn thing to put me in that position."

Direct shot.

All of that had happened and I hated the reminders. Tuesday Clark almost died in a house fire. Delaney was taken by a crazy bitch to a cemetery. And Quinn had been shot and thrown out of a moving car and had almost died. All nightmares my family had endured and so had Brady. He'd been there, too. He'd witnessed the trauma those situations had wrought.

I didn't want to be next. I also didn't want my

family to go through something like that again, and I seriously didn't want Brady to, either.

But it was more. I grew up shrouded in love. I knew what it felt like to be protected, and because of that, I'd been free to be me, to find my own way, become the person I wanted to be knowing I could take risks and if I failed I'd be okay. I also knew not everyone had what I had, therefore I appreciated it.

But this was different—it *felt* different.

Brady had my back. Not as a family friend but as *my* man.

The difference was huge. So huge, I wished we were in private so I could tell him how much it meant to me. But alas, we were standing in the library parking lot with my cousin in attendance so my vows of love and appreciation would have to wait.

But I could give him *something*, so I did.

"Okay, Brady. If I see something I'll call you."

"Thank you." His relief was stark and that made me feel something, too.

Another blessing.

And as soon as we were alone, hopefully in my bed, I'd show him my gratitude.

"That's my cue," Ethan muttered. "I'm going to the station. I'll be in touch."

"Thanks, E."

"Anytime, Had."

Chin lifts and "laters" were exchanged between Brady and Ethan. Then we stood and watched my cousin drive away.

"You still got time for lunch?" Brady asked.

"Yeah."

"Let's go."

"I need to grab my purse."

"Unless you need it for some reason other than thinking it's because your wallet's in there, you don't need it."

"So what you're telling me in macho-man, alpha, ape talk is, you're paying."

"Yep."

"I can pay. You bought dinner last night."

"Do you need your purse?" he asked, completely ignoring what I'd said.

"No. But I need to tell Ellen I'm leaving."

"Then go tell her, baby, I'll wait here."

"We're not going to discuss who's paying, are we?"

"Payback for lunch is cook dinner tomorrow night. BBQ pulled pork sandwiches with that coleslaw you make."

Pulled pork sandwiches were my specialty.

Everyone loved them, but my coleslaw was even better.

"Deal."

"Go, baby," he muttered. But the way he said it with his tone low and gentle made me shiver.

I loved it when he called me baby. I loved it when he gentled his voice. But I really loved when he did both of those and his eyes went soft. The trifecta of hotness. And it was hot because it was aimed my way.

15

I was closing down for the night eager to get to Hadley's for dinner when Drake walked into my office.

Stone-cold and pissed.

Fuck.

"The Lieutenant Colonel in charge of the 8th Special Forces Group just ate lead," Drake told me.

The 8th Special Forces Group was Liberty McCoy's unit. The Lieutenant Colonel, her company commander and the man we'd been investigating for months. The commanding general of Army CID had refused to dig into the unit, for reasons we all understood but didn't like. The Hell-raisers as the unit was called were a black ops team, meaning their missions weren't classified, they were nonexistent. Anyone looking into the Hellraisers would find they were an Intelligence unit under the Army's psychological warfare division.

There were so many layers of security we were barely scratching the surface. And the fuck of it was, Liberty had some of the information we needed but was bound by oath. None of us would put her in the uncomfortable position of having to choose between finding the person who had endangered her life and her vow of absolute silence.

"Self-inflicted?" I asked as Drake sat down.

"According to our sources, that's what the Army's prepared to rule it."

"Fuck. That's not good. Did he leave a note?"

"Nope. And there's more than a few things wrong with the crime scene."

I settled back in my chair and braced. I'd gotten to know Drake well over the last nine months he'd been with Triple Canopy. He was normally the most laid back of all of us except when it came to his fiancée. Then the calm slipped and deadly intent toward the person responsible for her capture and subsequent torture took over.

"Those would be?" I prompted.

"Greg Berkshire was right-handed. GSW to the left temple. There are also ligature marks around his wrists. His house was ransacked, and his computer wiped clean."

None of that coincided with a suicide. But I was more interested in how Drake knew about the Lieutenant Colonel's house being ransacked.

"You know this how?"

"We got word and Logan got his ass over there before CID could get there."

Logan had been Drake's second-in-command when they were in the teams together. So it was only natural now that they both worked for Triple Canopy. Logan would still be Drake's go-to person. Trey, Matt, Luke, Logan, and Drake made an exceptional team, which was exactly why Clark, Lenox, Levi, and Jasper wanted all five men to come aboard.

I wholeheartedly agreed. When an element worked, you did your best to keep them together. The pitfall to that was getting them to work with others outside their unit.

"You get approval to send in Logan?"

Drake's eyes narrowed and he leaned forward, gearing up to take my head off. But I beat him to the punch.

"Brother, you are not in the Navy anymore."

"Know that," he grunted.

"Right, which means you're no longer jammed

up with government procedure and rules. But you still have a chain of command and protocol you have to follow. That protocol's in place so if shit goes sideways we can take your back and not have to guess at what you were doing and why. We are all dedicated to finding the person responsible for what happened to Liberty. I get you feel like it's your duty as her man to shoulder the burden, but it is not. You have firepower at your disposal. Don't shut it out."

Drake held my gaze then jerked his chin. "Understood." He leaned back in his chair.

Now that that was over, it was time to move on.

"Did Logan get his computer?"

"Yeah. He gave it to Dylan."

Dylan Welsh was a computer genius. Natural talent that had been honed under Blake McCoy's expert guidance. Blake was also a natural but her skills had been sharpened by the CIA. Together, the two made an excellent team. However, like her husband Levi, she was supposed to be retiring, and like her husband, she was slowly doing that but not willing to completely step back until they'd found justice for her daughter.

"Then Dylan will find something for us. Any word from Liberty?"

"Yeah, she'll be home in a few days." There was no missing the terseness in Drake's voice.

"She see any action?"

He blew out a breath. "Always."

"Has she made a decision about reenlisting?"

"Not yet. She has awhile left on this contract."

I nodded my understanding. Drake wanted Liberty safe—ideally, that'd be her not signing another contract—but Drake knew better than to voice that opinion to her.

"We'll meet first thing tomorrow to go over whatever Dylan's found on Berkshire's computer."

"Copy that." Drake stood but made no move to leave. "Happy for you, Brady."

Since Drake had opened the door, I decided to walk through it.

"Liberty still have nightmares?"

Drake's posture stiffened and went on alert.

"Sometimes. Rare, but they still come." His gaze became knowing and he asked, "Is that what's held you back from Hadley?"

"Part of the reason, yeah. When they hit, sometimes I can wake myself up before they get bad. Other times I wake up when I crash onto the floor after twisting around in bed. I don't want her to see that shit but I really don't want to accidentally hurt her because I'm trapped in hell and have no control over my body."

"Have you ever thought about talking to someone about them?"

Jesus fuck.

Time for honesty.

"Tried that. Was in therapy for two years and the nightmares got worse."

"No, I mean talking to someone who knows, not some doctor who thinks they're an expert because they've learned about shit in a book. Clark would be a good person to start with. I don't think it happens to him much anymore but he'd understand. And I know Liberty would talk to you. Therapy helped her, but I think her openly talking to her family helped more."

Nolan Clark was an imposing man with a sharp bullshit meter. I respected him as a boss and as a friend. He was also Hadley's uncle and I needed to tread lightly talking to him about my concerns.

"Clark might not be keen talking to me about my issues, especially because after twenty years of burying them, I'm willing to face them only because I want my bed to be a safe place for his niece to sleep."

Drake grinned. "Yeah, I'd leave that last part out.

Though the man's not stupid, and since you've worked for him longer than I have, I reckon you know that. But I'd still talk to him. One thing I've learned about this family, and since they don't hide it I know you haven't missed it, they love hard. And they do it without blinders on. Clark might not want to think about his baby niece in bed with a man, but he also wants her safe and happy. The fact you're standing here breathing after you've claimed Hadley should tell you something. The same way they welcomed me, they're welcoming you. Only, you've been part of their family long before you and Hadley got together and that should tell you something, too. I think Clark would be pissed he knew you were battling demons, ones he could help you with, and you *didn't* reach out."

"'Preciate the wisdom." I stood.

"Anytime. Before I let you go, how's Luke's progress? Is he almost ready to take over classes with Matt?"

Matt Kessler had been a SEAL sniper before he joined Triple Canopy. Luke was his spotter. Together they made an incomparable sniper cell. Once Drake was unfairly discharged from the Navy, and Trey and Luke were medically discharged, Logan and Matt left the teams as well.

Matt and I had been teaching the sniper course, something I wanted to expand. That meant booking more classes but I could only do that if Matt and Luke took some of the class load.

I nodded. "He's there. His shot placements are excellent, but he still needs to build confidence, which will come with muscle memory. He still goes to glass with his left eye and when he does, it pisses him off that he's forgotten he's now a right-handed shooter. It's a hard habit to break, so he'll need time. But with all of that, I feel the best way to get him over it is to put him out there. So next week, he and Matt are taking their first group out to the range."

"You going out to oversee?"

"Hell no. That will defeat the purpose of throwing Luke into his new role. He doesn't think he's ready. I know he is, so I'm tossing his ass into a class as the lead instructor. Matt will be there to take his back, but each of them has a specific skillset to teach and Matt won't be able to hold his hand."

"I agree. Luke's damn good, and losing most of his eyesight in his dominant eye has fucked with his self-confidence. Only way he's gonna get it back is if someone forces him." Drake fixed me with another grin. "Glad it's you, brother, and not me."

"Don't thank me. Next week you have a group of

weekend warriors coming for tactical shooting 101. You're gonna hear enough lingo tossed around to wish you were deaf for the afternoon."

That got a chuckle. "No doubt. Have a good night with Hadley."

"Plan to."

Drake left and I finished closing down for the night.

Hadley and her famous pork sandwiches were waiting.

16

I was on my hands and knees clicking a board into place when I heard the knock.

"Come in!" I yelled and finished laying the plank.

"Babe."

At the tone of Brady's voice, I glanced around the floor and found my cell five feet away from me.

"If you tried to call or text me and it didn't go through then your phone's on the fritz because mine's right there, and I even made sure the ringer was all the way up so I'd hear you if you called."

Brady was silent so I craned my neck back to find his eyes had zeroed in on my ass. I cleared my throat and waited for his gaze to lift. This took a while, seeing as he was clearly enjoying the view.

That actually made me feel warm and squishy inside. Years, I'd wished Brady would give me a clear sign he felt the same attraction I'd felt. And finally, I was feeling it. And not because his eyes were glued to my ass—though I did like that part, too—but because he was standing in my living room and the reason he was there was to have dinner. A meal I'd cooked at his request. And he'd requested it because he'd eaten it before at family parties. Which meant there was already a layer of friendship that had naturally slid into an open intimacy.

"You didn't lock the door," he told me.

"What?"

"The front door, Hadley, you left it unlocked."

"Yeah. I knew you were coming over."

"Neighborhood's not shit, but it's not great. And just to say, even if it was great, you need to keep the door locked."

Sweet Jesus.

"Fine." I gave in not wanting to hear him extol the merits of locking doors. "But if you want me to keep the door locked when I know you're coming over then you better take my extra key. As you can see, I'm busy. I didn't want to have to stop and get up to answer the door. And just to add, I don't have a doorbell so if I'm upstairs it's highly unlikely

I'll hear you knock. Especially if I was doing something like say, taking a shower or blow-drying my hair."

"A key to your house?" He looked at me slightly dumbfounded.

"Well, I'm not offering you one to my car."

"Don't be a smartass."

"Then don't ask silly questions. Of course to my house."

Brady continued to study me. Now that he wasn't looking at my booty, I felt stupid on my hands and knees so I stood. Once I was on my feet, Brady closed the distance. Once he had me in his arms he leaned down, dropping his mouth on mine. I opened and he slid his tongue inside. Then Brady took a good amount of time building the kiss. Taking us from slow glides to seriously hot. By the time he broke the kiss, I was panting and hoping he didn't want to eat right away because I could think of a better way to occupy our time.

"A key to your house is a big step, darlin'."

His gaze was so intense it burned straight through me, heating me up from the inside out.

"Doesn't feel that way. It kinda feels like we've been in the slow lane for a lotta years and we're now finally going at an acceptable speed."

His lips twitched before he teased, "What speed is that, Mach 1?"

"If Mach 1 is us finally admitting we have feelings for each other, sharing meals, conversation, phenomenal sex, and flirty texts, then yes, Mach 1."

"Flirty texts?" He chuckled.

"Well, what would you call texting me to tell me to wear your favorite bra? And you can't call it your favorite when you've only seen four. I have better ones than the purple one you've requested. Though I'll confirm now I did fulfill your request even though it felt more like an order." I watched Brady's gray eyes flare and I liked that a whole lot. So much, I wanted more of it so I reminded him. "Though you don't get the matching panties because you already tore them off of me. But I did find a suitable substitute and I don't mind you ripping these, either."

"You need a couch" was his strange reply.

When he grabbed my hand and pulled me across the room, up the stairs, and tossed me on my bed, I understood his statement. And even though my lack of furniture downstairs delayed his plans, he wasted no time executing them once he had me in my room.

He tore off my shorts down my legs. Ditto with my t-shirt, only that was yanked up and over my head. He remained standing at the side of the bed, spread my legs wide, pushed my panties to the side, then his face was between my thighs. His mouth worked miracles—tongue flicks followed by long swipes and hard licks. It took him approximately five minutes to have me writhing on the bed, primed and ready to explode. So when he slowed what he was doing, my hands went to his head and I fisted his hair and lifted my hips.

"Almost."

With one last long graze of his tongue, he lifted his head and kissed my belly, then stood to his full height.

I didn't have time to appreciate the man standing before me. The man I'd fallen for. I'd taken one look at him and knew he was meant to be mine. The man I'd subsequently spent years falling further in love with. Brady's eyes held mine, but his hands were busy unfastening his jeans. Seconds later, he fell forward, his palms planted on the bed next to my head, and he surged in.

"Nothing more beautiful than when I'm first inside of you."

"Skin," I begged. Thankfully, he understood without further prompting.

He managed to get his shirt off, all the while still thrusting. When he accomplished that task, his next was to yank down the cups of my bra, exposing my breasts. If I hadn't been primed and ready to explode, I would've commented on this. But as he drove in and pulled out, each stroke bringing me closer, I was at a loss for words.

"Nothing feels better than you. Nothing, baby."

I was certain nothing felt better than him either, but I couldn't tell Brady that because he powered in harder. So hard, my body was jolting and his hands went to my hips, keeping me at the edge of the bed. At the same time, he yanked me down on his cock as he pitched forward. *Deep.* So deep, my back arched, my legs around his hips tightened, and I dangled on the precipice of a huge orgasm. So huge, I was afraid to let go.

"That's it, Hadley," Brady groaned. "Goddamn. So beautiful. Feels so good. Give it to me."

"Can't," I panted and tightened my inner muscles, trying to keep my climax at bay.

"Jesus," he grunted and pounded into me.

"Too much," I stuttered out.

Brady drove in faster, harder, until I couldn't hold back. Everything narrowed to him. To us. What he was doing between my legs, how he smelled, how he felt pressed against me, how his breath fanned over my neck, how full my heart was. Everything. It was already too much but his teeth grazed my shoulder, then moved to the sensitive skin under my jaw and I lost control.

Without me telling them to, my hips bucked, my body locked, and in a rush, I exploded.

This was not an orgasm, it was a full-body nuclear detonation. Hot and cold washed over my skin, my breath caught, my lungs burned, and my heart melted.

"Jesus Christ," Brady moaned and slammed into me, planting as deep as he could.

Absentmindedly, I felt his cock jerk.

Time stopped.

Everything stopped.

Then Brady moved, lifting his face from my neck. His beautiful eyes came to mine and I knew something had changed. The usual sadness that lingered was absent. But there was something else in its place. Whatever it was, wasn't good.

"Don't let me break you, baby."

"What?"

"Don't let the ugliness I got inside me break you."

Fear.

That was what I was seeing, the sight of it repugnant. Cruel and horrendous.

"You won't break me."

"Promise me, Hadley. Promise you won't let me ruin you. I couldn't live with myself if I hurt you. I know you don't want to see it, but you have to know. Deep down, you know I'm screwed up. I want to untangle all the shit in my head, I just don't know how. I'll do anything to protect you from it. Swear it, baby, I'll try to get rid of it for you. Just don't let me break you while I'm trying."

I felt my throat clog with emotion—mixed emotions. Some vicious in their loathing. Some gentle in their need to soothe him.

"I promise you won't break me. But you have to promise to let me help work out what's eating you. No man as selfless, as protective as you, should live with ugliness. I want the shadows gone, Brady. And I'll do my part to make that happen, but you have to let me. I'm strong, honey, and for you, I can be stronger."

I watched in rapt attention as Brady's eyes turned glossy. I didn't think there was anything that could make me love him more, but seeing that, knowing he trusted me so completely he'd allow himself to be so vulnerable, my love for him grew. Fierce, savage, brutal love that I would protect with my life. I'd burrow so deep there'd be no room for the demons that plagued him.

"You mean the world to me."

I love that.

Then I lost his eyes because he buried his face in my neck. I wrapped my arms around him, held on with my legs still around his hips, and I felt wetness leak from his eyes. I soaked up every last tear he shed. I'd take them all if it meant he let go of his pain.

It was a long time before he picked me up and carried me into my bathroom. I stood by the basin as he gently cleaned our combined release from between my legs, the act intimate. The gentleness of it overwhelming.

Maybe I wasn't done falling in love.

Maybe I'd fall more every day.

Maybe each day, he'd show me something new, something I didn't know I needed and it would surprise me and make me love him more.

There would be nothing better than falling more every day for the rest of my life until my dying breath.

That would be a dream come true.

Later that night after Brady raved about dinner, he helped me finish the floors, and tucked me in, staying long enough for me to fall asleep in his arms. I found that I was right, I wasn't done falling. Because when I felt his lips brush my forehead and heard his whispered "Sweet dreams, my beautiful Hadley" as he got out of my bed, my heart swelled even more.

17

Something was off.

Way, *way* off.

Brady was pulling away.

I was sitting in my office staring at the email I'd been drafting for the last hour wondering what had gone wrong. Everything had been going great—until yesterday. We were just us, but more. The teasing, friendship, easiness was all still there but it now included touching, kissing, sex, and open affection. Brady had come over every night since our first date. Sometimes he showed with takeout, sometimes I cooked, but however it came to be, we ate dinner together.

He'd helped me put in the new baseboards, making a tedious job fun. We worked well together.

He hadn't taken over even though he could've done it faster and probably better than me. He just let me work and kept me company while I did. Brady knew without me having to tell him, I wanted to accomplish the task. And after we were done, he praised my work in a way that made me feel good. He was genuinely impressed, not because I was a woman, but because laying flooring was hard work and I'd done a damn good job.

And every night we ended up in my bed watching TV, making out, having sex, then cuddling before I fell asleep and he left. Every morning, I'd woken up alone and each time it stung. But I was determined to give him time and address it in a few weeks.

But now something was seriously wrong.

Yesterday he texted me he had to work late because there'd been a break in something the team was working on. I knew it had to do with my cousin Liberty because my mom had told me my dad was happy that they'd finally had a solid lead. But what concerned me was he declined my invitation to come over later. And it wasn't the refusal, it was the way he dismissed me.

I spent last night and all day trying to talk myself

out of being concerned. Telling myself I was overreacting and being a needy girlfriend.

And no one liked needy.

But I wasn't overreacting. I knew I wasn't. And it wasn't because Brady didn't answer his cell when I called him this morning on my way into work. It was because it had been six hours and he hadn't returned that call or the text I sent at lunch. And when I phoned Triple Canopy, Lauren, the receptionist, told me Brady hadn't been in all day.

Now I was worried. I didn't want to call my dad, uncles, or brother to find out why Brady wasn't in because that was seriously not my place to do, but I was concerned enough I had to do something.

So even though it was pouring buckets and there was a storm warning in effect, I was going to drive to Brady's house and check on him. It was mid-summer in Georgia, and tropical storms and hurricanes were something I was used to. Thankfully, the storm hadn't been upgraded to a hurricane but it was blowing something fierce. That meant I needed to get on the road before it got worse. Once I got to Brady's, I'd stay there until the wind and rain calmed, and if needed, I'd sleep on his couch. But there was no way I wasn't going to check on him, not after the way he'd pulled away from me.

I hit send on the email I'd been working on as the first crack of lightning rent through the sky, lighting up my office. The following rumble of thunder was my cue to leave. I grabbed my purse and dashed out, calling out my goodbye to a volunteer named James, not feeling any remorse leaving him to lock up the library.

I knew he'd lock up but he'd stay and read until the storm blew past. Same as Ellen, he was retired. He, too, was in education, only he was a college professor. A man whose thirst for knowledge had not dimmed with age. He loved books, and if I had to guesstimate, I'd say he'd read eighty percent of the titles we shelved, save the children's section. I knew the man also read romance. We'd had deep discussions about women's psyches and why women lean toward the alpha male—if not in their real life, then he's part of their fantasy—and how romance feeds the need to believe that true love overcomes all.

Keys in hand, I jogged through the empty parking lot, wincing as the hard rain came down in sheets and the wind kicked up violently, blowing the low thunderclouds across the sky. I beeped my locks and jumped into my car soaking wet.

And that was when I felt the first warning. The cold chill that seeped into my bones telling me to go home. I dipped my head and glanced out the windshield and watched as the lightning flashed, brightly lighting up the dark sky. Thunder boomed, trees swayed, the gutters overflowed but I was Hadley Walker, determined if not a little reckless. Concern outweighed common sense. I started up my Camry, and not for the first time wished I drove a vehicle that sat higher off the road.

By the time I was halfway to Brady's, I was seriously contemplating my stupidity. I was driving twenty miles an hour under the speed limit, my wipers were on full speed and still, visibility sucked. I knew I was going to catch a ration of shit from Brady for driving in this weather. If my dad or brother found out, they'd lose their ever-loving minds.

A fifteen-minute drive had turned into thirty-five, and by the time I pulled onto Brady's street, I was white-knuckling the steering wheel. The storm had picked up, the roads were horrible—though thankfully empty because most people were smart enough not to go out for a cruise while mother nature was unleashing her fury.

I pulled into Brady's driveway, kicked off my heels, and tossed them in the passenger seat next to my purse. Leaving both my shoes and bag in the car,

I ran to the porch as fast as my bare feet would take me, splashing in ankle-deep water as I went.

I knocked then waited.

Then I knocked again and still no answer.

I glanced back at the truck in the driveway just to make sure I hadn't been hallucinating. After I ascertained that my car was indeed parked next to Brady's truck, I pounded on the door. The rain was coming down sideways. The overhang I stood under did very little to shield me from the torrential downpour.

I pounded on the door again, this time yelling Brady's name as I did. Concern grew into fear.

What if something happened to him?

What if he slipped and fell getting out of the shower and he's sprawled out on his bathroom floor with a bleeding head wound?

I was getting ready to find a way to break into Brady's house when the door flew open and there he was.

Disheveled.

No. *Destroyed.*

Eyes alight with grief.

I felt my chest start to burn. Something was *very* wrong. So wrong I saw it, I felt it, and he knew I did because he flinched.

"What the fuck?" His deep voice held a vein of menace but I ignored it and pushed past him.

"What the fuck?" he repeated. His tone no less dangerous but I ignored that warning, too.

I shouldn't have.

I should've heeded my earlier caution and gone straight home.

But stupid me didn't listen to anyone, not even myself.

I stood rooted in place as I took in Brady's living room. I'd been to his house three times in the last four years. And each time I'd been there it was OCD clean.

Now it was not.

The first thing I noticed was a box wrapped in birthday paper sitting on his coffee table. That by itself wasn't noteworthy, but the Care Bear wrapping paper looked old and tattered. Totally out of place. Alone, it would have been strange, but couple that with the photographs strewn around the box and it was *seriously* strange.

Next, I took in what looked like legal documents if the blueback and fourteen-inch paper was any indication. Not a few bound files but a lot of them. Some thicker than others. There was also more loose-leaf paper scattered on the floor.

"Brady?" I muttered.

"Fuck!" Brady roared.

I forced myself to stay calm even though the atmosphere in the room had gone from not so good to electric.

For once in my life, I was at a loss. I had no idea what to say or what to do. I heard Brady moving behind me, I felt him come to a stop beside me, but I couldn't stop looking at the Care Bear wrapping paper.

"You shouldn't have come here," he spat.

Yes, he spat out the words like they tasted bad and he sounded like he meant each one of them.

Still, I ignored the warning bells.

I shouldn't have done that, either.

"What's going on?"

"None of your fucking business."

My head whipped to the side—my soaking wet hair whipped with it—fully prepared to tell him exactly what I thought about him being a royal asshole.

But my words died a quick death when I took in his stone-cold face.

His tone was angry but his features were awash with sadness. So much leaking out of him it hurt to look at him.

"Honey—"

"Turn around and get the fuck out of my house."

Jesus, that hurt.

This was not *my* Brady.

Ugliness—that was what was pouring out. He'd said he had it inside of him. He'd made me promise not to let him break me.

For a week, I'd been happy. For a week, he'd shown me that we'd been worth the wait. But now, he'd taken himself away from me.

I drew in a breath and hesitantly asked, "Who's in the pictures?"

I started to step toward the table but stopped when he declared, "None of your business."

"Brady."

"Don't do this to us," he whispered, and I swear to God, it hurt to hear his tortured whisper.

Quiet pain that was so loud it scored through me.

My heart started burning.

"Please tell me what's going on."

"Go home."

"Please—"

"Jesus fuck, woman!" he exploded and I took a step back. "Clue the fuck in. I don't want you here. I'll give you a lot but you do not get this. You do not get Nicole. Especially not today."

Nicole?

I gazed into Brady's eyes but there was nothing there, not even the cloudy gray I'd seen for years. Not the sadness I was well-acquainted with. Blank. Empty. Bottomless. Nothing.

That killed.

That hurt worse than his refusal to talk to me, worse than him telling me to leave.

Brady Hewitt was undone.

Checked out.

And the hell of it was, he didn't want to check back in.

He didn't trust me to help him get him through whatever this was.

I stood there looking at the man I loved and wondered if he ever would.

Without a word, I headed to the front door.

He said nothing.

My hand went to the knob and I took my time opening the door, giving him time to stop me.

He said nothing.

I opened the door to the howling wind and sideways rain.

He said nothing.

So I did the only thing I could do. I slammed the door behind me and rushed to my car. I didn't feel a single drop of rain, I didn't feel the wind against my clammy skin. I didn't feel a damn thing as I drove down his street. I was too busy wondering if in my determination to get what I wanted if I'd taken into account what was good for me.

In the five minutes I was in Brady's house, the storm had gotten worse. My vision blurred, tears fell, and my heart burned.

I could handle anything but that.

I would guide Brady to happiness but I couldn't force it on him.

With tears in my eyes, my heart breaking, that horrible scene on repeat, and the unknown Nicole— a woman Brady obviously loved very much—on my mind, I had no business driving down flooded streets.

You do not get Nicole.

Who the hell was Nicole?

18

A crack of lightning.

I stared at the box, unseeing.

A violent rumble of thunder.

I blinked and looked around.

Hadley was gone.

The sound of the storm raging outside penetrated my haze.

Jesus fuck, what had I done?

I'd sent Hadley away—out into a storm she had no business driving in. Belatedly, her wet hair and soaked clothes hit me. And she'd been barefoot. What the fuck?

Wrong.

All wrong.

I jogged to my bedroom, tagged my keys, wallet, and cell, debating the merits of calling her.

No. The storm was too bad, all of her attention needed to be on the road.

I stalked through my living room, paused next to the table, and scanned the pictures of Nicole. Some were of her as a baby, some had my parents in them, some me and her. My eyes hit the one I wanted and I grabbed it off the table and stared at the old, faded image. My beautiful baby sister smiling bright and happy. I was standing next to her, her head tipped back looking at me and I was smiling back. Her last happy birthday. The one before my piece of shit father killed her. The last happy one she had. She'd only lived to see nine of them—nine birthdays, but only eight happy ones.

And happy was relative.

When your parents were deadbeats there wasn't a lot of happiness. But from the time I was old enough to do it, I always tried to make her birthday special. Even if I had to steal ten dollars out of my dad's wallet after he passed out drunk and court getting an ass-whoopin' if he caught me in the act— which he only did once—it was worth the risk to see Nicole smile. It wasn't like our parents were going to buy her anything, give her a party, bake her a cake, invite her friends over for a celebration.

No, not in the Hewitt house. Birthdays were just another day. Same with Christmas. My father would bitch about how holidays were made up by greeting card companies and toy manufacturers as a way to get rich. He'd drunkenly complain about how stupid birthdays were and how ridiculous it was to buy something for someone who'd done nothing.

His foul words never fell far from my mind. His anger. His twisted, pissed-off face when I was ten and asked if I could have a bike for my birthday.

"You think because your mother pushed you out of her twat you get a present? Are you dumb, boy?"

That was the first and last time I'd ever asked for anything.

But Nicole? I always got her something. She, too, knew never to ask for anything.

The only reason I had the picture in my hands was because our next-door neighbor, Mrs. Burk, had taken it. Hell, most of the pictures I had of my sister was because of Mrs. Burk. She knew how my parents were. She was a mom, one that gave a shit. She was good to her kids, so she knew just by looking at me and my sister, our parents were assholes.

But she also knew there wasn't anything she

could do about it. They didn't hit us, they kept a roof over our heads and food on the table. But nothing more. Not a hug. Not a kind word. Not a present. And certainly not love. They didn't even like each other. To this day I couldn't figure out why they'd had children. The best I could figure out was it was my mother's way of keeping my father.

Not that he didn't go out and carouse. He did and often. Then he'd come home, stumble through the door, my mother would be blitzed, and the fighting would commence. It would be loud, it would be ugly, and they'd hurl nasty insults back and forth. But it always ended the same. My mother would shout that my father smelled like another woman, my father would shout back he had to get laid somewhere, then doors would slam.

Sometimes the fights would wake up Nicole and she'd come into my room and crawl into bed next to me. When we were young, she'd curl her little-girl body next to me and we'd lie there in silence. When we got older, she'd lie beside me and hold my hand and we'd talk. Every conversation the same—making plans to escape the dysfunction of our parents. Vowing never to be like them. And at some point during our late-night talks, while our fucked-up parents shouted down the house, Nicole would always ask why they didn't love us.

I never had an answer.

Twenty fucking years later, and I still didn't.

All I had was a stupid fucking birthday present my sister never got to open because my piece of motherfucking shit father killed her, some pictures, and fucked-up memories.

That was what I had.

That was what they left me with.

That was what they left *in* me.

And now I'd turned into him—the man I hated more than anything in this world. I'd turned into a monumental dick and hurt the woman I loved because I was angry, grieving, and lost.

Jesus fuck.

I should have stayed away from her. I knew better than to let her in. I knew I had him inside of me, his filthy, tainted blood running through my veins.

I knew it but I couldn't stop myself.

I was out my front door and in my truck before I understood what I was doing. My need to get to Hadley to explain overrode all common sense.

No one deserved a woman as good as Hadley Walker. Me especially. I'd fought it. I'd denied it. I'd shoved it away. I'd run from it but I couldn't outrun it.

Five minutes into my drive, my grief-clogged mind cleared and I became painfully aware of how bad the streets were. Rivers of rainwater flooded the pavement, broken tree limbs littered the sidewalks and traffic lanes, thunder and lightning lit and rumbled.

Christ, Hadley's out in this.

I kept my eyes peeled for her car as I slowly made my way to her house. When I pulled in front of her condo, I was praising all things holy I hadn't driven up to an accident involving Hadley's Camry.

I parked in the guest parking and jogged to her front door and knocked.

No answer.

I knocked again, louder.

No answer.

Knowing she'd be pissed but having no other option, I used the key she'd given me and let myself in. The downstairs was dark. Not bothering to flip on the lights, I headed for the stairs and called out her name.

No answer.

The upstairs was just as dark as the downstairs and my heart started pounding in my chest.

Fucking shit.

I made my way back down the stairs, through the kitchen, and checked the one car garage she hadn't been able to use until just recently when they'd cleaned all of the scrap building supplies she'd been storing.

Empty.

Nausea roiled as Judge Patterson's angry words at my father's sentencing slammed into my chest.

"Mr. Hewitt, actions have consequences. Your unlawful and frankly despicable actions were the direct cause of Nicole Hewitt's death."

Actions have consequences.

I'd never forgotten that.

But twice now my actions had hurt Hadley.

She wasn't home.

There was a tropical storm tearing through the streets. Streets she was right then forced to be on because I'd kicked her out of my house.

I was no better than my father.

I was a fucking Hewitt.

Fucking Christ.

What would my consequences be for behaving like a goddamned weak asshole?

I was back out in my truck when I tried to call her.

No *fucking* answer.

I tried again and again, and in between calls I texted her, begging her to check in.

I got no reply.

Then I was back on the road aimlessly searching.

Hours passed and still no Hadley.

Hours of excruciating pain.

August 25th.

A black day always.

Nicole's birthday. The anniversary of her death.

But as I drove through flooded streets with the wrath of Mother Nature booming around me, I knew if something happened to Hadley I wouldn't survive my penance.

The rain had finally slowed to a light fall but the wind was still brutal as I pulled in front of Hadley's condo for the fourth time. The previous three times she hadn't been there. But she still wasn't answering her cell and I'd filled her voice mail with pleading messages, so I was checking again.

But I was not hopeful.

Just like the times before, from the sidewalk I could see that the downstairs was dark.

Fuck.

I let myself in and was preparing to yell her

name when the kitchen and dining room lights came on and I froze.

Then I could no longer keep my feet.

The pain of my knees hitting the wood floor didn't register.

Yet, there was no relief, even though Hadley was standing with a surprised expression on her face.

"Brady?"

"Jesus fuck."

My head dropped forward and I choked down the sting in the back of my throat.

I had to fix this.

I had to fix whatever was broken inside of me.

I had to do it for Hadley.

19

The surprise of seeing Brady in my living room took a moment to wear off. But even when it did, I remained frozen in alarm.

Brady was on his knees, ass to his ankles, head bowed, both palms now on the floor in front of him. He was also breathing heavily, his torso swaying with every breath.

The sight of that was all wrong.

Woodenly, my legs took me across the room, stopped a few paces away, and stared down at him.

"Brady?"

"I fucked up."

Strangled. Tortured. Terror-filled.

"I thought...you weren't answering your phone... the storm."

I bit my lip and didn't tell him I'd forgotten my phone on my desk at work.

It was a stupid thing to do, but in my haste to get to Brady, I hadn't picked it up and didn't realize it until after I'd left his place, pulled off the road into a shopping center, and parked. I also refrained from pointing out I wasn't a complete moron and I'd lived in Georgia my whole life, so it wasn't the first time I'd had to pull over and wait until a storm blew past. Thankfully, being the bookworm I was, my tablet was always in my purse, therefore I didn't mind sitting in my car because I had hundreds of books to read.

"I can't do this anymore," he rasped. "It's eating me up."

I took a deep breath and looked at Brady. Not at the wrongness of a strong man brought low, a man who should never be on his knees, but as a man who was in tremendous pain.

Hours ago, he'd cut me deep.

He'd refused to talk, he'd kicked me out, he'd been a total jackass. None of those things were okay, none of those would I put up with. But I knew down to my soul, that man back at his house was not my Brady.

I had to hold it together and deal with that later.

Now, it was time to get to the bottom of the issue.

"Why today?" I asked.

Silence.

"What triggered it?" I tried a different question.

Silence.

"Tell me."

My demand was met with a pain-filled hitch—the sound akin to the noise a wounded animal would make—but Brady spoke no words.

"Who's Nicole?"

Brady shot to his feet with shocking speed. I stepped back. He advanced. One hand went behind his back, then he shoved whatever he was holding at me. Waved it in my direction like it was on fire and he didn't want to hold it while it went up in flames.

I took it and looked down. Then I squinted at the photograph.

The boy in the picture looked like a mini version of Brady. No, a younger Brady with a mop of dark blond hair that was in serious need of a haircut. Not because it was curling around his ears but because it looked shaggy and unkempt. But that wasn't what had me holding my breath, it was the little boy's smile. Big, wide, genuine. He was looking at a little girl, and whoever she was, he loved her. It shone so brightly, so openly, it was so beautiful that it hurt to see.

"Is this you?" I whispered.

"Me and Nicole," he choked.

Nicole.

He still loved her now. Clear as day.

My heart started to ache, not because Brady openly loved someone else, but because he no longer smiled like that. Not even in the last week, and he'd smiled a lot. He'd laughed, he'd teased, he'd looked happy, but he did not look like he did in that picture. Not even a tenth as happy.

There had to be a reason he no longer smiled like that and I was afraid to hear that reason. I was scared that whatever had killed his happy meant something bad had happened to a beautiful little girl with a bright smile and gorgeous cascading blonde hair which needed to be cut and styled as well.

"Who's Nicole, honey?"

"My sister." Two words wrenched from his soul. Guttural. Emotional. Sad.

Sister?

Brady had never mentioned a sister. No one had ever mentioned he had a sister. My stomach bound into knots and the photograph started to shake in my hands.

With a heavy heart, I asked, "Where's your sister?"

"He killed her."

Oh, fuck.

Oh, no.

I had a bad, bad feeling I knew who 'he' was.

My dad's been in prison for twenty years.

Seven years after my dad went down, she successfully drank herself to death.

Brady had said they were alcoholics. No, he'd said they were mean, nasty drunks.

Oh, shit.

"Brady," I whispered, not knowing what else to say.

"Twenty years ago today, he killed her. And now he's getting out. He gets to breathe after he killed her. The only good thing I had in my life. His drunk ass killed her, stole her life, and that bitch knew he was drunk and shouldn't have been driving. Shouldn't have been allowed to take two children out on his boat. But she said nothing. Not a goddamned word when I told the bastard we weren't going."

Brady's gaze looked far away as he relived that day. "Not when he grabbed my sister and shoved her in the back seat. No way was I letting her go anywhere alone with him. That stupid, fucking bitch knew he was drunker than normal and she allowed her husband to drive to a lake with her two children in the car.

"But only one came home that day. The other lay dead in a morgue. Her piece-of-shit husband locked up. And her son forever broken after he tried but failed to save his baby sister from drowning.

"But do you think she offered a hug, a kiss, support, love, care, something, anything? Hell no. She hit the bottle. So she wouldn't feel anything. But me? I felt it all. I still feel it all. I see it. I hear it. I taste the lake water as I swallowed gulps of it down. I see her limp dead body. I see that bastard uninjured and swaying as he was handcuffed. But you know what I'll never see again?"

Brady's face twisted in extreme agony and it hurt so bad to see it I wanted to beg him to stop talking. "That," he grunted and jabbed his finger toward the picture. "I'll never see her smile again. I'll never hear her laugh, her voice, her singing. I'll never hug her. I'll never wish her another happy birthday. I'll never get to see her grow up, escape the hell we grew up in, and finally be happy. Never. I'll never get that. But Brett *fucking* Hewitt gets to live."

I was speechless.

He was correct on all accounts, and the unfairness of it, crushing.

"Fuck!" he roared, and I felt a woosh of air as Brady lunged for me.

I braced as his arms went around me and he shoved his face in my neck. His arms were so tight the air was leaving my lungs. But I wrapped him up as tightly as I could and I held on.

That was all I could offer.

"I don't want to be like him," he mumbled against my throat.

Be like his father.

Was he crazy?

"Honey, you are nothing like him."

"It's inside of me. The anger. The bitterness. The poison waiting to come out, hurting the people I love. I've turned into the man I hate."

What in the world?

"No, you have not." I squeezed harder, which was to say, just a fraction more because I was already squeezing as tightly as I could.

"I get you need to believe that, Hadley, but, baby, I don't know how you can say that after how I just treated you."

"Let me go."

His arms immediately dropped and he stepped back.

The quickness of his actions broke my damn heart.

"I see *you* need to believe that. I won't lie and pretend that you kicking me out of your house didn't sting." Brady flinched and closed down. "But you have to know I'm smart. You're not new, you've been around my family a long time, so it's not lost on you that my family has seen its fair share of tragedy, and with that comes the unfortunate flare-up of tempers. Do you think I love my cousin Liberty any less because she snapped at me when she got home after being held as a POW? Do you think I love my sister Delaney any less after she lost the baby and was so filled with grief she kicked me out of her hospital room? Or when my sister-in-law Kayla passed away and my brother shut down for years and refused to hear reason? Do you not think that he didn't say mean and hurtful shit to me? Of course, he did. He was hurting. He was grieving. He was in pain."

I took a deep breath. "But I forgave him. Wanna know why? Because I'm smart enough to understand when something is wrong. When someone is emotionally crippled and needs to be loved through it, not berated and persecuted because they're feeling pain so deep they can't keep it in.

"But just to say. The next time that happens, I will not be leaving. I will be holding your ass to the fire and demanding you talk to me. You want this to work between me and you, everything is my business when it brings you pain. Every last goddamned thing, Brady. And do not mistake me for some weak woman who'd stand by and let you use her as a punching bag. I am far from that. I'm damn strong. So strong I can stand up to you, stand beside you, and I can damn well carry you when you need me to."

Brady was silent but his eyes were not. They were communicating loudly. Every feeling he had swirled in his gray eyes, cloudy and turbulent.

One day, the storminess would be gone.

One day, he would smile that real, genuine smile again.

"Baby—"

"No, Brady. Not now. Not tonight. All of that can wait until tomorrow. Since I still don't have furniture we're going upstairs and sitting on my bed so you can tell me about Nicole."

"Had—"

"No lip, Brady."

"Bossy." His mouth quirked then he said, "I was gonna say thank you. Once again, I don't deserve your forgiveness but you're giving it to me anyway."

"The fact you think you don't deserve it is a problem. And fair warning, I'm gonna tend to that, too. And before you argue with me let me remind you of something. My father and my uncles are the best men I know. They are loyal, they are smart, they take care of those they love, so they would never let a wolf into their flock. They sought *you* out. They recruited *you*. They've taken *you* in and treated you like family from the moment you started working at Triple Canopy. You know them, you know the depth of their love for our family. Would they have brought you into the fold, kept you there, and protected you if *you* were not worthy?"

"Point taken," he begrudgingly mumbled and I let out a breath I hadn't realized I was holding.

Then I stared at Brady, really and truly studied him.

He was not fucked-up. He'd been neglected. He'd been emotionally abused. He'd been let down by the people who were supposed to love him the most.

Fuck those people.

Brady was ours.

We'd loved him the most.

The Walker, Clark, Lenox, and McCoy clans had more than enough love to spare.

He thought he'd claimed me, he thought I was his.

He was right, but he was also wrong.

Brady was mine.

All mine.

And *I* would love him the most.

20

"Baby?"

"Yeah?"

"I can't sleep in here," I told Hadley something she knew.

For the last ten minutes, she'd fallen quiet.

I didn't blame her—it was nearing midnight. Not only that, I'd emotionally put her through the wringer. We'd gone upstairs, she'd changed out of her still damp work clothes, settled us on the bed, then got down to her interrogation.

And she was thorough.

All the while, Hadley had burrowed in next to me. Her leg was thrown over my thigh, her arm rested over my stomach, and her fingertips gently grazed my skin as I spoke.

I was pinned down, and oddly, it was wholly comforting. I'd told her how Nicole and I had grown up, about my parents drinking, and finally about Nicole's last birthday.

It was hard to talk about. I'd spent twenty years not wanting to face my part in her death. Once my father had us on his boat, I should've demanded Nicole put on a life vest. I hadn't. Partly because I was fuming angry and not thinking. Bottom line was she was nine, I was eleven, and I should've been looking out for my sister better.

Hadley had pressed closer when I told her how my drunk father hit underwater debris but was so intoxicated that after the impact he hadn't stopped. Instead, he'd cursed and shouted and full-throttled the boat, damaging a large section of the hull.

It had taken seconds for the boat to take on water. I hadn't been paying attention to my sister as she made her way to the bow as the stern went under. It was shocking how quickly a fifteen-foot Boston Whaler can sink. But that wasn't what killed Nicole. Her feet got tangled in my father's old fishing net and she fell overboard.

I dove into the water after her. With zero visibility in the murky water, it took forever to reach her.

I'd had to come up for air twice. That was two times too many.

Too late.

Impossible to do CPR in the water.

Too fucking long did I float in the water holding my dead sister while that bastard bitched about his boat.

Not once did he ask if Nicole or I were okay.

I wished he would've died instead of her.

But through the whole disturbing story, Hadley remained still and allowed me to get it all out.

Now her head was heavy on my shoulder, her palm was over my heart, and her breathing had evened out. And I was completely drained.

I couldn't chance falling asleep next to her.

Not after all I'd shared. The nightmares would come.

"Babe," I prompted when she didn't respond.

"Will you stay?"

"Had—"

"I don't want you going home alone. Tomorrow, I'll go with you. I want to see more pictures of Nicole. Tonight was about tragedy, but, honey, tomorrow's gonna be about sweet memories you have of your sister. She was beautiful. You loved her. And I've seen one picture of her and I know she loved her big brother. I know that look because I have a big brother, one I love just as much as she loved you. Please. I can't bear thinking about you facing what's at your house without me."

"I'll stay in your guest room if you promise no matter what you hear you will not come in."

"I promise." She'd uttered the vow but made no move to disengage. "I'll stay in here but I want you to know I won't like it. My first instinct is to go to you. My first instinct is to help you. My first instinct is and always will be to stand beside you and I cannot do that from all the way in here."

Her words collided with my worries—freeing them, untethering them, until they started to lift.

"You're wrong. You safe in your bed, understanding, giving me what I need, is you standing next to me."

She sighed and nodded against my chest. There was one last thing I needed to give her before I went downstairs.

"I dream about more than my sister's death. Sometimes I dream about the battlefield, both real and imaginary scenarios. Sometimes I dream about being a civilian and walking into an active shooter situation, or I stumble onto a robbery. My mind never quiets. I don't always thrash around in my sleep, but when I do, I have no control and that's the part that scares me. I want you to know I had every intention of working this out before you and I got together. But then you kissed me—"

"Um. *You* kissed *me*," Hadley interrupted. Her tone teasing, her voice light, and I smiled.

"Right. I kissed you. Point is, after that, my plan went to shit. I spoke to Drake the other day and he suggested I talk to your Uncle Clark. I'm gonna reach out to him."

"Good."

"My father's getting out of prison." I had to stop and take a deep breath before I could get the rest out. "I don't know if he'll try to reach out to me. I hope to God he doesn't. But if he does, that's something you'll not be involved in. That's not because I don't trust you, that's not because I don't think you're strong enough to deal, it's because that piece of shit gets no part of you. And that includes him laying his eyes on you, hearing your voice, breathing your air, however it can happen, it's not gonna. So if he shows, calls, sends a letter, I'm asking you to please give me that."

"Okay."

"Okay? That easy?"

"Yes, okay. I'll give you that, but only because if I see him I'll throat punch him."

I barked out a laugh, then froze.

"What's wrong?"

"I've never, not once in my whole life, laughed when talking about my father," I admitted.

Hadley didn't say anything but she didn't have to. Not when she snuggled in closer and turned her head to kiss my chest.

That was it—all I needed to let go of some more of the bitterness.

21

Thank God for Saturdays. The library was open but I didn't have to be there. That meant I got the whole day with Brady.

It was early, but instead of rolling over and trying to go back to sleep I got out of bed and padded to the bathroom.

The sooner we faced the shit part of our day the faster we could get to the good parts. Those being dealing with what Brady had left behind at his house —the bad. Then moving on to anything but that—the good.

I'd just stepped into the shower and wet my hair, thinking about every heartbreaking detail Brady had shared last night, when the curtain opened and the man himself stepped in behind me.

Good Lord—delish.

All thoughts of neglectful parents, murderous fathers, and tragedy disappeared when Brady's arms slid around my middle and he pulled my back to his front. Which also meant he'd pulled my ass tight against his hard cock.

Now that was de-*lish*-ous.

"Morning, baby." His greeting rumbled against the nape of my neck before he pressed his lips against my skin, sealing in his words.

"Morning, honey."

Thankfully, I stopped myself before asking the gratuitous question, *did you sleep well?* I knew he hadn't. I heard him shout twice in the middle of the night. I couldn't make out what he was saying so I didn't know if his nightmare was about Nicole, the battlefield, or some other situation that Brady dreamed about. Both times it had woken me. Both times my heart thundered in my chest. Both times I desperately wanted to go to him. But both times I'd remained in my bed—alone. With the man I loved in the next room suffering by himself.

I hated it.

But I'd done it.

"Trying to pull a fast one, huh?"

"A fast one?"

"Sneaking into a shower without me."

Brady nuzzled my neck and the hands folded together on my stomach split—one glided up, the other skimmed down, both hitting their targets simultaneously with precision-timing and aim.

"Didn't know you'd want to join me," I moaned.

"Consider this an announcement."

One finger circled my clit while his other finger circled my nipple.

Oh, yeah.

"What exactly are you announcing?" I teased and rubbed my ass against his hard length.

"That anytime you're naked I expect an invitation to attend."

Brady's finger on my clit moved lower and plunged in.

"And if I extend this invite can I expect this kind of hospitable ministration every time?"

Brady didn't miss a beat. Two fingers were working between my legs—hard and fast, while he pinched and rolled my nipple with his other hand.

"No."

"No?"

My hips jerked and rocked against his hand.

"Sometimes you'll be greeted with my mouth. Other times, my cock. Sometimes I might just want to play with your tits or alternately, just your pussy. You never know."

"Then consider this your standing offer to join me wherever it is I might be naked."

Brady nipped the side of my neck before his tongue licked away the sting and his mouth moved to my ear.

"Grind your pussy on my fingers."

I did as he commanded and rocked harder. His hand left my nipple and slid to my ribs. Then I lost his hand along with his cock resting against my ass. I felt both moving behind me—his hand stroked his shaft while the head of his cock rhythmically nudged my ass.

That was so hot, I ground down hard trying to get his fingers deeper.

"I see you like knowing I'm stroking my cock while I got my fingers inside you."

"Oh, yeah," I panted. "Feel good?"

"Not as good as it's gonna feel when I get in your pussy."

"You should do that now."

Brady's mouth went back to my neck—licks, kisses, nips—all three so good I dropped my head to the side to give him better access.

"Almost," I warned.

"Don't. Not until I'm ready."

"Then you need to slow down," I begged.

He didn't slow down his fingers fucking me. He didn't slow his hand jerking his cock. He didn't stop grazing his teeth against the sensitive skin under my ear. All of that inched me closer and closer to climaxing.

And when he grunted right before he said, "Brace your hands on the wall, I'm gonna fuck you hard," I nearly orgasmed. But I managed to press my hands against the tile in front of me before he drove his cock in so fast, so hard, I came up on my toes.

The 'nearly' went out of "nearly orgasmed" and I exploded around his cock the second time he thrust in.

My eyes closed, my head fell forward, and Brady continued driving into me.

"Good God," Brady grunted and bucked harder. "Gonna come with you."

With one last stroke, he slammed home and stayed planted.

I had no idea how Brady knew I was still at the peak of my pleasure. But it wouldn't take long for him to tell me.

"When you come, baby, your pussy clenches so tight, you get so slick, so hot, it feels so good. Feeling all of that, I lose my mind. But what's better than all of that, Hadley, is knowing it's me giving it to you. It's my cock driving deep. It's me touching you." Brady's head dropped on my shoulder and he groaned. "Feel that?"

It took me a moment to understand what he was asking, but when his cock twitched I answered, "Yeah, I can feel it."

"That's what you do to me. I don't even have to move. Just knowing it's you my cock's in, your skin, your hair, your smell, it's you—just you."

I loved that—all of it.

I loved he thought it was just me.

I loved that he thought I felt good because I thought he felt good, too.

I loved that he'd stroke his cock while he finger-fucked me, making the whole thing dirty, but he could make love to me, too. I loved the sweet side of Brady just as much as I loved the dirty. I loved that he was brave and protective, but I also loved that he was damaged and man enough to let me help him.

Simply put, I loved everything about him.

About us.

"Wanna kiss you," he whispered, and I smiled.

I lifted my head and craned my neck until

Brady's lips touched mine and gave me a sweet, slow, toe-curling kiss.

And when he broke it, I really loved the way he muttered, "Love waking up knowing you're close."

I loved that, too.

But I reckoned I'd love it even more when that "close" became waking up next to me.

22

I was standing in Hadley's empty living room waiting for her to finish getting dressed so we could go to my house. Something I wanted to do only slightly more than I want my balls carved out.

But I was doing it. Partly because I owed it to Hadley, partly because she was right and I didn't want to face my pain alone, something I'd done for the last twenty years. Even when my mother was alive, she didn't acknowledge my sister's birthday one way or the other. It was just another day to her.

I'd bet Emily Walker wouldn't let one of her children do anything alone, especially not grieve. The same as I'd bet Jasper Walker would die before he let harm come to one of his children.

There was the crux of my problem. I needed

Hadley, but I didn't want her to know intimately that there were people in the world so callous, so evil, they'd kill one of their own children. I didn't want her exposed to that kind of sickness.

However, I hadn't fought her when she demanded to go with me to clean up the mess I'd left.

"Ready?" Hadley asked and I turned to watch her bounce down the stairs, bright, satisfied smile tugging her full lips up.

"Yeah. What time's your furniture being delivered?"

"Between noon and five." She rolled her eyes. "Though I did ask them to call me when they were on their way, but you know how it is. They'll be here when they get here and they may or may not call." She shrugged and stopped in front of me.

"Right. We'll hit my house and after that, I need to run by Triple Canopy and pick up a few files. We'll come back here, I'll drop you off, then I'll go out and pick us up lunch."

"Or alternately, we can come back here, I'll make us something for lunch, and we can use the time it would've taken you to go out to find something better to do."

"Like the way you think." I dipped my head and brushed my mouth against hers. I barely won the battle against taking a brush of the lips to a full-blown kiss, and straightened instead. "Let's hit the road."

"Okay."

Easy acceptance.

Pure Hadley—go with the flow, happy, skip-jumping down the stairs like I hadn't been a dick last night.

"Wait." I pulled her back, needing to tell her something before we left. "I'm sorry about last night. All of it. I was out of line. I said some horrible things to you, but sending you out into the storm was the worst. I put you in danger and I swear to you, promise, baby, that will never happen again."

"It's been said, a smart woman knows when to forgive and not hold a grudge. But a smart woman also knows when to kick her man's ass should he make it a habit of being a dick without seeking help for what's making him that way. I trust you. I forgive you. Now it's time to move on."

"It's not that easy, Hadley. I sent you out into that storm—"

"Don't borrow trouble, Brady. Yesterday was not the first time I've driven in a storm, it wasn't even the worst I've driven in. I'm not stupid. I knew to pull over and keep myself safe. I had my tablet and I sat in a parking lot and read. It was all good, and as you can see, I'm standing here just fine."

Thank God she'd been smart enough to pull over. The streets had been horrible.

"Why didn't you answer your phone?"

Her teeth sank into her bottom lip, her gaze went over my shoulder, and she tried to shuffle away from me. What she didn't do was answer.

"Hadley?"

"I forgot it on my desk at work. I was in a rush to leave to get to your house before it got too windy and I didn't grab it."

Jesus Christ.

My gut clenched at the thought of Hadley driving around in the motherfucking pouring rain without her cell, all because she was trying to get to me.

"New plan. We stop by the library before we come home so you can get your phone."

Hadley's eyes flew to mine and they widened. "That's it?"

"What do you mean, that's it?"

"No lecture?"

"Babe, after the way I acted I got no room to lecture you about anything. Though I will say I'm pissed you were out in a storm with no phone, but that's on me. If I hadn't pulled away, you wouldn't have felt the need to rush to my house. But please, *please*, keep your phone with you."

She nodded and gave her promise. "I'll buy one of those ugly phone cases that clips onto your belt and wear my phone from now on."

"You wear classy skirts to work, baby, that's not gonna work."

"Oh, right." Her nose scrunched, then she continued. "I'll just keep it in my purse from now on."

"Good plan."

"I love you, Brady," she whispered, and warmth hit my chest.

Sweet Jesus.

"Love you, too."

"What's in the box?" Hadley gently asked.

I was kneeling, picking up the transcript of my father's testimony I'd tossed on the floor. I'd long since stopped keeping it in order. I could read the documents forward, backward, from the middle to the end, or in any order, and still not make sense of why a father would operate a vehicle, a boat, or any mode of transportation while drunk. I'd never understood how a man allowed his brain to get so polluted with alcohol he'd put his children in danger.

I'd sat in the courtroom during his trial and read the transcripts and I still couldn't fathom it.

I glanced up from the papers I'd collected and looked at Hadley. She was on her knees in front of my coffee table sorting through pictures. So far, she hadn't commented but I knew what she saw. My childhood wasn't pretty. My sister and I weren't cared for. To her, we probably looked like two ratty, street kids. And we basically were.

"Nicole loved *Sabrina, the Teenage Witch*. Total obsession. Every Friday night she was in front of the TV watching and my ass was next to her. When she was seven and I was nine, it was torture being forced to watch. When I was eleven and Melissa Joan Hart started wearing crop tops and plaid schoolgirl skirts, I didn't mind so much."

"You were perving out on Melissa Joan Hart?" Hadley scrunched her nose and she looked damn adorable doing it.

"Babe, as I said, I was eleven. I was perving out on the JCPenney's catalog bra section."

"Right." She chuckled.

"There was a time when us poor teenage boys

didn't have the internet. We had to make do with what we could find. And every now and again, you could see a nipple poking under the material of a bra and it was an instant hard-on."

"You poor thing. No Pornhub, however did you survive?"

"Melissa Joan Hart and her plaid skirts. Alicia Silverstone in a tight latex bat suit. Jennifer Love Hugetits in pretty much any movie she was in. And my all-time favorite, Reese Witherspoon in *Cruel Intentions*—full-frontal nudity and at the time the hottest sex I'd ever seen. I rewound and paused that movie so many times I ruined the VHS tape."

"VHS?" Hadley laughed. Full-on, outright, belly-laughed.

And the unthinkable happened—I joined her.

Surrounded by all the ugly, all of the painful memories, the reminders that my sister was gone, I joined Hadley and laughed.

I didn't give one shit, she was laughing at me. That I was seven years older than her and she'd probably never owned a VHS tape, or that I'd admitted to jerking off.

What I did give a shit about was, it felt great.

I felt freer, lighter, and for once, optimistic about the future.

"Did you...did you just... seriously call her Jennifer Love Hugetits?" she sputtered.

"Babe. Seriously. They're huge. And if you think there's a man my age that hasn't perved out over her rack, you are wrong."

"No. I believe you. I've just never heard her called that. I also had no idea you were a boob man."

"I'm not."

"Well, you seem to like hers."

"Um, yeah, they're hard to miss. But I can take or leave big tits."

"Then what's your thing?"

"Legs. And before you ask, by and far, you've got the best legs I've ever seen. And when you wrap them around me with your thighs pressed tight to my sides, swear to God, Hadley, they feel so good there I lose my mind. Second to that is when they're over my shoulders. Third way I like seeing them is in your heels, and that's only because when you're in heels your ass sways when you walk and that's hot, too. But barefoot or in one of your five-hundred pairs of flip-flops strutting your ass at your uncle's pool wins out over heels—but only if you're in a bathing suit."

Hadley's face flamed red. The pretty blush on her cheeks had me fighting to control my cock. It had been less than an hour since I'd had her in the shower and I was ready to have her again.

"Thank you?" she shyly teased.

"Don't know how I got so lucky, baby, but you gotta know that I know I am."

Hadley's eyes dropped to the pictures still scattered on the table and murmured, "I'm glad you feel that way. And I hope you know, with time, I'm gonna make you feel luckier. We're gonna get you through this."

Fucking hell.

Just by her saying that, I already felt luckier.

"I don't want to take—"

"Stop." Hadley's eyes sliced to mine and her voice was stern. "In life, there's a time when you give and there's a time when you take. You've given me a lot, Brady, and you know you have. It's time for you to take. And in the future, you'll give. That's just the way it works. So stop worrying about me."

I stopped shuffling markers and thought about what she said. And as always, she was right.

"Sexy and smart. Yeah, I'm seriously fucking lucky."

Hadley went back to gathering the pictures but she did it with a smile on her face.

I, however, was not smiling when I finished

collecting all the legal documents. As if she read my mind, Hadley asked, "Where do you want these?"

I wasn't sure how to answer that but I knew where the papers were going. I stood, grabbed the folders off the table, went into the kitchen straight to the trash can, and dumped them in.

I'd spent twenty years living in a black hole. Twenty years carrying those stupid fucking papers around with me.

Two decades.

Too damn long.

Hadley smiled from where she sat.

It was time to start living.

"Salem the cat," I said in the truck.

Hadley gave me a puzzled look.

I shook my head when I realized I'd been lost in my head and had started a conversation from the middle. "That's what's in Nicole's present. I told you she loved Sabrina. Salem the talking cat was her favorite character. But she never got to open it. I was going to give it to her that night after our parents went to bed. I knew she'd be upset they didn't do anything, so I wanted to wait to give it to her."

"You're a good big brother," Hadley murmured. She grabbed my free hand and rested it on her thigh.

We drove in silence the rest of the way to Triple Canopy.

"You don't have to come in," Hadley told me when I cut my truck off in the library parking lot.

I couldn't say why I wanted to go in with her, just that I did. I had a weird feeling and it'd started eating at me as soon as we got close to the library. I was hoping it was simply because the last time I'd been here, I'd found the ruined books.

On that thought, I looked around the parking lot. No cameras.

"Any word about getting some cameras back here?"

"I put in a request but I haven't heard anything yet."

I was giving it a week then I was setting them up.

We got out and made our way into the building. I was surprised to see how busy it was. Several people were waiting to check out books, more were wandering around browsing the shelves, and still more sitting at tables.

A woman who'd introduced herself as Ellen caught Hadley's attention and I followed her to where the older woman was standing next to a cart.

"Hi, Ellen."

"Hello, dearheart, I didn't think I'd see you today," Ellen greeted. Then her eyes slid to me and she smiled. "Brady. Nice to see you."

"You, too, ma'am."

"I forgot my cell on my desk."

This statement was mumbled like Hadley didn't want to say it.

"Child. How many times do I need to tell you to keep your phone close? You can't be too careful these days." Ellen clucked and continued. "Even in a town as safe as this, there are still wackadoodles."

"I know," Hadley huffed. "I was trying to beat the storm."

"Bless. It was a doozie. We lost two trees and we can't get a service out until tomorrow."

"Do you need help clearing?"

"Absolutely not. You have better things to do." Ellen paused and suddenly she looked pensive. "There's no easy way to say this so I'm just gonna be out with it. This morning there was another book found."

Hadley's eyes slowly closed and her brows pinched together.

"Damn," she whispered. "Where?"

"A patron found it on the shelf and brought it to my attention."

"What?"

"The gentleman pulled it right off the shelf, took it to a table, and opened it up."

"This is getting ridiculous," Hadley seethed. "Where's the book now?"

"On your desk."

Without another word, Hadley turned and marched her ass to her office looking like a woman on a mission. I quickened my pace and closed the door behind me just in time for Hadley to start her rant.

"I am so over this shit. Who the hell does this person think they are? Total BS." She found the book sitting on her desk and picked it up. "You've got to be shitting me." Hadley turned with the book in her hand and violently shook it. "*The Chocolate War.*"

It was obvious she was red-hot pissed and it was entirely possible I should've known what *The Chocolate War* was about but I didn't have the first clue. Not that she'd given me the opportunity to ask before she exploded.

"Why are people dumb? Seriously? This..." She shook the book again. "These aren't just words on a page. This book isn't about entertainment, it's thought-provoking. The theme is entirely uncomfortable—peer pressure, the power of fear, manipulation. This book makes you stop and think. It might not change every reader's life, but you can't read this book and not wonder how as an individual and as a society we unknowingly get pressured into conforming."

Again she didn't let me get a word in edgewise before her face crumpled and tears brimmed in her eyes.

"I just don't understand how someone can be so close-minded."

There was the heart of her problem. Sure, she was pissed another book had been destroyed, but Hadley couldn't understand the reasons behind the vandalism. She couldn't comprehend how a person could be so intolerant, bigoted, or narrow.

"I know you don't."

"At least I can replace this book without the board knowing and Mrs. Stick-Up-Her-Ass finding out and forbidding the book from being re-shelved."

"Not a fan of you spending your money replacing books, especially when they get pulled or ruined after you put them back out. Is there a way to bypass Gayle?"

"Nope. The board has to approve all purchases. And her favorite thing to do is red-line any book that has ever been challenged. She'll go as far as citing a school district in another state if they banned a book from their high school library. She's ridiculous."

Gayle Gains had just gotten herself scratched onto my Monday morning to-do list. Hadley told me Gayle had been on vacation when the last set of books were found but that didn't mean she wasn't involved.

"We'll get this figured out," I told her.

She gave me a wobbly smile and jerked her shoulders, clearly still pissed and sad with a healthy dose of confusion mixed in there, making her smile not really a smile.

"I appreciate you wanting to help. But you have a lot on your plate. Mom told me you guys were getting closer to finding who was behind Liberty's kidnapping and that's more important than what's happening here. I don't want to take your time."

"Babe," I started, and made my way to her, hooking my arm around her waist when I got close. "We're gonna figure this out, yeah?"

Hadley nodded then dropped her forehead to my chest.

"Yeah."

"Grab your phone and let's get home. If memory serves, you offered to feed me and I'm hungry."

She nodded against my chest then slowly tipped her head back and said, "Depending on how long you mind waiting, I can make French Dips."

"Sounds good, baby, but I got something else I prefer to eat while we're waiting on your furniture."

"You got a hankering for pizza?" she teased.

"Nope."

"A salad?"

"Nope."

"Hm. You want tacos?"

"Might save time, you just grab your phone, get your ass back in my truck, and I take you home and show you."

"We only have an hour until the delivery window opens. How much time do you need to prepare this meal?"

Damn, she was cute.

"Normally, five minutes, tops. But seeing as you're being a smartass I feel like taking my time. I might need the full hour, eat you real slow like, get you close and back away, leave you hanging, begging for me to finish you off. Yeah, I like that idea—getting you right on the edge then making you wait until your couches are delivered before I make you ride me. Nothing like breaking in a new piece of furniture with an orgasm."

"Well, then, what are we waiting for?"

"For you to get your ass in gear and grab your phone."

"I can't get my phone while you're holding me, Brady."

"Right, I'll amend. We're waiting for you to kiss me first."

Hadley didn't hesitate. Her chin tipped up and she offered her lips. I gladly took her up on her offer and took it past a lip touch straight to deep. She gave me more and moaned into my mouth. I took it, memorized the sweet sound, then I gave it back.

Only, what I gave was silent—a promise, a vow, a pledge that I would even out the scales.

For now, I had no choice but to take until I could get myself sorted. And in return I'd give her anything she needed, everything I had, everything I could possibly give was hers.

We'd stay balanced.

I'd make damn sure of it.

23

I had furniture.

And just as I'd hoped, the couches looked great. The deep blue denim color popped against the light-colored wood floor, the cherry end tables gave the room contrast, and once I bought the mustard-yellow lamps I'd had my eye on, the room would be bursting with color.

I'd made the decision not to decorate the walls. Unfortunately, the room wouldn't be complete but the condo was meant to be fixed up and flipped. I'd already spackled and painted—it was a pain in my ass the first time I'd done it and I would rather live without artwork hanging than to have to go through that rigamarole again.

"Babe?" Brady called from the dining room table.

"Yeah?"

I finished fluffing a throw pillow and looked at him. His hair was a disheveled mess. The sight sent shivers down my arms and made the area between my legs tighten.

I'd done that to him.

It was my hands that had mussed up his hair as I gripped it while he ate me out. True to his word, he'd spent a good amount of time licking, stroking, and driving me to the edge, only to stop, let my climax wane, then start all over again.

When the knock came at the door—not the call that the store had promised, but a knock—Brady'd kissed each inner thigh and strode out of my bedroom, leaving me breathless and on the edge. I knew he wasn't entirely unaffected by what he'd been doing to me when he rushed the delivery men out the door, slammed it closed, dropped his pants, sat on my new couch, and instructed me to climb on.

It must be said a bossy, turned-on Brady was hot. Therefore, I obeyed gleefully and without delay. But once I was astride him, it was my turn to play. I'd ignored his demands to go faster. I disregarded his commands to ride him harder. Instead, I went slow and built our desire until need took over and my body would no longer allow slow.

Each and every orgasm Brady gave me was the best. Sometimes he held my gaze through the explosion, sometimes he kissed me through it, sometimes he shoved his face in my neck and sucked and nibbled. But there on my couch, while we simultaneously found pleasure with our eyes locked he wasn't just *looking* at me. It was profoundly different—not a moment of vulnerability, not a lust-hazed stare—complete and utter trust shone. No shadows of sadness, no grief, no wariness—absolute adoration and promise.

It was beautiful.

It was intense.

It was a look I was determined to see more of.

In other words, it was everything.

"Would you mind if I called the guys and asked them over?" he asked, pulling me from my thoughts.

"Not sure what guys you're talking about but you can ask over anyone you'd like," I returned.

Brady was studying me and I wondered if he was having the same thoughts as me, and those were: I liked him being in my house, I wanted him there, and not just as a visitor. Alternately, I liked being at his house, I wanted to be there, and not just as a guest.

I wanted more.

It was crazy. In most ways, it was too soon to

want to live with Brady, but in other ways, it wasn't. It had taken us four years to get here; that was a long time to get to know someone. We'd agreed what we had wasn't a fling, we weren't dating in the sense that we were feeling each other out, we were working on a future.

A future that would one day include merging our lives and living together. In that vein, I didn't like him having to ask if it was okay for him to invite someone over to *my* house.

"Hadley? Did you hear me?"

Hear him?

Oops.

"No, sorry. What'd you say?"

"You okay?"

He pushed his chair out and stood. The files he'd picked up from Triple Canopy were neatly arranged over the table.

I even liked seeing that—him working in the dining room with me putzing around the house. Neither of us talking, but we were close. I could look over and see him and he could do the same.

So I made a decision.

One that I didn't have to think about because it felt right, it felt natural, and I didn't need five hundred hours to weigh the pros and cons and contemplate whether it was too soon.

But maybe Brady would need time to think.

"Will you think about something for me?"

"What do you want me to think about?" he cautiously asked.

"I want to move in together," I blurted out and watched Brady go solid.

Welp, maybe it was too soon.

"Now?" His tentative question gave me serious doubts about just blurting stuff out ever again.

But that was who I was: I felt it, I said it.

And I'd said it so there was no going back.

"You don't have to answer right now. But I'd like you to think about it."

There, I'd given him an out. An escape hatch in case he didn't feel the same way I did. He could use it and not feel like he was hurting my feelings.

"I don't need time to think about it. I know what I want. But what I want and what's smart are two different things."

"Right."

That was a disappointment, something I'd dwell on alone when I could dissect, scrutinize, and analyze what he'd meant by 'smart.' I'd likely do this with a bag of greasy, over-salted chips and a tub of ranch dip. Some people worked through heartbreak and disappointment with wine and ice cream. While those two things work for others, my go-to was chips and dip, and if I was especially upset, I'd add in a few Snickers bars for good measure.

"I'm sensing you're misunderstanding me," Brady said but stayed across the room. "You'd be packing up your shit, including the furniture you just had delivered a few hours ago, and we'd be hauling it to my house this afternoon, *if*, when you got there you'd be sharing my bed. But until the time comes when we both feel it's safe for you to be there, we're gonna wait."

"I can stay in the—"

"Absolutely not." Firm. Resolute. No wiggle room. "No bullshit, Hadley, I want us living together and we will be soon. But for both of us, I gotta sort my head out first. I owe that to you. You might not need it, but I have to prove to you I'm making an effort. I'm gonna talk to Clark on Monday. I'm also gonna reach out to Liberty. And if I have to, I'll go back to seeing a doctor. Though it didn't help before, but truth be told, I wasn't all that motivated to get help. I am now. I want you in my bed, I want you in my house, and while you're there I want it to be safe and healthy. I'm asking you to let me prove to you,

you're worth the effort, you're worth the time, but more than that, you deserve to know your man will do whatever's necessary to keep you safe."

That right there was why I loved Brady. That was why when he'd shut me out and blown up at me, I knew there was something deeply wrong. And that was how I knew with a hundred percent certainty I could trust him.

"Okay, honey," I agreed.

I mean, what else could I do?

What woman wouldn't want her man to put in the time and effort to prove she was worth it?

When Brady remained silent I brought the conversation back to his earlier question.

"Who's coming over?"

"Just like that?"

"You keep saying that to me and I don't understand why."

"Because the Hadley Walker I know loves to argue."

Well, that was true. I could see his confusion.

"When have I ever argued with you about something you needed?"

"Fuck," he clipped. "Just when I think I've figured out all the reasons I love you, all of the ways you make me happy, you prove I haven't."

"Funny, the other night I was thinking about all the reasons why I'd fallen in love with you. But then I realized I wasn't done falling because you keep giving me new reasons to love you. Then I thought there'd be nothing better than falling more every day for the rest of my life until my dying breath."

Brady stood frozen, the look on his face easy to read—he liked what I'd shared, and by the way his chest wasn't moving, like he was holding his breath, he liked it more than a little bit.

I felt the same about what he'd said.

"We should stop talking," he weirdly suggested. "You gotta know I want nothing more than to take you upstairs and show you how much what you just said means to me. But I found something important about Liberty's case and I need to call my team over here to discuss it. If it wasn't about her, we'd be going upstairs and I'd show you how much I fucking love you."

God, I wanted that.

But Liberty was more important.

"Well, then, you better call your guys over so you can tell them what you need to tell them and I can be a bad hostess and not invite them to stay for dinner. Though, I am my mother's daughter so I'll set out some snacks and offer them a drink. But they ain't getting more than that from me."

"They don't need snacks and they are *not* staying for dinner."

"*Honey.*" I couldn't keep the horror-struck tone from my voice that he'd suggest such a thing. "I said bad hostess, not heathen."

Brady smiled and his body shook as he silently heaved with laughter until he could no longer hold back and it became audible. Deep, rough laughter filled my living room and I wanted to hear that sound for the rest of my life.

But I was also Hadley Walker so I was bound by the laws of nature to give him attitude when he was laughing at me.

"I don't see what's funny, Brady."

That just made him laugh harder.

24

"You've got to be shitting me," Matt seethed, not taking his eyes off the bank statement I'd handed him.

Luke, Logan, Trey, Matt, and I were sitting around Hadley's dining room table waiting for Drake and Carter. In the meantime, we were looking over bank accounts and printouts of emails Dylan had found. I was explaining the money trail when I heard Hadley's excited voice.

"Hey! You're home."

My gaze slid from Matt to the front door in time to watch Liberty walk in followed by Drake. His tired eyes came to mine and he jerked his chin in greeting.

"Got in this morning," Liberty replied.

RILEY EDWARDS

"Yo," Trey greeted and stood.

The rest of us followed, meeting Drake in the living room while Hadley hugged her cousin. She rocked her back and forth then scolded, "Shouldn't you be home sleeping?"

"And miss hearing all the latest gossip? No way."

"What, you got time for gossip but no love for me?" Trey groused.

Liberty disengaged from Hadley and stepped into Trey's widespread arms. A millisecond after Trey had closed his arms around Liberty, Drake grumbled at Trey to let go of his woman.

"You sure you're hung up on that caveman? You and I can run away and—"

"And I can kick your ass, you don't step away from my woman," Drake cut off Trey's good-natured tease.

"You could try, but even with a bum leg you know I'd take you," Trey volleyed.

Liberty patted Trey on the chest, stepped away, and asked, "You know, one day he's gonna pay you back, right?" Trey looked confused so Liberty continued. "When you find a woman, Drake's gonna hand you shit as payback."

Something flashed in Trey's eyes then he quickly

268

covered the look with one of his devil-may-care smirks.

"That's not gonna happen. I got a lotta love to spread around, too much for any one woman to handle."

"Swear to God, your comebacks suck, brother." Matt snickered. "A lotta love to spread? More like, a lotta—"

"*And* we're done," I cut in before the conversation deteriorated any further.

"I got your number, Trey Durum," Liberty rejoined. "One day, a woman's gonna swoop in and knock you on your ass and when she does, you're gonna have to admit I was right."

"Babe, that day's never gonna come."

"Bet," Liberty pushed.

"I wouldn't take that bet. Liberty is the worst winner out of all of us," Hadley piped up.

"Agreed. One time I let her win a shooting competition and she gloated for an hour," I warned Trey.

"You are full of shit," Liberty snapped.

She was right, but also wrong. I had absolutely let her win that day and I'd done it so she'd have something to smile about. Back then, Liberty's good days were coming more and more but there had still been an underlying fear. She'd gone through hell and had survived a traumatic event that very well could've broken her.

She hadn't actually gloated about her win for an hour. But that was only because ten minutes later, she was confronted by the man who'd taken her hostage. Then she'd been forced to kill that man while he pressed a gun against Drake's temple.

"Who's full of shit?" Carter asked as he walked in.

"Brady. He's still saying he let me win," Liberty griped to her cousin.

Carter said not a word but his chuckle spoke volumes.

"Rematch," Liberty snapped.

"Here we go," Delaney said from beside Carter. "It's a toss-up who's more competitive, Liberty or Carter. They're both sore losers and pouters so I think we should squash this now."

Good advice.

"Yeah, let's do that," I encouraged, then added, "How about we get to work? That way we can all get on with our afternoon."

"I invited Quinn and Addy over since I knew Liberty was gonna be here. Mom and Dad have

Emma for the rest of the day so I thought we could hang out." Delaney smiled and I held back a groan.

All four Walker girls together meant it was going to be a long day.

"Awesome," Hadley chirped and made her way to me. "Raincheck?"

"Delayed," I corrected.

"Delayed," she agreed and smiled. "I better figure out something more than snacks to feed everyone."

One arm went around her waist and the other moved to cup her jaw. When I had her close I muttered, "We'll order in. I don't want you in the kitchen making a bunch of food for thirteen people."

"Thirteen?"

"If Quinn's coming, Brice will be here. And if there's food, the guys are staying. So that's thirteen at the minimum, assuming Jackson and Tuesday, and your brother and Mercy haven't heard. Not to mention Nick and Meadow, and Ethan and Honor. We can go from thirteen to thirty and have to move to a bigger house or rent a reception hall in the blink of an eye. So we're ordering food, yeah?"

Hadley stared up at me, her eyes sweet with the soft look she gave me when I said or did something she liked. A look I loved, though I didn't understand what I'd done to deserve it.

"I love that you know that," she whispered.

"Know what?"

"Know my family. Know that one or all of them can stop by at any time. Know that an afternoon that was supposed to be just ours can and sometimes will turn into a family blowout. But mostly, I love that you don't mind."

I felt my chest start to get tight and I dipped down and pressed my lips to hers. When I straightened, she was smiling. That tightness turned into a burn.

"Family's everything, baby, and you got a good one."

"My eyes are bleeding," Carter complained.

"Even if they're nosy," I added, and Hadley smiled bigger.

"You're making out with my cousin. That's not nosy, that's just plain cruel."

"And they're annoying," Hadley mused.

"Can we please get to work?" Carter huffed.

"Jeez, Carter, keep your panties on," Hadley shot back, then rolled up on her toes and pressed her mouth to mine. "Thank you." She kissed the side of my jaw and rolled back down and stepped away.

"He's all yours," she proclaimed and strode back to Delaney and Liberty.

She did that with my eyes glued to the sway of her hips while I ignored the guys' comments. I gave zero fucks they were giving me a hard time about watching my woman—the show was spectacular.

Trey, Luke, Matt, Logan, Drake, Carter, and I were sitting at Hadley's eight-person dining room table. A table you gather around over Thanksgiving dinner. A big family table. There were papers spread across it but I wasn't seeing the bank statements, the background checks, the service records of the men Liberty both served with, and those higher up than her.

I wasn't seeing anything. My vision was blurred and my heart pounded in my chest.

Hadley came from a big family, and while we'd never talked about it, I was pretty sure she wanted to create one herself. It wouldn't be a stretch to think Hadley wanted kids, and probably a lot of them.

Kids that I didn't want.

Fuck.

"Good find, Brady," Carter cut through my anxiety-filled musings.

I blinked to clear my vision and found Carter's eyes on me. They narrowed but he didn't call me out on whatever he saw.

"Dylan found it," I reminded him.

Dylan hadn't been able to recover the information on Lieutenant Colonel Greg Berkshire's computer. Whoever had killed him had a deep understanding of computers, which explained why they'd felt confident leaving the machine behind. It was useless. However, when I'd asked Dylan to start digging into the virtual banking system, he'd hit pay dirt and found accounts in Greg's name, his wife's name, and one of his son's names.

Along with finding the bank accounts, Dylan had also found an address tied to an email account we hadn't known Berkshire had. An email account that Dylan was able to hack, which led to him finding emails between Berkshire and a Dr. Davidson, owner of the company Counterproliferation. CP was a privately-owned, government-funded company that's mission is preventing the proliferation of weapons of mass destruction and their delivery systems. Specifically WMDs and chemical weapons in Syria.

Liberty had been captured in Syria. Further, CP

had been trying to find the bomb-maker Lore for years with no luck.

The puzzle was fucked-up but the pieces fit.

"Yeah, but none of us thought to dive into virtual banks. I still can't believe people think it's smart to put their money in a fake bank somewhere in Hong Kong. Hell, you have to pay like two percent to withdraw money at an ATM."

"You're thinking like an old man," Matt put in. "The people who use virtual banks don't use cash for purchases. Their money's direct-deposited into their account and they use the debit card for everything. Hell, even vending machines have card readers now. They don't care there's no actual branch to walk into. Smartphone accounts are all the rage and it's only getting bigger."

"Dude, you're loaded," Luke started. "Would you keep your money in a fake bank?"

"Fuck, no. I like to be able to walk into a bank and count my money. But I have invested in virtual banks looking for startup capital and I've made a killing off of them."

"Now what?" Trey asked. "We have a dead lieutenant colonel with over two-million dollars split up into three accounts when the man makes under nine thousand a month as an O5. Not to mention he's got a wife and three kids. No way in fuck he just saved that money. You didn't find an inheritance. Did he win the lotto, win it gambling? Good investments?"

"No, no, no, and no. Dylan searched his family, his wife's family, tax returns, no windfall."

"Fuck," Carter clipped.

I turned to Drake, his face set to granite.

"I know we're doing our best to keep Liberty as far away from this investigation as possible but we need to know if she's ever had contact with Dr. Davidson, or if she ever saw Berkshire and Davidson together."

Wordlessly, Drake stood and went to Hadley's French doors leading to a postage stamp backyard where the women were visiting while we'd taken over the house.

Moments later, Drake came back with a wary Liberty.

"I know we gotta tread carefully, Liberty. You know I wouldn't ask if we didn't have a strong lead. I'm sorry, but I have to ask—how well do you know Berkshire, and do you know a Dr. Davidson?"

Her face turned a new shade of red. I doubted her rosy complexion had to do with the Georgia heat. She also looked pissed.

"As you all are well aware, there's a formal CID

inquiry still ongoing. So let's just say today's not the first time that name's been mentioned. But beyond that, I will not comment on the Army's efforts."

Thank Christ, we were finally on the right track.

"Fair enough."

Liberty blew out a long breath and took her time to collect her thoughts. Something I appreciated about her. She was walking a fine line and I admired how steadfast she was in her quest to stay true to her oath.

"It's a gut feeling," she sighed. "You have to understand we all wanted to find Lore, especially me. But Dr. Davidson was rabid to find him when Lore started making chlorine bombs."

Weaponizing chlorine was not only cheap but easy to deliver. They were often called a poor man's atom bomb. A barrel filled with cylinders containing chlorine gas was dropped from a helicopter. There was no explosion, just a deadly vapor as the broken canisters full of noxious gas leaked, causing respiratory failure, chemical burns, blindness, and a whole host of other issues.

"Anything else?" I prompted.

"Dr. Davidson is ambitious, and when I say that, I really mean obsessed." She paused again and pinched her lips, wanting to say more but under strict policy not to. "He wanted Lore by any means necessary. Some of the tactics he'd suggested went against the rules of engagement. When called out on those actions, he fervently argued that capturing Lore was more important."

"Who called him out?" Trey inquired.

"I did. And that was not the first argument I had with the man about his tactics."

"Fuck," Drake mumbled.

"Can you give us anything else?" I asked, knowing my question was futile.

"All I can tell you is Dr. Davidson spent a lot of time with the Lieutenant Colonel and he's not my biggest fan."

I glanced at Carter. He was studying his cousin carefully and looked like he had something to add but was holding back.

"What's on your mind, Carter?"

"Is Dr. Dickwad the type of man to hold a grudge?"

The air around the room turned stagnant. Most of the hostility was rolling off of Drake, but plenty was coming from Trey, Luke, Matt, and Logan. The men were close to Liberty, but out of those four, it was Trey whose eyes narrowed. Liberty and Trey were tight, they'd bonded after the bombing in

Lebanon that had ended Trey's naval career. Drake for obvious reasons had serious unease about his fiancée going out on missions with her special forces team while the person responsible for her capture was still unknown. Carter, too, had obvious reasons. But it wasn't until that moment I'd caught on to how deep that bond had dug in. We were all naturally protective, but Trey's large frame vibrated with anger.

"I don't know the man well enough to say for sure," Liberty said. "He doesn't like me. He didn't before I questioned him, but having the audacity to speak my mind royally pissed him off."

"Why?" Carter pushed.

With a long-suffering sigh, Liberty looked at her cousin and gave him a small frown.

"You know how it is. SEALs, Rangers, Special Forces, they're all the same in that it's a boys' club. I knew that going in. I knew I had a long row to hoe. I knew I had more to prove than any man there. I knew whoever I was paired with as my battle buddy was gonna think he drew the short straw. I'm not as strong as the men I trained with and I never will be. That's not a weakness, not when I'm smart enough to recognize that, work around it, and not try to front like I can carry a two-hundred-pound man five miles when I absolutely could not. Ranger school was a bitch, but I knew that going in. It took a while for the men around me to see I wasn't asking for special treatment. I didn't want my standards lowered because I was a woman. Eventually, every man came around but only after I proved my worth.

"Special Forces training was worse. Way worse. I caught shit and I had to eat it because I had no choice. I had to prove myself all over again and I did. No favors, no special treatment, no female standards —either I could do what the men had to do or I had no business being there. But in the end, it was worth it, I proved something. Not to them, to myself. But even though I demonstrated—repeatedly—that I'd earned my place the same way every man had, there are still those who believe that the Special Forces community should only allow men into the club. And that goes across all branches in the military. But it is not my job to change their minds. My job is to complete whatever mission I'm sent on. And that first clusterfuck of a mission notwithstanding, I am damn good at my job."

"So, he doesn't like you because you're a woman?" Carter bit out.

"He doesn't like me because he's one of the good ol' boys who still believes a woman has no place in battle. He couldn't hide the fact he hated that I'm a female lieutenant in the Army who happens to be the OIC of a special forces element and I don't take shit from suits who sit behind a desk in Washington, shit all over our chain of command, throw out rules that will not leave his ass swinging but my team's. But there again, it's not my job to care what he thinks, my job is to carry out the mission. As far as I'm concerned, Dr. Davidson can kiss my ass. I don't need his respect or his approval. He's not the one putting his ass on the line and it won't be him taking my back when bullets are flying. He can dislike me, hate me, think women should sit at home and knit afghans. His opinions are not gonna stop me from strapping on my vest, my gun, and doing my job."

Sour hit my gut and I knew every man in the room was feeling the same thing I was. Liberty might not care. And was damn well right not to give a fuck what some dickhead thought about women in Special Forces. I may've let Liberty win our shooting competition but I'd *barely* let her win. Considering I had years of sniper training and more years of long-range training, it was damn impressive she could keep up with me. Something no other man at Triple Canopy could do. Not her father, her cousins, nor her uncles could outshoot me.

But that feeling in my gut had nothing to do with her rightly standing up for herself and everything to do with evidence suggesting that her commanding officer had been a traitor, and some dickwad with a hard-on for her had paid a man who she'd trusted to off her.

Which now put a whole new spin on her capture. She was *not* just bait to draw out Roman, she was meant to come home in a pine box because she'd dared to be a soldier while female.

"You need—"

"No," Liberty cut Carter off.

"No?"

"Don't," Liberty spat. "Not you, too. Don't treat me like a woman. You all know how hard I've fought to earn my place. How hard I fought to come back from what happened. I fought hard, Carter. Don't shit on that, disrespect me, and tell me I need to stand down. I'm your equal. I'm active duty. I'm an officer. Treat me as such because I damn well deserve that."

After that, Carter looked properly chastised and my respect for the lieutenant grew. That was saying something since I'd already held the woman in the highest regard.

"You're right," Carter mumbled.

"We still need to trace the origin of the deposits. A few emails between Davidson and Berkshire's not enough if we're gonna prove Berkshire took a payoff. And no disrespect, Liberty, but there's over two million dollars, no way in fuck—"

"Are you saying I'm not worth two million dollars, Brady?" Liberty smiled.

"You're worth more than that, darlin'. But the two million wasn't paid in a lump sum, the payments are spread out. Did all two million come from Davidson? Or was Berkshire selling information to others? The no disrespect part is, you're gonna have to dance the line, look at these statements, and hark back to what missions you were on during those dates."

"I would, but I was captured on my first mission out. I have no knowledge of what came before me."

"Fuck, I forgot."

"We're gonna have to call and ask General Wick. He'd have the answers, though he won't give them to us. My suggestion is to have my dad call him," Carter suggested.

General Wick was a close friend of Levi, Jasper, Lenox, and Clark. They'd served together back in the day. I, too, knew the general well. Something I was almost positive my bosses didn't know about, and information I'd prefer they didn't find out.

My gaze slid from Liberty to Drake then back to Liberty. She was still out bravely serving, doing so with a possible target on her back.

Fucking shit.

I had no choice.

Liberty's safety was more important.

"We'll meet with the guys on Monday, get him up to speed, and ask him to call the general."

"Great. So we're done?" Trey asked, not masking his impatience.

"Yeah."

"Great. I'm gonna head out."

"Head out? Hadley just ordered a crapton of food and everyone else will be here in a minute," Liberty argued.

"There's six other men here to eat all that food. Trust me, Liberty, it won't go to waste."

Proving once again that she was sharp, Liberty took in Trey standing, yet leaning slightly, taking some of the weight off his bad leg. Her eyes got squinty.

"Why are you rushing out of here? Is your leg bothering you?"

"I'm not rushing. I got shit to do and my leg's fine."

His leg was not fine. He was rushing. Though he might've had shit to do.

"Hey," Adalynn Walker called from the front door and Trey jerked and his body went solid.

My gaze sliced from Trey to watch Hadley's twin walk through the living room.

It had long ago stopped giving me pause seeing Hadley's double, but that didn't mean that sometimes it still hit me that there were two of them. They were identical—in other words both gorgeous— but from the beginning, I could tell them apart. Hadley carried herself differently. She was sass and attitude to Addy's shy and sweet.

But right then, the thunderous look on Addy's face didn't say sweet. It said, ballbuster.

"You missed PT yesterday," Addy snapped.

Oh, shit.

"Yep," Trey snapped back, his expression matching Addy's.

There it was, the rush to leave.

"So, what, you're a quitter?"

"Can we not do this here?" he growled

I wasn't sure if it was Trey's angry tone or if Addy remembered they had an audience, and as Trey's physical therapist, she shouldn't be discussing his care openly.

"Yeah, Trey, we'll talk Monday at four when you meet me at the gym." And with that, Addy strutted her ass to the back door and Liberty followed.

Well, it seemed Addy could be full of sass and attitude, too. That was, if she had the right man to pull it out of her.

The back door slammed, Trey's eyes turned to ice, and he mumbled his goodbye.

Then I watched him hide his limp as he made his way out the front door.

"That's gonna be interesting," Matt muttered.

"No, it won't," Carter grunted.

"Dude, Addy's hot," Luke put in.

"Warning—I wanna hear shit about how hot my woman's twin sister is even less than Carter wants to hear it."

"Shit, brother, I didn't think about that." Matt laughed. "So, seeing as Trey was absolutely enjoying—"

"Don't go there."

Luke and Logan joined Matt laughing like a bunch of fools.

I wasn't laughing. Neither was Carter. He looked pensive. And I wondered which cousin he was worried about—Hadley, Addy, or Liberty.

25

I took one look at my sister's face then glanced through the back windows into my dining room just as Trey ambled across my living room.

"Oh, shit," I said at the same time Liberty asked, "What was that about?"

"Don't 'oh shit' me when you haven't returned my calls in two days," Addy snapped.

Oops. I hadn't called her back, but things had been extreme with Brady and I hadn't had time.

"It's only been twenty-four hours," I corrected. "And I forgot my phone at work. Brady took me this morning to go and get it. I was going to call you but then Delaney showed and said she'd invited you and Quinn."

"Don't throw me under the bus," Laney complained. "And stop forgetting your freaking phone at work."

"Swear. To. God. One more person bitches about my phone I'm gonna lose it. Now, accept my apology for not calling you back and spill. Why are you pissed and why is Trey running out of my house?"

"He didn't run." Addy's hurt-filled eyes came to mine and I clamped my mouth closed.

Damn.

How in the world had I missed my sister falling for Trey? And how in the hell had that even happened?

"Adalynn?"

"Don't. I don't want to talk about Trey."

"Okay."

Shit.

I liked Trey, he was a great guy. But my sister had spent years licking her wounds after her boyfriend, Jake, dumped her before he left on deployment. She hadn't dated anyone seriously since then and that was almost five years ago. Trey didn't strike me as a man who understood commitment. It was a shitty thing to think, but the man was beyond hot and he knew it. Why he'd joined the Navy instead of moving to Hollywood I did not know. He wouldn't have had to audition, all he would've needed to do was show up and he would've been cast.

No one cared if a man that good-looking could act—pretty face, hot bod, you're in. Case in point, Josh Duhamel. Smoking hot but can't act worth a lick, and considering Trey was much better-looking, he could've been a movie star.

The last thing my sweet twin needed was a *dawg* out to get laid. That was not my sister's style. I hadn't asked, though I'm almost positive she would've told me since we told each other everything, so I was pretty certain she hadn't gotten herself any since Jake the Jerk dumped her.

So, yeah, Trey would chew her up and spit her out. Quinn...now Quinn was a different story. If she wasn't already very much taken by her hot-guy-firefighter, my older sister would chew Trey up and teach him a lesson. But not Addy.

Damn.

"How's everything with Brady?" Addy changed the subject, and even though I'd just henpecked my relationship with Delaney and Liberty before my twin had arrived, I was willing to do it again to stop the unconcealed hurt on her face.

I didn't give details that were not mine to give

but I explained why the last twenty-four hours had been intense and why I hadn't found the time to call her back.

Without the whole story and leaving out the parts about his sister which would elucidate the situation, I watched Adalynn's eyes get squintier and squintier as I continued.

"I hope you know what you're doing," she mumbled.

"I do."

"None of that sounds good," she noted.

"Because it wasn't good, it was horrible. You know I walked into this with my eyes open. I knew something was eating at him. I know what that is now and it's worse than what I'd imagined. *The* worst, Addy, something none of us sitting here can imagine, not even Liberty, it's that bad. What I can tell you is, down to his soul he's in pain and he's been avoiding dealing with it for twenty years. But now he's ready to face it because he thinks I deserve the best and he knows he needs to sort his head and be healthy to give me that. It sucked hearing the man I love tell me to get out of his house, but you know what sucked worse? Looking at him, knowing he was in agony and not being able to reach him. Not being able to protect him from that. So, I'll take that suckage if it means I get to stand by him as he works this out. I will not give up on him."

Something flashed in Addy's eyes, something I recognized not only because we were halves of the same whole, not only because I knew her, but because I saw that same exact look in the mirror when I thought about Brady.

Oh, shit.

Adalynn was totally in love with Trey.

"Addy," I murmured.

"Don't say it," she whispered. "I know it's not right."

"What's not right?"

"I'm his therapist."

Yep. She was in love with Trey.

"So?"

"It's not right. It's not professional."

Liberty snorted, obviously understanding the veiled conversation.

"Trust me, you cannot help who you fall in love with, Adalynn. You cannot control when, you cannot control where, and you cannot control how it happens."

My cousin would know. She'd fallen in love with

the man who'd rescued her from the pits of hell while in a war zone. She'd outranked him, making their relationship not only inappropriate but against military regulations. Lucky for her, he'd fallen just as hard. In an effort to protect her from losing her commission and everything she'd worked hard for, Drake had taken an undeserved dishonorable discharge from the Navy. And not a single day had gone by that Drake had regretted that decision.

"I don't want to talk about this," Addy grumbled.

"What'd the guys need to talk to you about?" I asked Liberty.

"Nope. We're not talking about that bullshit, either. I've been gone for weeks. I need more gossip. Anyone knocked up? Thinking about getting knocked up? Secretly ran away and got married? What's new in the Lenox-Clark-Walker-McCoy clan?"

"I know something juicy," Delaney chirped.

"Spill," I demanded.

"Okay, this is top-secret. But, I think Mercy's pregnant."

"Seriously?" Addy breathed.

We'd been waiting for my big brother and his wife Mercy to get down to baby-making.

"Well, I'm not sure. I overheard Jason telling her

not to forget to take her vitamins and she was only allowed one cup of coffee. So it's a reach and more of a hopeful guess."

"Mom and Dad would be so happy," I stated the understatement of the year.

"They would be," Laney agreed. "And one more secret. This one's super, top-secret, swear on the sisterhood you will not utter a word." Once Laney had our solemn promises, she continued. "I'm three weeks late. I took a test this morning and it was positive."

My heart swelled so big I thought it was going to burst. Being an "aunt" to my cousins' kids and Laney and Carter's Emma, was the coolest thing in the world. I adored my nieces and nephews.

"Ohmigod." Addy clapped. "Carter's gonna be so happy."

"Yeah, he will," she agreed.

It was then for the first time I started wondering how many kids Brady wanted. I hoped at least four. I'd compromise at three but I really wanted five.

Growing up, our house was busy, loud, and chaotic. Admittedly, I now sought peace due to the chaos. But I wouldn't have wanted to grow up any other way. A house full of noise, love, and laughter.

The opposite of what Brady had had. Something I wanted desperately to give him.

So I'd settle on three kids, but I was going to push for six.

"I THINK I have permanent hearing loss," Brady complained.

We were in my bed, both of us on our sides facing each other, the length of me pressed tight against the length of him. Maximum touching, post seriously-hot sex. His hearing loss could've been due to me screaming my last orgasm so loud even my ears were ringing. Though he could've been talking about the decibel level rising when Quinn, Brice, Jason, Mercy, Jackson, and Tuesday had shown up, because seriously, my family was loud and my condo was small so it didn't help we'd all been packed in like cattle.

"Which part damaged your ears, honey? The general volume of my family? When Jackson and Brice started arguing over Tom Brady leaving the Patriots? Or when Quinn and Laney started shouting over who was doing the dishes? Or when my brother announced his wife was finally pregnant and everyone shouted?"

"All a' that," he said, and his eyes danced with humor.

Oh, yeah. I loved that look.

"I'd say I was sorry but this isn't your first rodeo, cowboy. You knew how loud they can be yet you stayed."

"Indeed, I knew."

"Did you have a good time save the damage to your eardrums?"

"I always have a good time when I'm with your family."

God, I *loved* that.

I was happy, sated at the end of a good day hanging with my man and my family, learning that my brother and my sister were both going to give me more family to love. Though Delaney didn't announce this because she was planning something special for Carter involving Emma and a big-sister shirt. So the only thing making the end to the day not perfect was that I knew Brady was going to leave. He'd wait until I fell asleep but then he'd go home.

I didn't like it one damn bit. But I wasn't going to let it ruin my good mood.

"Can I ask you something?"

I felt Brady's body go stiff before he relaxed and said, "Ask away."

"How many kids do you want?"

His reaction was an immediate shutdown.

Vacant.

And not his normal blank stare—a catastrophic, all-systems failure.

"I don't, baby," he told me gently. But there was no amount of gentleness that would soothe that crushing blow.

"You don't?"

"No."

How could a single, softly spoken word feel like a slap in the face?

"And since we're already talking about this you should also know, I don't ever want to get married."

It seemed the more words he delivered in that gentle, velvet tone, the more they hurt, because that felt like a dagger to my heart.

"What? I thought you wanted forever."

"Forever. Not marriage. You want my ring on your finger, it's yours. You want me to wear yours, I will. But, Hadley, baby, you're gonna have to find it in you to be happy with my promise I'm yours forever. Because I do not ever want to get married."

"And if I can't find it in me?"

I didn't think it was possible, but Brady closed down more.

Lights out.

Gonzo.

"Then I'll have to find it in me to step aside so you can find a man who can give that to you, because, baby, I love you down to my soul. I'll give you everything that's in my power to give you. But I know that's not something I can give."

My blood froze in my veins.

Step aside.

Step aside so I could find a man who could give that to me?

I could feel my feet slipping on thin ice, I could hear it cracking, and I was scared that at any moment, I'd fall through into the icy water and die a slow, cold death.

Yet, I still had to know.

"Why?"

Brady was silent for a beat, then he commenced shattering my heart.

"Because I promised myself I'd never saddle a good woman, the woman I chose to love and cherish for the rest of my life, with that piece of shit's name. It's bad enough I have to live with the Hewitt name.

No way in fuck will I ever infect you with the moth-erfucker's name."

"Brady," I whispered.

"Not gonna strap you with that, baby. Not gonna tie kids down with it, either. I want to give you forever, but that only comes with my vow right here, right now. I promise I'll be faithful, I'll work hard to give you a good life, I'll love you until my dying breath. But I'm never giving you my name."

I let every heartbreaking word crash over me. I let them settle low in my belly, each word piled up like a mound of rocks, making my stomach ache.

It was on the tip of my tongue to argue, to rail and tell him I didn't care who gave him his name, I still wanted it. I wanted to be tied to him every way I could be. I wanted to have kids and give them our name. But now was not the right time. It was late, he was tired, and the sting of his sister's birthday and the anniversary of her death was still fresh.

So instead of doing what I always did, pushing and arguing, I found patience.

No, that wasn't right. I remembered how much I loved Brady. I thought about all that was swirling in my mind, the hurt and devastation his parents had wrought, and how hard it was for him to face that.

Yet, for me—for us—he was going to face those demons.

Then I thought about his promises. Forever. Faithfulness. Happiness. Love. Protection. I wanted that. He'd give me a ring and wear one himself but I'd never have the piece of paper that legally bound him to me. Did I *need* that paper, or did I just need him? I wanted both. I wanted it all. But what I needed most was him—so I could live without the paper.

I wanted kids. I wanted them badly. Giving up that dream would be beyond devastating—it would be earth-shattering. But now, us lying in my bed face-to-face, our bodies pressed tight, arms around each other after a long day, with everything that had happened yesterday still weighing heavy on Brady, it was not the time to try to talk him around to giving me at least one.

"That's a lot to think about, Brady," I stated, then asked something I shouldn't have because it was borderline pushy. "How firm are you on all of that?"

"Firm."

Quick. Decisive. Blank.

Heartbreaking.

"Right."

"You want me to stay until you fall asleep?"

God, I hated that he had to ask.

"Always."

I saw up close and personal—with our noses only inches apart it was hard to miss—relief followed by sadness.

I hated that, too.

26

It had been nearly a week since I'd told Hadley I never wanted to get married. Six days of her acting like I hadn't seen the disappointment wash over her features when I told her. Six fucking days of her pretending I hadn't gutted her when I said I never wanted kids. Six great days of us being together. Four of those nights were spent at her house, me leaving after I'd tucked her into bed and she'd fallen asleep. But before that, our nights included dinner together, watching TV, laughing, conversation, and mind-blowing sex. Last night, we'd switched it up and she came to my place. It had been more of the same, with the only switch-up being that I didn't want her driving home, so I'd left her in my bed and slept on the couch.

During last night's dinner conversation, she'd told me she was going to start the renovation on the kitchen and forget about redoing the master bathroom, which was the last update she'd make before the condo would be ready to sell. Then she told me she wanted to sell as quickly as she could. This had surprised me. The market wasn't shit, but she hadn't been there very long, and the smarter thing to do would be to hold on to it a few more months and wait. I expressed my thoughts, however, she was adamant. She wanted a bigger place with a backyard —a family home—then she'd swept her arm indicating my living room and said, "Like this place. If we'd been here last weekend, we wouldn't have been packed in like sardines. And your backyard is perfect for a family blowout."

It had taken so much out of me not to demand we address the gigantic fucking elephant in the room it's a minor miracle I'd held it together.

Six more days of falling harder, drowning in her, tying her tighter, loving her more than breath.

I needed her to make a decision.

What I hadn't had time to do was seek out Clark and have a much-needed sit-down with him. This was partly to do with me wanting to spend every free minute I had with Hadley so I could soak up those minutes and stockpile them just in case she decided to walk away.

The fuck of it was, I'd let her go. I loved her too much to hold her down. She deserved marriage and babies and family blowouts with her children running amongst the gaggle of kids her brother, sister, and cousins were popping out.

I was selfish enough to ask her to give that up so I could have her. But I was not dick enough to force it on her or beg her to stay with me if she couldn't find it in her to give all of that up so we could be together.

The other part of why I hadn't found the time to connect with Clark was because, after our meeting on Monday with all the principals of Triple Canopy in attendance, I'd laid out everything we had on Berkshire and Dr. Davidson. Levi, Jasper, Lenox, and Clark had all agreed it was time to call in General Wick and ask him to come to Georgia. Which had left my gut in knots. I respected the general and I knew he respected me. Further, I knew he wouldn't and couldn't explain how he knew me, nor could he tell anyone the missions he'd sent me on and what I'd done during those operations. But my bosses were smart, they were aware, they were watchful, and they, too, were former Delta. They'd know. They'd see the familiarity between me and

Wick and it would take a nanosecond for them to put the pieces together.

I hadn't *just* been part of the Combat Applications Group, I'd been General Wick's one-man fire team. His weapon of choice when a team couldn't be sent in or when our government needed complete anonymity and deniability. Darker than black-ops, so dark there wasn't an attributable agency, code name, or mission brief. Not a single document detailing my mission objective. Layers of protection set in place when the orders were passed down, so by the time Wick gave his verbal instructions, not even he knew who'd put the order in motion.

But Wick knew where he'd sent me and what I'd done.

Levi, Clark, Lenox, and Jasper were not stupid, they wouldn't miss a beat. They wouldn't know the particulars but they'd know. And what they'd know meant they'd have a clear understanding I was Wick's assassin. Something I never wanted them to know, especially Jasper. He'd given me his blessing thinking I'd walked in his shoes, I'd taken lives, I had deep marks on my soul. But under all those marks he still saw some good or he would've told me in no uncertain terms I'd be eating my balls if I dared to touch his beloved daughter. But he'd given that blessing without all the facts.

And now that Hadley was mine, unless she set me out, I wasn't giving her up. Not even if it meant Jasper and his brothers castrating me.

Something else I hadn't discussed with Jasper was Hadley's situation at the library. Nothing new had happened this week and it was Hadley's assumption whoever was behind the destruction had burned themselves out or had moved on to another branch, though Hadley had been in touch with other librarians in the area to warn them and no one had reported back to her that they'd had any issues. Yesterday she'd gotten word from the commissioners they didn't have the budget for cameras. It was time for me to talk to the guys about using Triple Canopy resources. Considering the top shareholders of the company were family or soon-to-be-family, I knew no one would have a problem but I still had to run it by them. And even though Jasper, Lenox, Levi, and Clark had officially retired, the "official" part of that statement was pretty loose considering they were very much involved with the investigation into who was behind letting Liberty's ass swing in the wind. They just didn't see to the day-to-day operation of the company.

But Jasper would want to know what was going on with his girl.

I needed to find that time, but seeing Nick Clark stop outside my open office door told me I wouldn't be finding that time. At least not now.

"Wick's here," Nick told me. "We're meeting in the conference room."

Fuck.

"I'll be right there."

With a jerk of his chin, Nick continued down the hall and I shot a text to Hadley telling her I'd be late.

I wasn't even out of my office when my phone chimed with her reply.

It was simple and to the point but made my stomach clench.

Yours or mine?

I wanted to type back ours. But seeing as we had a whole host of shit to wade through before we could circle back around to talking about living together, I couldn't.

You pick. Going into a meeting but text me what you decide.

I hit send and silenced my phone.

I'd given her a key to my place. Her reaction to the gesture hadn't been the same as mine. She hadn't dragged me to my bedroom and fucked me senseless, but her eyes had gone soft and her smile told me everything I needed to know. She liked having a key to my pad, but more, she liked what it said—full access, complete trust, no hiding.

I liked that, too.

I scanned the conference room as I entered, noting Luke and Trey were absent but Dylan and General Wick were present.

"Where's Trey and Luke?" I asked.

"Trey's at PT and Luke's still on the range," Jason answered.

"Brady, son. Good to see you," Wick boomed.

Wick was a good man, a good leader. Loyal to his country, to the Army, to the men who served under him. But seeing him brought back the bitter taste, the past I couldn't escape, the blood I'd spilled, the marks I'd willfully and readily earned. A past I didn't want Hadley to ever know about. In other words, I respected the man, I liked him, but I'd never wanted to see him again. Yet, there he was.

"You, too, sir," I said, and locked eyes with the man who'd sent me places where no one else could go, had me carry out missions no one else could.

And I hoped to God what he was silently

communicating to me while he held my stare was that he'd keep our secrets just that—secrets.

Unfortunately, Drake was sharp and perceptive and jumped on the familiarity. "I didn't realize the two of you knew each other so well."

"We've crossed paths," Wick smoothly covered. "I don't have much time, let's get down to what's so important I needed to get my ass on a plane for a face-to-face."

Since Wick had set the tone that he wasn't in the mood for chitchat, I didn't waste the opportunity to move the conversation away from how well I did or didn't know the general.

"Dylan," I prompted, and our IT wizard launched into his brief.

It took under thirty minutes for us to lay out several months' worth of work. When we were done, Wick's expression was thunderous, his voice no less stormy as it rent through the silence like a gunshot.

"Stand down."

Two words. That was all it took for the room to go electric.

"You knew my daughter's commanding officer was a fucking traitor and Davidson was behind what happened to my daughter and you didn't say anything?" Levi's question matched Wick's tone and volume—angry and loud.

"I suspected something was up with Berkshire but I didn't have proof. And more than that, I didn't want to think a man I served with, a man under my command, would be a traitor. But I can't say I didn't suspect it. It was nothing more than a gut feeling, but not until I spent some time thinking back after Berkshire was murdered did I clue into Davidson being a part of that. Dr. Davidson had millions of dollars in government contracts. He's expected to deliver. And he's known to run a shady operation."

"So, you're not buying the suicide story either?" Drake inquired.

"Not for a second."

"Are you willing to look at the bank statements?" I asked.

Wick's gaze snapped to mine and I didn't like what that was non-verbally communicating.

"No."

"No?" Levi growled.

"For more reasons than one, I know I can't tell you what to do, Levi. You've got your daughter wrapped up in this mess and I know you want to see the man responsible brought to justice and he will be. I also know it's a waste of my breath and time to tell you to stand down because that's not the type of man you are, but I'm doing it all the same. Stand down. You've got my word I haven't forgotten what happened to Lieutenant McCoy and I'm working on my end to see this gets done."

"Mess?" Levi thundered. "This isn't a goddamn mess. My daughter's life was endangered. She was taken, beaten, mentally tortured, and left to die. Would've died if Drake and his team hadn't found her when they did. And after my girl endured that fucking nightmare she decides to stay in the Army, further swinging her ass out there. First, my girl does that because unlike those motherfuckers Berkshire and Davidson, she takes her commitment to her country seriously. And, Wick, you know my daughter so you know I speak the truth when I tell you her other reason for staying in is because she does not back down and she will not be cowed. Even if that means every time she goes out there's a possible target on her back."

Levi stared down Wick. "I want that target removed. I want the man who put that target on my daughter's back not breathin'. I believe you haven't forgotten. I believe that when you close your eyes at night you see my girl beaten to shit limping across the airstrip after her rescue. I know you also remember the little girl you bounced on your knee when she was a baby. But what you do not see is what I see, what Drake sees, and that's because while you care for my daughter and you respect her, you do not love her down to your bones the way Drake and I do. So I believe you're working hard, but you will not work as hard as we will."

He regained some of his composure. "Now, I'm asking you as my friend, as a man I served with, as a brother whose back I had on the battlefield, to look over the statement and tell Brady and Dylan what missions were happening around those deposits. We got enough to tarnish the memory of Berkshire. We will find the connection to Davidson making those payoffs, but I do not want more ghosts. We learned the hard way and it's a lesson we'll never forget."

No one in that room would forget the lesson that had almost cost Liberty her life. It was a lesson in revenge, but more, it was a lesson to never leave loose ends. Davidson's plan would never have worked if there hadn't been history. At the time when Levi, Jasper, Lenox, and Clark killed Roman's father they wouldn't have killed the boy or his mother, but they sure as fuck would've kept an eye on the situation. But they left shit unchecked, important stuff that years later had bitten them in the ass.

Wick nodded. "I'll take the paper copies back to my hotel and go over them. I don't want any electronic footprint. And that's not me covering my ass, it's me covering yours. I'll look them over but I can already tell you, it won't matter if I remember every single troop movement to match these dates, Dylan's not going to find the source of the deposits."

Fuck.

Fucking hell.

"How do you know that?" Carter asked.

"Because I've already tried."

"So you knew about the accounts," Levi stated. "Knew Berkshire had turned traitor. Knew that motherfucker Davidson had it out for my girl. What else do you know?"

"A lot. And you know I can't tell you." Wick's gaze sliced to Dylan. "Give me what you have. I'll be back at oh-six-hundred. My flight leaves at noon."

The room went silent, but the quietness did nothing to snuff out the hostility rolling around. Dylan gathered the papers and passed them to the general. Once he had the thick stack in hand, he looked at Levi. "You're right. I see all of that every night when I close my eyes. But I also see something you don't because you were not there. But Drake was. So was Logan, Luke, Matt, and Trey and I think it's important for you to know. Lieutenant McCoy is her father's daughter. She is intimately aware that target's on her back. And when this one is no longer there another will be in its place and she still won't back down. She's a McCoy, she's a Hellraiser, and you, Levi, made her that then you gave her to the Army. You gave her to me and that's something I take seriously. So, I'll leave you with one last thing because I know Liberty has not and will not give this to you. She knows more than you think she does, she's closer than you think to ending this, and I personally have fed her what she needs to end this herself. My advice to you is to give her her head and let that happen."

Holy shit. Liberty McCoy's been holding out on us.

Son of a bitch.

And by the murderous look on Levi's face, Wick should've kept that last tidbit to himself.

Wick started to make his way to the door, stopped by my side, and lowered his voice. "Whatever it is you're feeling right now, that worry I see in your eyes. Let it go. You tell them what you need to tell them and you'll find you're in good company."

Goddammit.

And with that, Wick left the room, closing the

door behind him.

It took approximately two seconds for Drake to break the silence. When he did, the walls shook.

"What in the fuck?" he roared.

"Liberty wasn't used for bait, she was marked. Berkshire fucked that up thinking he could mastermind some scheme, bringing down multiple players at once."

"Are you saying that fuckwad Davidson put a hit out on my woman because he didn't like her?" Drake seethed. "And gave that hit to her commanding officer to carry out?"

"Yes."

"You're shitting me," Nick grunted.

"I think Dr. Davidson didn't like Liberty calling him out. But more, he didn't like that she wasn't willing to break the rules. That made her a liability. And since he'd expressed his desire for her and her team to break those rules to complete the mission that made her a bigger liability. If what Liberty says is true, and I've seen it firsthand so I believe her, he had a huge problem with her being a woman and in a position of power. Wick said Berkshire was conniving and Davidson's known for running a shady operation. I can't say I understand the plotting, planning, and extreme effort it took to put that kind of operation into place when personally, I wouldn't have gone through the hassle."

"What's that mean? The hassle?" Jason asked.

I took a moment to consider lying to Hadley's brother, which would have the added benefit of not making myself sound like a cold-blooded killer in front of her dad, uncles, cousins, and the men who I needed to work with.

But in the end, I didn't need to say anything. Clark did.

"Because four bullets would've been faster, easier, and cleaner with a guarantee Liberty, Roman, Lore, and Roman's uncle were dead. Setting up that mission was risky, and as it turned out, didn't work. Liberty was left alive and so was Roman until he showed up here. And there wouldn't have been casualties."

Clark was correct, I would've simply taken out my targets. Berkshire fucked up planning that mission, though he might not have had a choice.

"Davidson took out Berkshire for fucking up?" Logan asked.

"That'd be my guess. Or he took him out because he was pissed he fucked up and Berkshire was stupid enough to threaten Davidson or push back. Making Berkshire a wildcard so Davidson put him down."

"Where's that leave us with Liberty?" Carter asked.

"Doesn't leave this room that we know—"

"Jesus Christ, Levi. I'm not letting my woman outta my fucking sight until Davidson's put down!" Drake shouted and stood.

Animosity clouded the air as the two men faced off.

Two men who fiercely loved Liberty. Her father and her man.

"No shit," Levi snarled. "She gets called out on a mission, you're her shadow. It's gonna piss her off and I don't give the first fuck. That will be on me and I'll deal with her." Levi turned to Dylan and continued. "I want both of her phones tapped. Personal and work." He took in a long inhale through his nose that didn't look like it did much to clear his mind. "Pissed as shit at Wick. I get it but I'm still pissed, and part of that is because he's right. We have to give Liberty her head the same way we'd give any man in this room his. But that doesn't mean she won't have backup if she needs it. No one mentions what Wick said. That's gonna suck for you, Drake, but you're gonna have to find a way. When this is over, she's gonna be pissed, but you have my word I'll take your back on that and let her know it was my idea."

"We done?" Drake asked, not bothering to try to conceal his anger. It rolled off of him, filling the room so thick it was hard to breathe.

"We're done," Levi confirmed.

Drake moved to the door but stopped with his hand on the knob. "It goes without saying, respect all around but I want this shit done. I wanted it done months ago before Liberty went back to work. Now I'm stating it plainly—Wick, us, CID, Liberty, I don't much give a fuck, but if it's not over in the next five days, I'm taking a leave of absence and I'm taking a trip to D.C. and I'll be personally ending it and I'll be doing that on my own without any interference from any of you."

"Drake—"

"I can't fuckin' sleep." Drake's strangled voice cut off Levi. "If her ass isn't in that bed next to me, I do not sleep. I close my eyes and I'm back in Syria, only I'm standing across the room and I can't get to her. All I can do is stand in the corner and watch her fade away. It was *me* who breathed life back into her. It was *me* who carried her outta that shithole. It was *me* who cleaned her. It was *me* who held her in the helo. And it was *me* who had the fucking honor of watching her muster up the last of her strength and with only *my* socks on her feet walk off that helicopter. You know what she said to me? 'Stick close, just in case I start to take a header.' It was then I promised her I would never let her fall."

Drake pointed around the room. "I get you're her father. I get they're her uncles. I get they're her cousins. But she is *mine*. Mine, Levi. Five days, then *I'm* taking the fucker out. This has to end."

With that, Drake left the room and slammed the door.

A ragged "fuck" came from Levi. His brothers moved closer to him and Carter stood.

"I'll go talk to him. He was—"

"He was right, Carter. He didn't say anything that wasn't true," Levi told him. "This has to end."

Carter jerked his chin to his uncle and left the room.

I took in the rest of the men at the table and said, "We've got less than five days to make sure Davidson goes down. Dylan, get on tapping Liberty's phone. And I don't care what Wick said, find the origin of those deposits. Nick, you got any friends at the FBI who could help, now's the time to call in those markers. Jason, you know the dark web better than any of us, start digging. See if CP is out there hunting for intel they can buy."

Wordlessly, Nick and Jason nodded and left.

"Logan, Matt, you're on Wick."

"Wick's clean," Jasper told me.

"I know he is. I also know we're getting close. Davidson's gotta be feeling the heat. Wick's smart, but he doesn't have eyes in the back of his head."

"You think Wick's put the pressure on Davidson?" Clark asked.

"If I was Wick and I was getting impatient I'd get word to Davidson I was getting close. I'd want him sweatin', scramblin', forcin' him to make a mistake. Since Wick taught me most of what I know, I figure he's done just that. Which means Wick needs someone covering his ass."

I felt Jasper's eyes boring into me, seeing more than I wanted him to see.

"More than just crossed paths," Jasper mumbled.

Here goes nothing. "Wick was my handler."

Jasper's knowing gaze held mine.

If he changed his mind and didn't want me near his daughter, he wasn't getting his way. And if Jasper changed his mind, that meant Hadley's brother would follow. Then every man in the room would back his play and I'd be up against a battalion of badasses.

But I'd win.

Hadley was mine.

27

Wick

General Wick sat in his rental outside Triple Canopy and engaged his cell phone. He had to make this call now, before his phone, hers, or both were tapped.

That was what he'd do, so he knew he didn't have time to waste the thirty minutes it would take him to get to his hotel.

There were closer places to stay, but he'd chosen the rundown, out of the way, pay by the hour motel carefully. They needed this done but also needed civilians safe. So Wick had rented three rooms, that way no one would be in the adjoining rooms. There was no telling how Davidson would come at him and the general didn't want bullets going through a wall and striking an innocent bystander.

"How'd it go?" Liberty immediately asked.

"About as well as expected. Your dad took a pound of flesh and your man looked like he wanted to wring my neck."

"I know they're gonna be pissed when this is over, but they'll understand. I'll talk to them. Are you on your way to the motel?"

It was still hard for the old man to reconcile Lieutenant McCoy was the cute baby he'd rocked. She'd grown from a beautiful, smiling little girl to a competent, strong, beautiful woman. An officer in the U.S. Army. She was one of the best soldiers he'd ever commanded, save Brady Hewitt. No one, not even Jasper, Lenox, Clark, or Levi, could compare to Hewitt's superior skills. Battlefield tactics came naturally, his rifle an extension of him, his focus laser-sharp.

It had been one of the best days of Wick's life when Hewitt told him he wasn't re-enlisting. There comes a time in a man's life when he needs to stop running and start healing, and Wick knew exactly who could help the man heal.

There was no better family than the one his former teammates had created. They loved ferociously, they were rabid about loyalty and love. If anyone could help Hewitt face what that mother-fucker of a father did, they could.

And when Liberty had told him Hewitt had finally stepped up and admitted he was in love with Hadley Walker, that was the second-best day of his life. Even better than the day he had the honor of witnessing Liberty McCoy realize her dream and become a Ranger. Even better than the day she'd become a Special Forces soldier. Better in the sense that Hewitt might've thought he was claiming Hadley, but one does not claim a Walker. They claim you. And when they did, that is forever.

So, finally, Hewitt would heal and move on.

"I'll be on my way to the hotel soon," Wick answered Liberty. "But there's been a change. You sit tight. No doubt Drake will be home in the next fifteen minutes."

"What?" she snapped.

Pure McCoy. Just like her father, she didn't like last-minute changes.

"They know you know more than you've let on. Drake's not feeling too happy about that. He'll be leaving here and coming straight to you."

"That's impossible. I was careful and fed them

just enough for them to think I was helping but walking the line of OSPEC."

"Know that, girl. I told them. Now, you're out. You sit your behind at home with your fiancé and let me finish this."

"I cannot believe you," she hissed. "You still need backup. I'm meeting you there."

"No need. Hewitt will have men on me."

"You can't know that unless you told them everything."

"Trust me. I know Hewitt."

"General—"

"Trust me, girl. You've done your part. Now you let me do this."

"If he doesn't—"

"Then I'm dead and you'll have everything you need to take down Davidson and his company. Stay home and that's an order."

"Not an official one, Stewart," Liberty balked.

"You're right. But it's a request from an uncle to his beloved niece so I'm begging you, sweetheart, stay home, stay safe. And let me finish this. You've done good. You've set everything in motion. Thank you for that. I gotta hit the road so Logan and Matt can follow me and do that thinking I don't know they're doing it."

"Fine. But only because I trust Logan and Matt. But if you get to the motel and they didn't tail you, call me and I'll come back you up."

"Sure," he lied.

"I know you're lying," she sighed. "Love you, Uncle Stewart. Please be safe."

"I haven't spent over half my life in the Army to be taken out in a dirty motel room by a piece of shit with zero combat training. I'll be fine."

He hoped that wasn't a lie.

"Call me when it's over."

"Will do."

Wick disconnected and started his rental. Then he drove to a shitty motel with Logan and Matt trailing him four car lengths back. They were good, he wouldn't have noticed them if he hadn't been the one to train Hewitt.

Now all that was left was to wait.

28

I was in the lobby checking my phone to see whose house I was heading to when I heard Levi call my name.

"Need a minute," he told me when I turned my attention his way.

"Only have a few of those. Hadley's waiting on me."

"Then we'll make this quick."

Without waiting for my answer, Levi headed down the hall that led to his office. I followed wondering when the semi would leave semi-retirement and the men would actually retire. That was supposed to happen months ago.

I stopped in front of Levi's empty office, heard

voices coming from the one next door, and continued down the hall. My chest started to get tight.

I entered Jasper's office, took in the space, and bit back a grin. Not a single item had been packed up.

"Just a question, Jasper, but when you actually retire and leave this place, are we leaving your offices set up as shrines to the four old men, or are you planning on clearing out so we can do something useful with the space?"

Jasper's mouth twitched and the other men chuckled.

"Can't speak for my brothers but my shit's staying as a reminder."

"What's the reminder?"

"Anyone thinks to slack off, I can and will be back."

He was full of shit. Not a single man who worked for the company would ever slack off. For most of the employees, it was their birthright, their legacy. The rest of us were loyal through and through, so Jasper was absolutely full of shit and it was he who couldn't let go of his baby.

"Levi said you needed a minute. I told him, and now I'm telling the rest of you, I don't have much time. Hadley's waiting on me."

That earned me another twitch of Jasper's mouth that led to an out-and-out smile.

"Right, then I'll start," Clark said and I braced. "And in the effort to save time I'll say it straight. Before today, we knew you were close to Wick and we'd suspected what that relationship was. That was one of the reasons we recruited you."

"And what relationship did you suspect I had with Wick?" I asked even though I didn't want to have this conversation.

"Exactly the one you confirmed," Jasper said, and that tightness in my chest intensified until it compressed my heart, making the muscle work double-time. "Wick was your handler and you were running ghost ops for him. You were the best on your team. Natural talent. Wick wouldn't let that go to waste. He'd see it, recognize it, and use it. And we recognized it because we'd seen it before. That's not what Triple Canopy does—the company will never descend into the darkness—but that doesn't mean when we were looking to bring a man on, we didn't want the best. You ever wonder how we got word your enlistment was up, you weren't staying in, and how we knew where to find you?"

A dull roar in my head started at the knowledge

that Jasper knew exactly who I was and all the things I'd done.

"I figured you had friends in high places," I answered Jasper.

And that was the truth. I'd never thought much beyond the men's connection to the Army and Triple Canopy's proximity to post meant they probably still shared an occasional beer with someone in my chain of command. It wasn't top-secret information that I was getting out of the Army.

"Wick." That came from Lenox and my back snapped straight. "Told us he knew someone getting out. Someone who understood teamwork, commitment, and loyalty. Told us you were the best and he was worried about how you'd transition into civilian life with no family at your back and without the Army giving you a purpose. He spoke highly of you and did it for a good long while. So we looked into you."

What the fuck? They'd taken me on because they felt sorry for me that I had no fucking family?

"Get that look off your face," Jasper commanded. "We hired you because Wick was right. You were the best. Not only the best on your team but the best of any school the Army sent you to. You're one of the few men I know who's as good as you are, yet has no ego. You don't brag about it, you don't draw attention to it, you're still a team player even though in any given room you're probably smarter than the rest."

He motioned to everyone else. "And looking around this room with all the talent and experience we got, that still holds true. We know you scored a ninety-eight on your ASVAB and you could've done anything inside or outside of the military. But you chose to serve because you had a shit family, no money, and no options, and there is no shame in the reason why you enlisted. You had to get away from what you had to get away from."

Jasper's voice actually softened. "Before we approached you we knew about your father and what he'd done to your sister. We also knew about your mother's issues. None of those we cared about beyond the fact they were tragic events in your life. We didn't judge you for their deeds. We brought you on and you proved to be more of an asset than we'd thought, and we had high expectations.

"Now that you know we didn't recruit you because Wick was worried about you, but because we wanted you, I'll confirm that we had our suspicions Wick used you to run his ghost ops. As you know, Wick is tight-lipped so he never actually told us he was running them, but since I, Levi, Lenox,

Clark, and Wick had all worked the program back in our day, we're smart enough to put it together. You can take from that, that none of us had an issue with it. And that includes me and all the personal shit we got going on."

Some of the tightness started to leave my chest. But when Levi spoke, that loosening was short-lived.

"The question is, after all these years, with us proving to you you're more than an employee of Triple Canopy, you're family—how is it you can be standing there looking like you're getting ready to run the gauntlet?"

I looked from Levi to the wall decorated with photographs in an effort to free myself from the hurt in his stare. Hurt that for some reason, even though I'd caused it, felt so fucking good it burned my heart. The burn was so good, it was second to how Hadley made me feel when I got one of her smiles.

"Because until I met the four of you I didn't know what family was," I admitted and looked back at Levi. "Because up until you welcomed me into your family, not only did I not want to be a part of one, I knew I never wanted one of my own. Not once growing up was I shown care or concern. When I joined the Army I was given a team. When I was Delta I was given brothers. When Wick took me under his wing I was given a mentor. But nowhere in any a' that was I given a family."

I looked back at Levi. "And no disrespect, Levi, but you misread my hesitation. I wasn't trying to hide who I was or what I'd done from the men in this room. I wanted it hidden from my woman's father so he didn't change his mind and take the only good thing I have in my life away from me. And that extends past Hadley to all of you and the family you've given me. It was me not wanting the woman I love to know what I'm capable of and the body count I have on my conscience."

I looked at all those good men in that room. "So, yes, I was part of Wick's ghost team, but you have to know I wasn't only a part of it, I was his go-to. I have more hits on me than the other four he used put together. And that's something I never want Hadley to live with."

"I am not that motherfucker," Jasper barked, and my torso jerked back at the forcefulness in his tone. "I'm not gonna give you one of the most precious things I have in my life then take it away and leave you shattered. We've had this conversation, but it bears repeating: I love my daughter. I would maim and kill to protect her. I would lay my life down for her. As well as you know me, do you think I'd ever hand her to a man I didn't believe was capable of doing the same?"

"No," I bit out, only saying that one word because I could say no more with my heart in my throat.

"Damn right, I wouldn't. I know the man you are, Brady, and you know I love my kids, so you know I don't say this lightly when I tell you I'll be smiling when I walk her down the aisle to you."

Jesus fuck, that felt good.

Even if that would never happen.

That lump in my throat was getting hard to choke down.

"Why do you look like I just kicked you in the balls?"

Christ.

"Hadley knows this so it's only fair you do, too. I'm never gonna marry her."

"Come again?" Jasper growled.

Fuck.

"I already told her, me and her are forever. She's got my promise, she'll have my ring, I'll have hers, but she'll never have that paper. If she finds it in her to live with that, she'll be mine in every way that's important. I'll vow in front of you and God to take care of her always. But she's never taking the motherfucking prick's last name. Fucking guts me every time I have to utter it, you think for one second I'd take all the beauty that is Hadley Walker and make her say that cocksucker's name when she introduces herself, sign that fuck's name? Hell fucking no. *I* don't even like doing that shit. I love your daughter, I'm hers always. But we will never get married."

If I'd thought Jasper's features had been set to stone when he learned I'd never marry his daughter, they turned to granite upon hearing my reason why. Then the room turned radioactive when Jasper stalked from the room.

Fucking hell.

"That wasn't about you," Clark told me.

"It sure as fuck was."

"We've had you four years, Brady. Time for you to wake up and start paying attention. You do that, I guarantee you those nightmares you have will ease."

I stared mutely at Clark because I'd been putting off an important conversation I needed to have with him and he'd opened the door, but I couldn't find it in me to walk through.

I'd find out that the man Nolan Clark was, I didn't need to walk anywhere. He'd carry me through.

"I lived with my nightmares so long most days it

felt like I'd been born with them. I couldn't think back to a time I didn't have them. The more I fought them the worse they got. The more I tried to bury shit the worse it was until one night I had Reagan on the floor pinned under me, begging me to wake up. It was in that moment, completely wrecked, I knew I had to unpack all the shit I was burying."

He looked around the room. "My brothers helped me with that. They listened when I needed to unburden myself. My woman helped me, too. So this is where you need to open your eyes and see us. See what we've given you. Then see what you've earned. That's a place in our family. Long before there was you and Hadley, we'd taken you in, we'd claimed you. You are not that motherfucker's son. You're ours. *All* of ours, Brady. We claim you. You wanna marry Hadley and the only thing holding you back is giving her the Hewitt name, then give her Clark, give her Lenox, give her McCoy, give her Walker. Any of us would happily give you our name. No, son, it would be our honor to give that to you. You're smart, so after you think on this for a while you'll come to understand Jasper's reaction. And it had nothing to do with you and everything to do with the asshole whose seed made you but gave you nothing else, then took everything from you. For men like us, we cannot fathom how a man could do that to his son."

My jaw started to ache I was clenching it so tightly in an effort to stop my chin from wobbling. More emotion than I knew what to do with rushed to the surface, making me feel like I was going to come out of my skin.

"Never had a father. Never had a woman who cared about me. Never had a family beyond the sister I adored, but she was taken from me," I rasped. "So I hope when I tell you I appreciate you taking me in and giving me what you've given me, it means something to me. And that comes from my soul. But you're right, it seems I missed some stuff and I need to spend some time thinking about that. If the offer's on the table for me to talk my shit out, I'd like to take you up on that."

"The offer's on the table," Clark confirmed.

"That offer stands with all of us," Lenox told me.

"Appreciate it."

My cell rang, interrupting the heavy conversation. I pulled it from my pocket, saw it was Hadley, and took the call.

"Everything okay, babe?"

"You tell me. You said you were on your way home thirty minutes ago."

"Sorry, got held up. Leaving in a minute."

"No worries. I was just calling to make sure you hadn't run off with a hot babe. And if by some chance you did, I'm telling you you're missing out on the new purple panty and bra set I found. And I bought it on sale so I don't mind if you rip them off me tonight. As a matter of fact, I'll be disappointed if you don't."

"I should've led with this but I'm in a meeting with your uncles. Maybe we can talk about this when I get home, yeah?"

"Then I take it you don't want to hear about the lacy—"

"Hadley," I growled in warning.

"Tell the uncles I said hello," she chirped happily, like she hadn't just given me a hard-on.

"Will do. Love you, baby."

"Does that 'love you' mean you're not mad at me?"

"No, that love you means I love you, but it's also meant to cushion the conversation we're having when I get home. Now, I'm standing in front of your uncles, baby, so, you want me to explain how that conversation's gonna go or do you wanna let me go so I can say my goodbyes, get home, and show you?"

"I think they know the conversation we're gonna

have when you get home." She giggled and that did nothing to help my current state.

"No doubt, but I can clear it up for them in case they're not crystal clear—"

"No! Don't clear anything up. See you when you get home."

Hadley disconnected and I smiled.

"Thank fuck I have boys," Clark mumbled.

"Copy that," Lenox added.

"You best get home." Levi chuckled. "And count your blessings her father wasn't in the room to hear his girl telling her man she bought—"

"Christ!" I cut Levi off, making a mental note to turn the volume down on my phone when Hadley called so the room couldn't hear her.

I exited Jasper's office and was in the lobby when I paused to listen.

Yep, I could still hear the roaring laughter.

That made me smile.

29

I heard Brady's garage door go up, then down, and a minute later I watched him walk into his kitchen. His boots stopped two feet inside the door, he crossed his thick arms over his wide chest, and stared.

I stared back.

I did this mainly because Brady was hot as fuck but also because he had a playful glint in his eyes and I'd never seen it before.

It was a sight to behold.

"Good day?" I broke the silence.

"Total shit."

"Um. I'm sorry. You wanna talk about it?"

"Total shit...until you called with the news you bought me a new pair of panties to tear off of you.

Shit timing but after the day I've had, welcomed news."

"So, the glitter I see in your eyes is because you're thinking you're gonna get yourself some?"

"First, I'm a man, my eyes don't glitter. Second, I'm not 'thinking' anything. I *know* I'm gonna get myself some because you called to tell me to get my ass home because you wanna give it to me."

Wait a minute.

I did not call and tell him to get his ass home.

"I didn't tell you to get your ass anywhere."

"You might not have said the words but you sure as fuck did, telling me about purple panties, a bra, and something lacy. That's akin to you ringing the dinner bell for a hoard of starving people."

That made me smile.

And I wish it was that easy to make Brady's eyes dance with happiness just by telling him I'd made a new purchase and an invitation to rip said purchase off me while engaging in dirty sex. But alas, we'd already participated in such sex and it had not made his eyes glitter, which they most certainly did right now even if he was a man and said otherwise.

"Well, I'm glad you brought up starving people because I'm hungry. Dinner's done, so you're gonna have to wait a little while longer to see what I bought."

Something seriously beautiful flashed across his face and I didn't understand it. He'd said he had a shit day. He was almost two hours late getting off of work yet he was standing before me looking happier than I'd ever seen him.

What the hell?

If I was a different kind of woman, and Brady wasn't the kind of man he was, I'd straight-out ask him if he had a woman on the side that gave world-class blow jobs and she'd spent all day under his desk alternately icing her jaw so she could give him more.

"Need me to set the table, or are we eating in the living room?"

Who was this man? We'd never sat at his table.

"Table."

He went to the sink, washed his hands, and asked, "How was your day?"

"Happy to report it was boring. I finalized the summer schedule for the day camps that come to the library and that took up most of my day. Then I just did my normal work. Nothing exciting. No defaced books. The highlight of my day was watching a man pluck up the nerve to check out *Fifty Shades of Grey*."

"Seriously? Men read that shit?"

Shit?

Was he crazy?

"First, it's not shit. It's a beautiful romance between a very traumatized man and a woman who's strong enough to not give in, and in doing so leads him to the light." *Shit. Shit. Shit. Maybe I shouldn't have said that.* "And...um...well, with hot sex thrown in."

"And men read that?"

I couldn't help it, he looked so flabbergasted at the thought of a man reading a romance book that I laughed and I did so for a long time. So long, he called my name and I was still chuckling when I told him, "Yes, Brady, men read romance. They especially read erotic romance. But this particular man was finding it difficult to bring the book up to the circulation desk to check it out."

"How do you know?"

"Because I've seen him twice this week, pick up the book, take it to a table, and read it while intermittently looking at the desk waiting for James to be there so he could check it out. He finally got that opportunity today, took it, then was out the door like a shot."

Brady's face screwed up and I barely bit back my

laugh this time when I said, "I know you, my alpha stud, cannot imagine a man reading sexy romance books but I promise you, they do. A lot of men check them out."

"Alpha stud?" His lips twitched and those stormy eyes danced.

Yeah, there was something different about Brady tonight. Good different but different all the same. I really wanted to ask him why but I didn't want to ruin the mood.

There was a lot we needed to talk about. Marriage and kids on the top of that list but I decided I was going to wait it out. That was not me burying my head in the sand and it wasn't me being a coward. It was a calculated decision to wait until after he'd started dealing with the loss of his sister and his nightmares. Maybe after he sorted those two things he'd feel differently. If he didn't, then I'd deal with what my next move would be.

"Thought you were setting the table," I prompted.

"Alpha stud?" he parroted.

I rolled my eyes and turned back to the stove to stir the spaghetti sauce. I felt heat hit my back. Brady's arms wrapped around my middle, giving me a squeeze before his lips pressed just behind my ear.

Nice.

"Later tonight when I'm rippin' those panties... no..." He paused. "When I got my face between your thighs, you can tell me if I need to pick up one of those sexy romance books."

I rolled my eyes but stayed quiet.

"I heard about that book. Maybe it's time we start exploring me tying you to the bed."

"Or maybe we should explore *me* tying *you* to the bed," I teased.

"You want that?"

I thought about it for about a nanosecond, which was a nanosecond more than I needed because I knew my answer.

"No."

"Right, but you want me to tie you up?"

I shivered. What I didn't do was verbally answer because Brady felt that shiver. "Yeah, my Hadley wants me to tie her up."

My Hadley.

I *loved* that.

His mouth lowered and he kissed the sensitive skin below my ear. Then in a deep, rough, lust-filled voice that felt like silk as it glided over my neck, he said, "Not tonight. I have panties to tear off. But soon, I'm gonna bind you to my bed with you up on all fours. That way I have access to your pretty ass while you're helpless and begging for my cock."

Sweet Jesus.

I'd totally be begging, but still I said, "I don't beg."

"We'll see."

Brady nipped my neck and slid away. He went to get plates out of the cabinet so he could set the table. A table we'd never sat at before.

Yeah, something was totally up with him and I wanted to know what that was. But first I was enjoying dinner with my man sitting across from me.

With his eyes glittering with nothing but happiness.

"Brady," I gasped as he entered me from behind.

One could say he liked my new purchase. He liked the lacy purple panties so much he hadn't taken them off when he'd gone down on me. He'd just pushed them aside and ate. It wasn't until I was on the edge of my second orgasm when he lifted his head and shredded the lace, tearing them clean off.

It was hot.

Off the charts hot.

Then he wasted no time covering me with his big body and drove home, filling me so full in one long hard thrust all the air whooshed from my lungs. He'd kept at me a good long while, slowing his strokes every time he felt me close to coming.

Now I was on my hands and knees, so turned-on from being kept on the edge I was ready to lose my mind.

Brady folded over me, his mouth to my neck when he muttered, "Think how good it's gonna be when you're tied to my bed, baby. Helpless. No choice but to take everything I wanna give you."

It was good now. No, it was fantastic, but still, I wanted him to tie me up.

One of his hands left the bed and went between my legs and fingered my clit. My hips bucked in response and Brady growled. I was so close, so ready to explode, I cried out when he slid his hand lower and cupped my sex while his cock was gliding in and out.

"Feels so good." He nuzzled my neck. "Feeling you on the inside, feeling us connected, my cock dipping in and coming out wet. Want this for the rest of my life. You and me, baby, forever."

"I want that, too," I panted.

"You ready to come now?"

"Yes."

"How bad you want it, Hadley?"

"Please, honey."

"Mmm," he purred.

Yes, big, strong, alpha stud Brady purred in my ear and I swear to God, my nipples, which were already tingling, felt like they'd been electrocuted.

His hand moved back up. He honed in on my clit and pressed hard, rolling, circling, rubbing until my climax was upon me. But he didn't stop, he kept at me until my back bowed, my neck craned back, and I incoherently begged him to stop.

"More," he grunted.

"Can't."

"More, Hadley. I want more. I want it all. Everything, baby. Give me everything."

I didn't think I had more to give. I was going to fly apart if he didn't stop. My muscles ached, my lungs burned, my heart pounded.

His hips powered forward, driving his cock deeper, so deep it was near-pain, but it was stopping. Something was building, something brighter, hotter, something more, and it was so big I couldn't contain it.

"Fuck, yeah."

"Brady."

Sweet Jesus, was that my voice?

"Give it, Hadley. Let go."

There was nothing else I could do. I let go.

And when I did, my arms gave out and my cheek hit the bed, making my ass tip higher. I vaguely, in an out-of-body experience type of way, felt his palm smack my ass, detonating aftershocks, and I cried out again. This time so disjointedly I wasn't sure if I was pleading with him to stop or never stop.

I didn't know what I wanted.

My brain and my body were no longer one.

"Mine," he roared and I quivered.

A full body quake that I was sure registered on the Richter scale as an eight-point-five.

Then my eyes closed, and the next time I opened them, I was draped over Brady's chest tucked close to his side.

"You okay?"

"I think I died."

I felt his body shaking under me and I stiffened.

"Are you laughing at me?"

"No."

"Then why are you laughing?"

"No reason."

"No reason? So you often laugh after sex?"

"I do when my woman passes out."

"So you are laughing at me."

I was starting to get annoyed. And that annoyance stemmed from Brady screwing up the afterglow of an orgasm so big I thought he was right and I'd passed out.

"No. I'm pretty fucking happy you came so hard you sounded like the possessed girl in *The Exorcist* while you begged for me not to stop."

"I didn't sound like *The Exorcist*," I snapped.

Though I was pretty sure he was right about that, too, because my throat felt scratchy. But I wasn't admitting that he was pissing me off.

I started to push away but didn't get very far when his arm went super tight around me and he dipped his head so his face was close to mine.

"I'm teasing you," he whispered.

"Well, stop."

"Okay, baby." He kissed my forehead. "Now that you're awake, gonna clean you up."

Brady squeezed me, let me go, and rolled out of bed. I lay on my side watching him walk away. I was staring at his perfect ass, wondering if I indeed did pass out or if I'd been so exhausted I just went to sleep. Same thing with a minor shade of difference. I stopped caring one way or the other when Brady exited the bathroom carrying a washcloth.

"Spread, baby."

"Spread?"

"Open your legs, so I can clean you up." I was so focused on the tender look on Brady's face I hadn't moved when his hand gently tapped my thigh. "I'm wiped, baby. Open so I can clean me off you and we can get some sleep."

I knew he loved me. From word and deed, he'd made that clear. Before he loved me he'd cared deeply for me. He'd given me gentle looks before, but never tender. Never like I was so special he wanted to tend to me.

So I opened my legs.

Brady didn't make a big deal of it as he wiped my inner thighs and between my legs. His ministrations were soft, not fast nor slow—he didn't take a year to wash me but he didn't rush. He simply took care of me. When he was done, he went back to the bathroom, came back, got into bed next to me, and that was it.

He rolled me back so I was pressed to his side. His hand at my hip lightly grazed my skin, and he did this silently.

I knew he was tired, he'd told me as much, and I was, too. But that didn't mean I wasn't freaking out inside.

"What changed?" I whispered.

"Told you I had a shit day. Part of that was talking to your dad and uncles. It doesn't make a man feel real good when he realizes he's been a dumb fuck. I told Clark I'd think on some stuff, and on my way home I started to do that."

"Wanna share what you thought about?"

His hand on my hip stopped grazing so he cupped my ass and pulled me closer.

Closer.

I loved that.

"I have a good family," he declared, and I felt my brows pinch together in confusion. "It just so happens I didn't find that family until I was twenty-seven. I was so caught up hating the man who made me I missed the four men who'd come into my life. I missed what they'd given me. I was so caught in guilt about not being able to save my sister I missed what they were offering. I fell in love with you then spent four years thinking I'd never be worthy of you. I missed something huge—your father giving me his blessing. Not that I didn't take advantage of his approval, I did. As soon as he gave it, I came straight to you begging for a chance. But I never fully let that sink in, what his blessing truly meant. He said he wanted a good man at your back. But he also wanted a good woman at mine. That's what I was thinking about driving home to you tonight. I have your back, Hadley, always. You have all of my love and protection. And part of that was me thinking I needed to protect you from me."

I was still stuck on Brady finally coming to the realization that my family, *his* family loved him and how unbelievably happy that made me. So I almost missed his body stiffening under me.

"The night of Nicole's birthday I know you heard my nightmare." Before I could say anything, his arm tightened then relaxed and he went on. "Know it was hard for you to stay in your room and I know you did that because I asked you to. It fucks me to talk about this but I need to. I have to tell you so you can have my back. I dream about Nicole dying. Sometimes I can wake myself up, sometimes I can't. I dream about things I've done while I was in the Army. Those dreams aren't for you. I will not share those but I will take Clark up on his offer and talk to him about them."

Thank God.

Thank sweet baby Jesus he was finally letting me all the way in.

"What'd you dream about the night of Nicole's birthday?"

Brady's arm went tight again but this time he didn't loosen it when he said, "You."

"Me?"

"Same dream, me watching Nicole get tangled and fall overboard, me hearing her scream before she hit the water, trying to get to her, trying to find her. But instead of it being Nicole it was you. I saw you, I heard you, I couldn't get to you."

"And I died," I surmised.

"You were dead," he confirmed.

We both fell silent and I waited a good long while until Brady's chest stopped heaving in oxygen before I softly told him, "Nothing's gonna happen to me."

"I know."

"Thank you for telling me."

That earned me a tighter squeeze but no words.

"I want you to sleep with me tonight."

"Had—"

"If I feel you moving, I'll get up. I promise. I won't try to wake you. I won't touch you. I'll get up and leave the room. Please give yourself this. Give *us* this. You have my word, I'll get myself safe."

Brady didn't answer. I braced for his refusal while reminding myself this wasn't about me or how much he loved me. It was about him wanting me safe, and even though I hated it, I needed to give him time to work through it.

"Sleep, baby."

"You'll stay?"

"Yes."

I released a ragged breath and relaxed.

"Love you, Brady."

"Love you, Hadley."

Yeah, he did.

He loved me a lot.

He'd love me forever.

Knowing that, I realized I could live with him never marrying me. But not having kids would be harder to give up.

By the time I started to drift to sleep, Brady was still awake, protecting me, loving me, afraid to sleep himself because he wanted me safe. So, as my eyes closed I knew I couldn't give up the dream of having kids. Not only because I'd dreamed of having a big family all my life, but because I wanted to give that dream to Brady. I wanted my kids to have a father who would love and protect them the way he loved and protected me.

But that would be a conversation for a different day.

And when the phone rang in the wee hours of

the morning, Brady didn't jolt awake. His voice wasn't thick with sleep, he was alert and cognizant.

I didn't ask, but I didn't need to.

My Brady hadn't slept a wink, so I could sleep next to him.

Yes, I wanted my children to know that kind of devotion.

30

"Bayside Motel. Now," Logan clipped.

A call at three-forty-two in the morning was never good. Logan telling me I needed to get my ass to the motel Wick had checked into—really not good.

"Update."

I gently but quickly rolled Hadley off of me and got out of bed.

Logan continued. "Davidson made his play. Shocked as shit he came himself. We clocked him the minute he got out of his car, but waited too long. We needed him to gain entry, he did, we were right behind him ready for the takedown but Davidson wasn't fucking around. Neither was Wick. Gunfire was exchanged. Wick was clipped in the arm, Davidson took one to the forehead."

"Fuck," I rasped and yanked my jeans up. "Wick okay?"

"Man is pissed as shit Davidson got the drop but Wick was ready for it. Silver lining is, Davidson's very dead and Liberty's safe."

There was that. But we still needed confirmation it was Davidson behind Berkshire trying to kill Liberty.

"I'll let Wick fill you in on the rest. But I will warn you, Levi's on his way and what he knows means he's off-the-rails pissed, so brace, brother, if Levi's pissed, so are Clark, Jasper, and Lenox. We got four men we have to lock down so Wick doesn't end up like Davidson."

"Fuck," I repeated and pulled on my socks. "Gotta talk to Hadley, then I'm on my way."

"Right. See you in ten."

I tossed my phone on my dresser and finished lacing up my boots before I turned to Hadley now sitting up in bed with only a sheet pulled up covering her naked body.

"I gotta go, baby."

"What's happening?"

"I'll explain everything when I get home. I don't have a lot of details but just so you can get back to sleep, everyone is safe. Wick was injured but from what Logan said he's gonna be fine. Now, I gotta get going."

"My Uncle Wick's in town?"

"He is. We needed his help on Liberty's case so he flew in yesterday. Now I really need to go. I'll be home as soon as I can."

"I work today."

Fucking shit.

"If I'm not back before, call me when you get to the library."

"Okay."

Okay.

Simple as that, even though she was scared and unable to hide it. But she knew I was in a hurry and was giving me what I needed to get out the door— easy acceptance.

I pulled my t-shirt over my head and made my way back to the bed. Hadley didn't move anything but her eyes as they followed me until I bent forward and kissed her.

The kiss was quick but thorough, and when I pulled back, she was no less scared but no longer looked freaked.

"I promise everyone is safe. Totally safe."

"Okay. Go. Call me when you can or I'll call you when I get to work."

"Love you, baby."

"Love you, Brady. Be careful."

"Always."

Then I turned on my booted feet and walked out of my bedroom leaving my woman in my bed after I lay awake for hours feeling her pressed tight.

I hadn't lain awake because I was afraid I'd have a dream. I stayed awake because I was living a dream come true with my arms full of Hadley while she slept next to me.

LOGAN HAD BEEN WRONG.

We weren't going to have to lock down Levi, we were going to have to cuff and sit on Drake.

After Wick explained the trap that he and Liberty had set—which, there was no denying, had been a good plan, since Dr. Davidson had bought it and was now in the back of a coroner's van—Levi seemed to calm.

Drake, however, did not.

In the waxing morning light, Liberty's man looked like he was going to have a shit hemorrhage.

"Drake," Wick called out.

Drake turned back to face Wick, who was still

sitting on the ambo's bumper after refusing to climb inside, making the EMTs on site not only uncomfortable but confounded *and* uncomfortable. Wick was refusing all medical care except for the bandage now wrapped around his bicep.

Army CID, local police, including Ethan Lenox, were all at the scene doing their thing. Liberty was among the Army personnel. Her presence there was in an official capacity, so she was inside the motel room talking to the CID team instead of part of our huddle.

"Not now, General," Drake angrily returned.

"You got something to say, say it. But just to point out, that fuckstick's in a body bag. It might've been my bullet but it was Lieutenant McCoy's plan. Proving the woman's not only good on the battlefield but off. And at no point was she in danger tonight. Her behind was home in bed with you."

Wick paused, and in the flashing blue and red lights all around us, General Wick disappeared and Liberty's Uncle Wick took his place. Everything about the man changed. Pride and love shone brightly in his features but there was a hue of concern.

"I can imagine it hits you square in the gut. A man like you, to know that the woman lying next to you is keeping secrets. But, Drake, you gotta dig deep and let that go. You know why she had to keep this from you and you know she's gonna have to keep more from you while she's in the Army. One day, I'm gonna lose her. I figure that will be the day her contract ends and she doesn't re-enlist. I also know when that day comes, Triple Canopy will be gaining a new employee. And even then you're gonna have to find it in yourself to let her be her. She is not—"

"I know who the fuck she is," Drake snapped. "I know it and I'm damn proud of her. And you're very wrong, it's not her lying next to me keeping secrets that's a kick to the gut. And it's not me who has to dig deep to work anything out. It's my woman who's gonna have more shit piled on her. She's the one who's gotta come to terms with someone she trusted being a traitor. It's her standing in that motel room with that fucker's blood fresh on the carpet at six o'clock in the morning giving her statement. And me being the man I am, you know I want to cushion that for her and I cannot. So how about you cut me some slack, let me walk off my temper, so when she's ready to go, I can give Liberty what she needs instead of being pissed as shit I can't protect her."

Drake didn't wait for Wick or anyone else to cut

him anything. He turned and strode off so he could cool down, leaving the rest of us staring at his back.

My first thought was how grateful I was Hadley was a librarian and I'd never have to deal with what Drake had to deal with when his woman was called out in the middle of the night to leave for a mission. Not knowing where she was going or when she'd be home but having a deep understanding wherever she went she'd be in mortal danger.

Though it wouldn't take long for me to learn that, librarian or not, Hadley was a Walker. In other words, she was crazy-brave and reckless, meaning all the peace of mind I felt was a façade. If there was trouble to be had, my woman would find it.

And the trouble she'd find would put everyone to the test.

31

Four days later, I learned there was a downside to my determination.

Four glorious days of sleeping next to Brady, him opening up and talking to Clark, opening up to me and telling me about his conversations with my uncle, learning the difference between mourning his sister and keeping a wound that would never completely heal gaping and bloody to torture himself for something that was not his fault.

But through all of that, the four days had been peaceful. We hadn't talked about kids, marriage, our future, we'd just fallen into a serene rhythm. Brady had been coming to my house after work. I'd decided I wanted my condo on the market as soon as possible so I needed to fix up the kitchen and as inexpensively as possible re-do it, and Brady was all-in helping me.

Work had settled down for him, everyone was relieved the case they'd been working on for months was closed. Wick had gone back to his post in Washington and Liberty was free and clear.

Work for me had been what it always was, uneventful save some asshole defacing books.

That was, until today.

Then I'd made a horrible, awful mistake.

It went like this.

I was in my car after work texting Brady to tell him I was picking up dinner on my way home.

Yes, I had my cell, and no, I hadn't forgotten it once since the night of the storm. Though I learned a cell phone didn't do much good when the owner of said phone was an idiot.

I had just hit send and tossed the phone back into my purse because everyone knows you don't ever look at your phone while you're driving. I glanced in my rearview mirror in preparation to reverse out of my parking spot, when a white Ford Focus stopped in front of the drop-off bin. I patiently waited until the car pulled away and that was when I saw it.

My blood boiled.

At least a dozen books were dumped. Not inside the bin, but on the ground in front of the bin.

I didn't do what I should've, which was to put my car in park, get the license plate, grab the books, call my cousin Ethan, and get back into the library.

Nope, not me.

And considering my current predicament, it's safe to say I wasn't just an idiot, I was a fucking idiot.

Instead of doing what I should've done, I allowed the fire burning through my veins to lead me astray. I reversed, pulled out of the library, made a right out of the parking lot, and followed the Ford Focus. I continued to follow the car, stupidly thinking I was doing this like a boss (I'm a Walker!) five car lengths behind. I followed the Focus into a residential neighborhood and watched it pull into a driveway. I glanced at the mailbox to get the house number and drove past, stopping down the block. It was only then I reached for my phone and made the call.

What I hadn't done was check to see if someone was following *me*.

My call to Ethan was cut short when someone opened my car door, because I was not only a fucking idiot, but apparently The Fucking Stupidest Woman to Ever Live and didn't bother to lock the door.

I'd barely told Ethan the address before I was yanked out of my car by my hair and thrown into a van.

Now I was screwed.

And I didn't have my cell because during my abduction, it had fallen onto the street and the asshole who was doing the abducting stomped on it.

Totally screwed. And now I didn't have fire coursing through my veins. I had ice.

I was not scared, I was terrified.

Completely and totally.

I didn't know my location but it hadn't taken long to get there. Once we arrived, I fought, kicked, and screamed. None of this affected the two men who were dragging me into a big white building. Before they could get me inside, I wised up enough to look around. Then it hit me why they didn't care I was shouting at the top of my lungs. We were in the middle of nowhere. For as far as I could see, it was dense trees. I vaguely noted a large pond off to the side of the building with three sets of bleachers flanking it.

We entered the building and my fear skyrocketed.

Gleaming white walls, so glossy the overhead lights reflected off of them, making the room ultrabright. Rows of dark wood pews to the right and left created an aisle up the center of the large room.

As the two very large men dragged me down the aisle, I did my best to plant my feet in the plush cobalt blue runner but I was no match for them. They didn't miss a beat as my heels dug into the carpet. What felt like an eternity later, the men stopped in front of the dais and my blood pressure went through the roof.

"Kneel," one of the men commanded.

I didn't kneel. I was frozen solid as I took in the altar before me. It was massive, at least six feet long. The dark wood matched the pews behind me, but it was the words carved into the wood that had me mesmerized: Do This In Remembrance Of Me.

Then my eyes went beyond the altar to the large statue of Jesus on the cross. Crown of thorns, spikes protruding from His palms and feet, head bowed.

"You will kneel," the other man demanded, and when I made no move to do as he asked, my feet were swept out from under me and I unceremoniously dropped to the floor.

The pain of my knees hitting the hard surface didn't register.

We warned you and you didn't listen. You must be cleansed of your sins.

Ho-ly shit.

Holy shit.

I had no idea what being 'cleansed of your sins' meant, I just knew I didn't want to find out.

At that moment, I found I could beg and I would plead for forgiveness and salvation if it meant I never learned what these people meant by 'cleansed.'

"Please. I'm sorry."

Neither man said a word, their silence scaring me more than the pressure they were both putting on my shoulders to keep me on my knees between them.

A door to my right opened and a good-looking, older man wearing a blue choir-like robe with gold stitching casually walked through like there was nothing unusual about a woman kneeling against her will. Though, maybe he didn't know I was there against my will. Maybe—

"Is this her?" the man in the robe asked, and my hopes he'd help me died a slow, agonizing death.

"Please. I don't—"

"Silence," he seethed.

"Yes, Bishop, this is her."

Before I could plead my case, the man they called Bishop stepped behind the altar and picked up what looked like a bronze cowbell. Seconds later, he rang the bell and I heard murmurs behind me. I craned my neck to see people dressed all in white entering the sanctuary.

"You will face forward and bow your head," Bishop insisted.

Slowly, I did what I was told, trying to hold back tears while thinking of a way to get myself out of this.

"Come." Bishop's voice boomed. "It is a splendid day. The Heathen is before us."

There were boisterous cheers from behind me and I screwed my eyes closed and prayed.

32

―――――――

"Yo!" I heard Drake shout as I made my way across the Triple Canopy parking lot. At the same time, two squad cars came squealing to stop in front of the entrance.

Ethan jumped out of the passenger side of one of the cars and jogged back to the building.

"What's up?"

"Hadley."

That's all Ethan had to say.

All I had to hear for my world to tilt and acid to fill my gut.

I shoved past him to find Carter, Luke, Trey, and Drake in the reception area.

Looking visibly shaken, Ethan raked his hands through his hair as he said, "Ten minutes ago I got a call from Hadley. She didn't get much out before the call disconnected. Only thing I got was that she'd followed a white Ford Focus and an address where she was. I sent a couple of squads to the address and came here. There's an active shooter situation at First Union bank. SWAT and our only hostage team are on sight. I have authorization to—"

I had my phone out with Hadley's name pulled up. I hit go and went straight to voice mail.

"What's the address?" I cut Ethan off, not giving the first fuck what was authorized.

"Got people en route."

"And you know she's not gonna be there. What's the address?"

I ignored the burn in my stomach, ignored the fear, ignored the overwhelming homicidal thoughts threatening to take over and focused what was left of my intellectual capacity to find her.

"Let's—"

"If someone took her, she won't be in that house and you fucking know it," I interrupted. "What'd you get on those books?"

"What books?" Carter asked.

"Someone's been destroying books. Dropping them off in the bin outside or putting them back on the shelves," I answered then turned back to Ethan.

"One of them said heathens need to be cleansed. You have any religious fanatics on radar?"

"No. I ran the checks myself. Closest thing I could find was a Baptist church, but their focus is on drug addiction. Even still, I went around and talked to them about their outreach program and they're more activists for getting junkies in faith-based recovery programs. I wouldn't call them radicals."

"Get them to go back." I pointed to the two uniformed officers inside the door. "This time, ask them about other churches in the area. Extremists. Maybe a cult. Anything. And give me that address."

Ethan rattled off the address. I took off down the hall to my office, hearing boots pounding behind me. I hit my desk, powered up my computer, and lifted my eyes to find Carter glaring down at me.

"Need you to call in the others. The team needs to be ready to roll out as soon as we have a location," I told him and looked back down at my computer, which was taking a fucking year to boot up.

"You wanna explain why you didn't—"

"Call in the fucking team," I roared and Carter took a step back.

"Jesus, Brady, we'll..."

Carter abruptly stopped and jerked his chin in my direction before he turned and left.

Two minutes into my search, I really fucking wished Dylan was in the office. Not only was he better at this than I was, I didn't want to be sitting behind my desk. I wanted to be out looking for my woman but I needed to know where to look. And I knew, she wouldn't be at the address she'd give Ethan.

"Just got a call in," Ethan said from the doorway of my office. "They found Hadley's car down the block from that address, still running, door left open, cell on the ground smashed."

The tightness in my chest increased, making it hard for my heart to beat.

"John Swanson owns the property." I glanced from Ethan back to my screen. "My take, it's a rental. He's got five others in his name. Four in not so great neighborhoods, one in a gated community. But I can't find the rental agreements."

"Move," Dylan said, coming into my office. I gladly got up from my chair and let him sit. "Did you find anything else?"

"No."

"I need twenty minutes."

"Make it ten," I snapped and followed Ethan down the hall into the conference room. I ignored

Carter and Drake and went straight to the whiteboard.

Once I had the books I remembered written on the board, I pulled my phone out and scrolled to the pictures I'd taken and tossed it to Carter.

He caught my cell and his gaze went to the screen. "That's what we're dealing with. *Lolita, The Handmaid's Tale, Sex is a Funny Word, The Garden of Eden, Thirteen Reasons Why*. There were more books defaced but the two books I'm most worried about are *The Garden of Eden* which had "Godless heathens be warned" scribbled in it and *Thirteen Reasons Why* which had "We warned you and you didn't listen. You must be cleansed of your sins" written in it."

"What the fuck." Carter's grimace swung from me to Ethan. "Why didn't you bring this to us?"

"We're not discussing that right now. What we're doing is finding Hadley. Dylan's working on locating a rental agreement. Once we have that, we can look into whoever's name is on that contract. In the meantime, have you read those books?"

"No," Carter snapped.

I hadn't either and I really should've found the goddamn time to.

"Where we at?" Logan asked as he entered the room with Matt behind him.

I took the time to get them up to speed, and when I was done, Dylan was coming into the room with his laptop in hand, Clark and Jasper following behind.

I didn't acknowledge the newcomers, I didn't even look in Jasper's direction. I was hanging on by the tips of my fingers. I did not need to see his fear, his disappointment, to know I'd let him down.

I had to find Hadley.

I'd take what I deserved from her family after she was safe.

"John Swanson," Dylan started. "He owns Swanson LTD. In the last year, he's run background and credit checks on Iliana Thornburg, Ricardo Chavez, and Beth Heinz. Beth and Ricardo's credit reports show they live in two of his rental properties. Iliana was denied. I'm still searching the address to see if I get a hit, but so far I'm not finding anything, not even renter's insurance. Also, there are no rental agreements online. It might be faster if someone goes and talks to Swanson and asks him about his tenant."

"I'll go. Luke, you're with me."

"I'm going with you," Ethan put in.

"Levi went to the Baptist church," Jasper

informed the room. "Lenox went to the address to have a look around."

A muscle jumped in Ethan's cheek. "I got uniforms on the scene. My dad goes into that house without a search warrant, anything he finds cannot be used—"

"Don't give a fuck what can or cannot be used. All I want is Hadley."

My thoughts exactly.

"Do you know what's going on?" Carter asked Jasper.

"Hadley had a word with her mom. Emily filled me in. Pissed as hell books in her library were being ruined. She also said she reported it to Ethan. Had a word with Ethan, he was looking into it. Hadley wasn't freaked out or scared, just mad, so yes, I knew what was going on."

"Why didn't *you* bring it to us?" Carter pushed.

"Same reason Brady and Ethan didn't."

"I don't—"

"Liberty," Drake cut in. "We were neck-deep in Liberty's case," he correctly guessed.

"Put that out of your head, Drake. If any of us thought there was a real danger we would've brought it to the table and split our resources. No way would Brady let my daughter swing if he'd known. Nor would Ethan, nor would I. None of us took it seriously."

Right. It was time to stop talking about shit that couldn't be changed and time to start looking for Hadley.

"Dylan, text me Swanson's address."

I was almost to the door when Jasper stopped me.

"This isn't your fault."

"Jasper—"

"This is not your fault. Emily told me about the books. Ethan knew as well. Now's not the time to feel guilt."

"The only thing I'm feeling right now is the need to get to Swanson. She's been gone an hour. That's sixty minutes with a bunch of freaks who think she needs to be cleansed. I should've kept a better eye on this, I didn't, and that's mine to deal with. But not right now. Right now I want to get in my truck, go talk to Swanson, then get my woman. And while I'm doing that, do my best to keep a lid on the desire to snap someone's neck."

Jasper's eyes flared and I knew he was doing his best to keep a lid on his anger as well. A better man would've had a mind to his fear and helped him work through it. I was not a better man. I was a man who needed to get his woman safe so I could start doling out punishment.

You must be cleansed of your sins.

It would *not* be Hadley's perceived sins that would be cleansed, but someone's sure as fuck would be.

"Ethan, you're staying here with Clark. Levi gets a bad vibe about the Baptist church, he'll call it in. You, Clark, Logan, and Matt roll out and we'll meet you there."

"Uncle—"

I heard no more because I was out the door.

THIRTY GODDAMNED MINUTES LATER, Jasper, Luke, and I stood in John Swanson's study. That loose hold I had on my temper was slipping and it was slipping fast. And I wasn't the only one. Jasper looked like he was ready to blow.

We'd explained the situation to Mr. Swanson and his response was, "I can't say I'm surprised but I sure am shocked."

That was when my temper started to flare. It full-on caught fire when John continued, "Never could put my finger on it. I thought they were just very conservative. You know, God-fearing types. But Tammy, she seemed subservient, not shy, not afraid, maybe cowed in a way. But Colin, he doesn't seem like the type to take a hand to his wife. He's a big man, but soft both in word and gesture."

That was Colin and Tammy Rivers. I'd already texted Dylan with their names and within minutes, Dylan had texted back that their background check had come back clean. Which meant it was going to take him time to dig so we needed more from Mr. Swanson.

"Did either of them mention the church they went to? Friends?"

"No. Though last summer Colin asked if I knew a tree trimming service. Now, I take care of the property, all maintenance including a gardener. I learned if I want my properties maintained I need to—"

"No disrespect, Mr. Swanson, but we're in a hurry," Jasper thankfully cut the man off. None of us gave two shits why he included a gardener in the rent he charged. "Did Colin tell you why he needed a tree trimmer?"

"Yes. He said his church had purchased a parcel of land but before they could build they needed to clear some trees to make room for the new sanctuary."

"Did you give him a recommendation?"

"Yes. A friend of mine, owns Clear Tree."

For the love of Christ, why hadn't the man led with that information?

I had my head dipped down looking at my phone, sending a text to Dylan, when John asked, "Would you like me to call my friend and ask if he did the work?"

"That would be helpful, thank you," Jasper grunted.

I finished sending my message and glanced at Luke who looked like he was losing patience as well, but definitely had more of a handle on it than I did.

My phone beeped and Jasper asked, "That Dylan?"

My eyes dropped back to my phone. "Yeah. He's still digging."

"Harold." John's voice boomed. "How's business?"

I gritted my teeth in an effort not to explode.

"Good, good," John continued. "Last year, I sent one of my tenants to you. His church was looking for some..." There was a pause. "Glad that worked out. What was the name of the church, do you remember?" Another pause. "No, no problems. The missus and I were thinking about trying a new church."

Another pause, this one longer. My nerves were getting harder to contain when John spoke again, "Yes, you're correct. Doesn't seem like a place we'd be interested in. I'll let you get back to it. Let's set up a game soon."

Mr. Swanson put the phone back in the cradle and slowly lifted his head. And when he did, my stomach pitched at the look on his face.

"He didn't give me a name but said the property is at the end of Millers Road."

"What else did he say?" Luke prompted.

"Said I wouldn't be interested because he didn't get the feeling it was a church as such, more a cult. Said there was housing on the property and he thought it looked like a compound and they weren't very open to outsiders. When he and his crew showed up, women and children made themselves absent. And only the pastor would speak to him."

How in the hell had a cult gone unnoticed?

"Thank you for your help, Mr. Swanson. We appreciate it."

We were making a hasty exit when John called out, "Will you let me know?"

"Mr.—"

"I don't want a member of a cult in one of my houses."

"We'll let you know," Jasper agreed.

We were back in Jasper's truck when he said, "Your call."

"Say again?"

My mind was so wrapped up in finding Hadley I had no idea what Jasper was talking about.

"Your call," he repeated. "The three of us can hit Millers Road alone or we can call in the team for backup. We call them in, Ethan's part of that."

Fucking shit.

That cost Jasper. I knew it did. Not even the fog of wanting to get to Hadley was thick enough to block out the tone of Jasper's voice. Hadley was Jasper's. His daughter. But he was giving me the call. What he wasn't saying was, if Ethan was there, everything had to be done by the book.

I turned slightly in my seat and craned my neck to look at Luke.

"Call in the team."

"Brady—"

"Luke, call in the team," I repeated. "Priority is getting Hadley out. Everything else is secondary."

"Call them in," Jasper told Luke. Then in a low, menacing tone, he said, "When the time's right, I got your back."

I jerked my chin but didn't comment or commit

to Jasper's offer. If I didn't get my shot today, when the time was right, I would handle what I needed to handle and I'd be doing that alone.

I heard Luke calling in the team.

I watched the scenery go by in a blur.

And I did both of those with more fear than I'd ever felt in my entire life threatening to pull me under. I couldn't allow myself to think about what could be happening to Hadley. I couldn't allow myself to think about her being scared. And I seriously couldn't think about the possibility she'd already been injured or worse.

What I did do was allow the inferno to sear deep. I let all civility slip away and I became the man I once was. The man I never thought I'd be again. The man Hadley needed me to be.

Ruthless. Brutal. Cold.

33

Deep down in my heart, I knew Brady and my family were looking for me.

I knew it, but it did nothing to calm my fear.

The truth was, I was scared shitless.

More scared than I'd ever been in my life, including when I'd waited hours to hear if my sister Quinn was going to pull through surgery after she'd been shot.

That probably made me the worst sister in the entire world but I knew, *knew* this was not going to end well for me.

I'd been stripped of my clothes. I fought this. I'd cried and begged as the two men who'd dragged me into the sanctuary held my arms and a third man was holding my feet, preventing me from kicking, while a woman—a goddamned woman—stood in front of me and cut my clothes away.

She would not meet my eyes, she didn't look at the men, she didn't utter a word as I pleaded with her to help me. I begged her not to take my clothes. Fucking begged with tears in my eyes and she didn't look at me.

But others did.

There wasn't any available seats on even one of those pews in front of me. Men, women, children, all dressed in white, sat and stared.

None helped.

Not a single one made a move to protect my clothes from being stripped away.

"We've come together to cleanse," Bishop announced. "And give thanks the Heathen has been delivered."

"Please," I whispered. The man to my right wrenched my arm back until my shoulder popped and I shouted in pain.

"The demons within her are strong. They must be cast out."

"Don't do this. Please, this is wrong." My left arm was twisted and pain shot from my shoulder blade down my spine.

My vision started to swim and I willed myself not to pass out.

The woman gathered my blouse, skirt, and heels and disappeared from my sight. My bra and panties weren't much but they were something.

"Temptation comes in all forms," Bishop continued, and a chill pierced my heart. "Come and test your faith."

"No!" I shouted when the men in the congregation stood. "No!"

I struggled until one leg broke free from the man holding my ankles and I kicked as hard as I could.

"Heathen, be still," the man snarled and punched my back, making me cry out in agony.

My ankles were recaptured and I whimpered when my arms were tweaked.

The first man approached. He took a knife from his pocket and carefully lifted his blade, placing it under the material in front of my bra. He paused, then removed his blade without slicing the silk.

Thank God.

Thank you, God.

One by one the men approached, pulled their knives, and repeated what the first man had done.

I didn't struggle.

I didn't dare move a muscle.

It wasn't until the eleventh man approached, his eyes glistening with disgust and something that looked like lust, that my bra got sliced open.

"Temptation," the man roared and slapped me across the face.

It took several long moments for the shock and pain of the slap to wear off.

And when it did, I could no longer keep my tears from falling.

This was worse, so much worse than books being ruined.

I was so stupid.

I should've listened to Simon when he told me I needed to take the threats seriously. I should've listened to Brady when he wanted to involve Triple Canopy. I should've calmed down and called Ethan before I followed that car.

I should've done a lot of things.

But I didn't.

Now I was standing mostly nude in front of a line of men.

This was worse than bad.

"Please," I begged again when the next man stepped up. "Please help me."

"I am faithful," he spat. "I do not give into the

temptation of flesh. A whore's lure is the devil's work."

Ho-ly shit.

Holy shit.

It wouldn't be until the last man came before me with the same look in his eyes as the man who'd opened my bra that I would speak.

"I'm dirty," I told him when his knife went to my hip and slid into my panties. "Please, stay faithful."

His eyes snapped to mine. I saw the muscle in his jaw tick and I pleaded some more.

"Don't give in to temptation. I'm dirty. I'm a whore."

His eyes sparked and I gave up begging him not to cut my panties and instead started praying.

34

The smell of pine and freshly cut wood filled my nostrils as I made way through the thick forest known as Hoppers' Woods. It was a twenty-five-acre parcel of land at the end of Millers Road.

Dylan had found the land was owned by a church that called themselves, Faithful. No website, no phone number listed, no social media presence.

Nothing.

Nada.

Which meant the church was not a church but a cult like Harold had told John. Churches are about outreach, building their flock, helping the community.

Faithful was not about any of those things. And if I hadn't already been sure, I was very sure when

Clark had radioed he could see approximately fifty women and female children all dressed in long-sleeved white dresses that went to their ankles leaving the main building.

It was summer in Georgia.

Hot and humid and the women were covered from the neck down. At least the fabric was white so it would help some, but not much. Those women and girls had to be hot as fuck.

Luke had taken a high sniper position to the east, Logan to the west. Which meant the rest of us fanning out had coverage.

Still, I didn't feel good about this.

I was coming out of the woods to a clearing when Luke's voice crackled in my ear.

"Ground team, hold fast."

I stopped moving and waited for Luke to continue. When he did, my pulse spiked.

"I've got eyes on Hadley." There was a beat of silence then, "Carter, what's your twenty?"

"What's wrong?" I asked.

"East side far corner," Carter returned.

"Luke?"

I got nothing but silence.

Fuck.

"Anyone else have eyes on Hadley?" I inquired and got eight nos.

Carter and Luke did not report in.

I started advancing when Luke came back. "Hold fast, Brady."

"What the fuck's going on?"

Nothing.

I counted to ten and was ready to explode when I heard Carter say, "Locked down."

What the fuck?

A moment later, a panting Carter said, "Proceed."

Okay, now what in the actual fuck?

"Brady, keep your shit," Luke warned and I braced. "Carter, Ethan, Lenox, Clark, Jasper, and Levi are out of play."

"Why?" Trey clipped.

"Hadley's...fuck..."

"Luke," I growled and cold slithered down my spine.

"Lock it down, Brady, or I'll send someone to lock *you* down. Two men are dragging her out the back of the center building."

Fucking hell. I broke out into a jog, cleared the last of the trees, and from where I stood about five hundred yards away I could see the building. I couldn't make out faces but I could see what looked like bleachers. People were filing up the steps and finding seats.

That cold chill turned to molten lava.

"Where are they taking her?"

"Looks like a huge pond. Three men are flanking her, a dozen standing on the bank. More are taking seats. Brady, you and Trey are the only two that have a shot at getting across that field undetected."

Pond.

Water.

Viciously and swiftly, terror suffused. I was transported back twenty years. Visions of Nicole drowning tugged at the corner of my mind.

"Brady," Drake snapped.

My eyes wandered to the field in front of me and I scanned the area, planning my course of action. A scattering of trees and an outbuilding that would put me less than twenty yards from the bleachers.

I took off, made it to the first set of trees, glanced to my left, and saw Trey. To my right, there was nothing but a wide-open field, leaving Matt and Drake no cover.

"Logan, do you have a visual?"

"Negative on Hadley. I have power lines in my way but I have eyes on you and Trey. You're clear."

"Brady," Drake tried again to get my attention and again I ignored him.

"Luke, what do you see?"

"Five feet from the pond. Ethan and Carter are taking Jasper, Lenox, Clark, and Levi around to the front gates. Once you have Hadley, they'll come in."

Once I had Hadley.

Get to Hadley.

I shoved all thoughts of my sister out of my head, glanced back to Trey, and gestured toward the building.

He took off and a second later, I followed. We met at the building and I immediately noticed him favoring his good leg.

"You good?"

"Are you?" he lashed out. His jaw ticked.

"Fuck," Luke muttered and I peered around the corner of the ramshackle outbuilding.

And that was when I got my first look at Hadley.

Fury hit my chest, cracking the ice that encased my heart.

So much fury, there was no way I was going to be able to contain it.

A motherfucker in a blue robe was dragging a near-naked Hadley into the water. Her bra dangling from her shoulders opened in the front, breasts exposed, panties on, and a look of pure fright was on her beautiful face.

Locked down.

That was why Luke had called off her father, uncles, and cousins.

Hadley, nearly nude.

My beautiful woman violated.

"Luke, do you have a shot?"

"Negative."

No?

How the hell was that possible?

"Do you have a clear line of sight?"

"I..."

"Brother, I *need* you to have this," I pleaded.

"Women and children are—"

"You won't miss. Luke, you will not miss."

The man in blue had swung Hadley's limp body into his arms and turned them toward the crowd. Waist-deep water surrounded them and the hair on the back of my neck stood on end.

Every muscle in my body was tight, ready to strike.

Ready to kill, maim, harm.

"He's baptizing her. Cleansing her," I mumbled, and the man dipped Hadley's head back into the water.

"Matt and Drake have two seconds to get to where they need to be before I go in," I radioed.

"We're ready when you are," Matt announced.

Thank fuck.

"Logan, do you have a shot?" Luke asked and I didn't miss the tremble in his voice.

"You got this, Luke," Logan replied which meant he had no shot and Luke had to get his head straight.

"In three," I broadcasted.

But before I could count down, the man holding Hadley shifted. His right hand came out of the water brandishing a long blade and my blood turned to ice.

I didn't call out the order to move. I ran and I did it shouting.

A moment later, the man holding Hadley was no longer holding her, because he had a bullet between his eyes.

Then Hadley disappeared underwater.

35

I heard him.

The rebel yell.

I heard Brady and I waited.

Not that I could do anything else since I was fairly certain either both my shoulders were dislocated or they were broken.

The pain was otherworldly. The fear only exacerbated the physical hurt.

I was being cleansed.

Cleansed of my demons. Bishop had deemed me a temptation. He'd proclaimed I had one chance to release the evil inside of me and if I didn't, I would be sacrificed.

I wanted to fight this, but my arms would not work. I'd tried. I'd summoned up all the willpower I had and they still wouldn't work. Each step I took toward the "baptismal pool" was excruciating. I couldn't help myself. And I feared no one was going to find me in time.

Bishop pulled a dagger and brought it high, readying to plunge it into my body. Then over Bishop telling me the devil needed to be cast out, I heard Brady.

A moment later, I heard the gunshot and sucked in as much oxygen as I could, preparing to go underwater. I couldn't use my arms to swim but the water wasn't deep and I could stay under and wait. Brady would come.

I hit the water and sank.

I felt hands on me. Not gentle, they were tugging me to the surface. I couldn't see, all I could hear was muffled voices, but I knew. I didn't struggle as I was pulled up and held close.

"I got you."

Three words that had me sagging in relief.

But he didn't take us back to shore, he was swimming us out farther into the water.

"I can't swim. My shoulders are broken."

"I got you."

I didn't have time to think about how stupid I'd

been. How reckless. How I'd put myself and others in danger. Brady had me. I was safe.

And I finally, I gave in to the pain.

"Hadley, no, baby, stay awake."

"Hurt everywhere."

"I know. Just a little longer. Stay with me."

I didn't want to stay with him. I wanted to close my eyes and sleep for a year. I wanted to hide under my bed and not face what I'd done.

"I'm stupid."

"No, you're not."

"I'm so sorry."

Brady said something but I couldn't hear him over the sirens. I picked my head up off his shoulder and saw more police cars than I'd ever seen in my life drive straight onto the grassy area. Then uniformed officers were out of their cars swarming the area.

"What are they doing?" I asked as I watched in horrified fascination all the men huddle together as the women scurried around them to form a circle, dragging children with them.

"Good Christ," Brady grumbled in disgust.

And that was when I got it. The women were being used as a shield. A human barrier so the police couldn't get to the men.

What the hell?

"You're good," Trey shouted from the embankment and Brady started moving us that way.

Brady hadn't taken us across the pond but he'd taken us off to the side, away from the mayhem.

"Toss me your shirt," Brady clipped and I remembered my state of undress.

"Oh, God."

"Shh. You're safe."

Brady tagged Trey's shirt out of the air and brought it to my chest.

"I don't suppose you can put this on?"

"No way. Can't move my arms."

"Okay, baby. I'm gonna cover you the best I can."

"Please don't let my dad see." Brady's body went solid and I quickly rushed out. "It looks worse than it is. No one touched me like that."

"Did you ask for your clothes to be removed?" he snarled.

"God, no."

"Then it is worse than it looks. No one. No man, no woman, makes you take off your clothes without permission."

Okay, so he was right, but he was also wrong. *I* hadn't removed my clothes but I didn't think it was the time or place to tell him the specifics.

Trey was in the water, helping Brady carry me

out, keeping his eyes locked onto mine. When Brady adjusted the shirt, I understood why.

"Thank you," I whispered.

Trey jerked his chin and looked away, stepping in front of us. It's worth noting, Trey still had his firearm in his hand and a shiver of fear washed over me.

"No one's gonna hurt you, Hadley."

With each step Brady took, nausea roiled in my stomach. My shoulders burned, my arms tingled as they hung unnaturally.

"I'm sorry, Hadley."

"It's fine."

"Hang in there, baby, we're almost to the ambulance."

With all the strength I had left, I picked my head up and we were indeed close to an ambulance. The back doors of the rig open, EMTs and police waited for us to arrive.

I scanned the area and didn't see my dad. Thank God.

"You're not gonna leave me, right?"

"No, I'm not leaving your side."

Thank God for that, too.

"You shouldn't've moved her," one of the EMTs groused. "Bring her in."

Brady stepped into the back of the ambulance, gently laid me on a gurney, then everything was a blur.

I was peppered with questions by the medical professionals about my injuries, and to my horror, Trey's shirt was removed—silver-lining, a woman did it. She did a quick but thorough scan of my body before she covered me with a blanket.

"Right side, shoulder dislocation. Possible separation on the left," the EMT called out. "You said you have a headache. Were you hit in the head?"

"No."

"What happened here?" She gently glided a gloved finger over my cheek.

Shit. Shit. Shit.

My gaze skidded to Brady and I was rethinking wanting him by my side.

Furious didn't begin to cover the look on his face. Devastated was closer. Destroyed closer still.

"I'm sorry. So sorry."

"Baby, you got nothing to be sorry for." I had to hand it to him, he did his best to sound soothing but his anger came through loud and clear.

"Hadley?"

I looked back at the EMT and answered. "I was um...slapped. Not hard enough to give me a concussion or anything. The guy was kinda small so there wasn't much power behind it." That was a lie. It'd hurt like a son of a bitch. "I think my head hurts because my shoulders hurt so bad."

"All right. We're gonna give you something to dull the pain."

"Before you do that, we need to ask her some questions," a police officer said.

"No." That came from Brady. Firm. Unrelenting. "You'll wait until she's been checked out at the hospital. Then you'll wait until she's ready to talk to you."

"That's not—"

"Pearson," Ethan cut the officer off and I closed my eyes. "Not now."

"Lenox, I understand Miss Walker is family. But you know we cannot hold all thirty-five men. We need her to ID the two who took her."

"Only two out of the thirty-five are dressed in jeans and t-shirts. I think we got who took her."

"And the man who physically assaulted her. Do you have him?"

I felt it.

The air in the back of the ambulance went electric, but more, the air surrounding the compound sizzled. I didn't know how it happened, I didn't know when he'd materialized, but I felt my father's presence bearing down on me. I looked at Brady for help. I wasn't sure what I wanted him to do, possibly defuse the situation. Tackle my father before he did something that couldn't be undone in front of a million cops.

But whatever it was I was looking for in Brady, I did not find. He looked positively homicidal. And that was when I made my decision.

One last stupid thing.

Then I was done and I'd live the rest of my life in whatever bubble they wanted to put me in.

But for now, I was going to save my man and my father.

"I'm fine. Let me up so I can ID him."

"Absolutely fucking not," Brady ground out.

No help.

I looked at Ethan and gave him my best pleading stare. Some of the hardness shifted from his face but he shook his head.

"Ethan, please," I implored.

There was a tick in his jaw and I knew I had him. He was smart. He knew what it meant if the man who'd hit me was not safely tucked away behind bars. *He knew.*

"I get you, Hadley—"

"I'm getting up and I'm ID-ing the men who took me. I'm ID-ing the man who hit me. So either one of you can help me or I'm asking Pearson here to walk me over. Your choice."

"Motherfucking goddammit," my dad hissed. "You're going to the hospital, Hadley. The rest can wait."

"Help me up?" I asked the EMT.

"Doll, I understand why you want to do this. But I cannot help you out of the back of this ambulance. You're injured and it's against regulation."

No help.

Fine.

I struggled to sit only using my abdominal muscles and silently cursed myself for not going to the stupid yoga classes with Addy.

"Core muscles are important for back health."

How many times had I heard my twin tell me that? Too many to count.

The pain was extraordinary as I fought to get up.

"Jesus Christ, Hadley. You're gonna hurt yourself worse." Brady leaned over me to stop me from moving.

"Then help me."

"No. You're—"

"Help. Me." Brady's cold eyes bore into mine.

Storms once again darkened his beautiful gray eyes and I hated I'd put them there. "I won't let you do it."

"Hadley—"

"You know I won't. You saved me, Brady. You pulled me from the water. I know that was hard for you, honey. But you did it and you saved me. I'm not gonna let you do anything else. So either you help me one more time or I do it alone. But I'm doing it."

None of the fire left his gaze as he stared down at me.

I was not stupid, at least not about this. I knew what Brady had to have been thinking about when he saw me in that water. I knew he had to fight demons to get to me. I knew he was seeing his sister as he pulled me up.

I also knew with a hundred percent certainty the man he was, he'd exact revenge. He wouldn't allow a man to hit me. Neither would my father.

I couldn't save myself.

But I would save them.

36

Walker determination.

Christ.

Relentless.

I tucked the blanket around Hadley and her scowl deepened.

Fierce.

"It's cute you trying to shoot laser beams from your eyes, baby, but they're unnecessary."

I started to pick her up when the EMT stopped me.

"You can't take her out of here."

"Move aside," Ethan commanded and Hadley smiled.

Time to burst her bubble.

"You have two minutes, then you're on your way to the hospital."

"But—"

"No buts. You're getting your way. You got two minutes."

I glanced over at Jasper, his face hard as a rock, his posture stiff, his jaw grinding.

"Brady," he clipped as I started to move.

"It's my call," I reminded him and his glare hardened.

"No one's gonna hurt you," I reminded her.

"I know."

No hesitation.

Jesus.

She trusted me. Fully and completely.

"I love you, Hadley."

"I know that, too."

A new burn started. One I welcomed. The kind that made you want to never forget the moment, even if everything else about the moment was fucked.

But I'd never forget, not for a second, the trust, the certainty in her voice. After everything that had happened to her, she was standing strong.

Well, not technically standing.

But...

"We got the men separated," Ethan said from behind me. "Fucked-up shit seeing those fucking cowards hide behind the women. But worse seeing those women place the children in front of them."

Fucked-up didn't begin to cover it. Neither did cowardly. There was a special place in hell for men like these. And hopefully, with Hadley's help, I'd have the three I wanted to dispatch first.

A line of officers kept the men corralled until Ethan directed them to let us through.

It took Hadley less than two minutes to point out the three who'd harmed her. Though in their own way, every person who belonged to Faithful had hurt her. The women had stood by and done nothing. Not a single one of them had spoken up or helped.

But it wouldn't be until much later. Until Hadley's shoulders were reset and the determination was made she wouldn't need surgery. Until after she'd been given pain relievers that had put her to sleep. And later still, until after she woke and told her story to the police, that I would come to understand the severity of what happened to her.

And not a single motherfucking person had helped her. Not a woman, child, or man.

Through the police interview, I remained silent, supporting Hadley the way she needed.

I held her hand, I wiped her tears, I kissed her cheek and encouraged her to finish. What I didn't tell her and what she'd never know was, the more details she gave, the more fuel she added to the fire raging within.

Ethan gave me a poignant look as he exited Hadley's hospital room, following the two cops who'd taken her statement.

I knew he was worried and he should've been.

I was going to burn those motherfuckers to the ground.

"Brady?"

"Yeah?" I stopped looking at the door and glanced back down at my woman lying in a hospital bed.

Jesus Christ.

"We need to talk about what happened."

"We will. But first, you need more rest."

I wanted to rehash what had happened, never. But I'd listen as many times as she needed.

"No, now. Before it builds inside of you."

"Me?"

"I want you to let this go."

I carefully blanked my face and nodded. "Okay."

"You're lying."

"Get some rest."

"Do not lie to me," she demanded in a low tone.

My pulse started to pound and my temper ignited. "I'm gonna say this as gently as I can, Hadley. But you know I can't let that stand. Not any of it. Not those two fuckers taking you. Not that cunt taking your clothes off, not those bitches standing around watching, and most especially those goddamn men lining up to look at you. They wanna use God to play their sick fucking games, they're gonna learn the true meaning of hellfire and brimstone. They're so keen on worshiping and casting out the devil, I will gladly lead them to their maker. Then they'll receive their judgment."

"I'm scared," she whispered.

"And that right there is why what they did cannot stand."

"No, Brady. I'm not scared of them. *You're* scaring me. I'm scared *for* you. I'm scared my father, brother, cousins, and uncles will follow you down this dark path. I don't want that. I don't want any of you to be taken away from me."

"I won't ever—"

"Yes, you will. You go through with whatever you're planning, you'll be taken away from me. It won't matter if you're never caught and you're free to go to work, walk the street, drive your truck, come home to me, sleep next to me. You, my Brady, will never be free again. It will haunt you. Which means it will eventually take you from me. I'm begging you, help me heal the only way I can truly get over what happened. Stay with me."

Hadley reached out, grabbed my arm, and yanked me forward. My other hand shot out and hit the mattress near her hip and I braced.

"You're gonna hurt yourself."

"My shoulders were dislocated, not broken." The reminder felt like a knife to the gut. "I was scared, Brady. I knew I screwed up. I knew what I'd done was stupid. I swear to you, I will never do anything like that again. But hear this. I was scared shitless when I was standing in front of all those people but I knew you'd come. It wasn't pleasant having my clothes removed but I survived. It was creepy and disgusting having those men line up to look at me, but I survived. I did not want to be baptized into some sick cult, but I survived. Now listen to my words: *I survived*. What I will *not* survive, is losing you. You go through with whatever you have planned, you will be lost to me and I will not survive that."

That knife she'd plunged into my gut twisted.

"Baby," I rasped brokenly.

"I won't survive it, Brady."

Fuck.

My head fell forward and a war waged inside of me.

You will be lost to me and I will not survive that.

Jesus.

The door opened. I heard Emily call out, "We can come back."

"Thanks, Mom."

"No." I lifted my head. "Come in."

"Brady."

"Your family's waited long enough, baby. Let them come in."

"Brady?" Hadley's hand clamped around my wrist. Her eyes searched mine. But it wasn't either of those that made me come to a decision.

"You won't ever lose me," I told her.

"Promise?"

"Promise, Hadley."

"You won't—"

"I won't," I confirmed.

"Promise. Promise me. Swear it."

I moved to cup both her cheeks. Her fingers still

RILEY EDWARDS

wrapped around my wrist meant her arm came up, too, and there were no signs of pain.

"I swear to you. You will never lose me, not in any way. I'm yours forever."

"Thank you."

I closed the inches between us and brushed my lips against hers. "I love you, Hadley."

"Love you."

"Visit with your mom. I need to talk to your dad."

A twinkle of fear flashed in her eyes before it disappeared and she nodded.

"Okay."

She didn't ask me to promise again. She let me go and turned to look at her mom.

"I'm okay," she told Emily.

"I can see that." Emily smiled and caught my arm as I passed, pulling me to a stop.

She didn't say anything as she rolled up and kissed my cheek.

I received more of the same from Adalynn, Quinn, and Delaney as I moved to the door.

Unfortunately, the welcome out in the hall wasn't so warm.

As a matter of fact, it was damn right arctic.

"Waiting room," I said as I strolled past the men.

The short distance to the thankfully empty waiting room did not give Jasper time to calm down.

As soon as Carter shut the door behind him, Jasper launched in.

"I want a full workup of every member—"

"No."

"No?"

"That is not what Hadley wants."

"Hadley doesn't get a say," he spat.

"If you'd calm down and think, you'd realize she does. Actually, she's the only one who gets a say."

Jasper's torso swung back and he leveled me with a scathing stare. "And when you get your head out of your ass—"

"Stop." Clark stepped in and Jasper turned his anger toward his friend. "You need to take some time, brother, and think."

The deep freeze dragged on as each man in the room attempted to get a handle on their tempers.

I tried to keep my tone even. "I know it goes against every fiber of what makes us, us. But we're gonna stand down. And we're gonna do it because your daughter is scared as shit she's gonna lose us. But more, we don't listen to what she needs, we're gonna lose her. And there is nothing in this world I would do that would give her a reason to take herself from me. She straight out begged, pleaded with tears in her eyes, for me not to leave her. She does not want you to leave her either. I can't tell you what to do, I can't tell anyone in this room what to do. But I will not be a part of anything that she doesn't want. With that said, a single move is made on my woman, I will not hesitate."

"And if that move means that she's hurt?" Jasper asked sharply. "Taken again, only next time you're too late? You willing to take that chance?"

"Willing to? Yes. Do I want to? Fuck no. But am I going to listen to my woman? Yeah, Jasper, I am. I don't think you heard me. So let me give you her words: *you will be lost to me and I will not survive that.* That came out of my woman's mouth. Your daughter. When I tell you I will protect her, I mean that in every way. Every goddamn way, and not just physically. You do what you have to do, but do it knowing Hadley doesn't want retribution. She wants to heal."

The room went silent and after a few beats, I broke it.

"She's being discharged. I'm taking her home. Obviously, we'd like you all there. But if you're pissed at me and don't wanna be there, I get it. I'll do my best to cushion that for Hadley."

And with that, I walked out the door.

I said my piece. I let Hadley's wishes be known.

I couldn't do more than that.

And as hard as it was to swallow my own need for vengeance, I chose Hadley.

37

I now understood Quinn, Delaney, and Liberty.

I'd had a much smaller dose than they'd had and I was already over my family hovering.

When Quinn was released from the hospital after almost dying, my mom was way worse than she was behaving now. She'd looked at Quinn like she was made of glass. But she was looking at me like she was plotting something.

Every now and again I'd catch her staring. Then she'd look away and my normally pathologically sweet mother looked murderous. I wanted to ask my dad to have a word with her but he was in Brady's backyard with my uncles.

They'd been out there a long time. Brady thankfully was in the kitchen unpacking the bags of takeout that'd been delivered. Quinn and Addy were both in there helping him. But Addy's sidelong glances at Trey limping had not gone unnoticed by me.

He normally hid his limp the best he could, so obviously he was in severe pain. Pain that was my fault. But I couldn't let my mind wander to that right now. I needed to sort my dad and uncles out.

"Hadley, honey, you should stay in the house," my mom called out as I approached the sliding glass door.

"No, Mom, and I'll tell you straight, stop thinking about whatever it is you're thinking about. Actually, everyone in this room, stop thinking about it. I did something incredibly stupid and I learned my lesson. Don't pile more guilt on top of what I'm already feeling. I put enough people in danger today. Trey's hurt because of me. A man's dead and someone in this room made that happen. I could guess who it was but I know no one will tell me. So whoever it was that took that shot, make no mistake you saved my life. Bishop was going to cast out the devil with that knife. I appreciate you taking that mark on your soul so I could live. That's guilt I'll live with because I'm stupid. And if anyone in this room thinks I want to live with the guilt I'll feel if someone does something else, you are wrong."

With that, I opened the door and heard my dad and uncles arguing. They immediately stopped and four sets of eyes swung my way.

"Please don't stop yelling at each other on my account."

"Honey, you should be resting," my dad told me.

I didn't move.

"Hadley. Go back inside."

"Look at me, Dad."

"I am, honey. You should be resting."

Sweet mother of God, I had a whole lot of respect for Quinn and Delaney. If I heard one more person tell me to rest, relax, take a load off, or ask me if I needed something, I was going to scream. I loved how they loved me, but we'd been home less than an hour and I'd heard those things no less than seven hundred times and I wasn't exaggerating.

"You're not looking at me."

"I am—"

"No, Dad, you're not seeing me because all you're seeing is your fear. Because if you were truly seeing me, you'd know I was fine. You'd know I'm stronger than what was done to me. You'd remember I'm your daughter and you made me this way. And lastly, if you were looking at me, you'd remember you love me more than anything and that's including your selfish need to avenge a wrong that was done to me. Now look at me."

"Hadley—"

"I did not want you to see me like that," I whispered. "Brady, he loves me a different way. He loves me as a woman. You? You love me as your little girl and I always want to be that to you. I didn't want you to see me undressed."

My dad flinched and actually took a step back. Uncle Clark's hand went to my dad's shoulder to steady him.

"I'm gonna tell you the same thing I told Brady. I was scared. No doubt about it, I'd never been so scared in my whole life. But I knew Brady would come. I did not want you to come, Dad. I didn't want Uncle Lenox there. I didn't want Uncle Clark. I didn't want Uncle Levi. Not my brother, not Carter or Ethan. Not because I don't trust you, but because I love you and I knew any of you seeing me like that would destroy you. I knew there'd be no hope of me stopping the rain of fire you all want to ignite. But I'm asking you all to give me this."

My father made a strangled noise and I knew I was close to talking him down. My dad loved me.

And under all that alpha, bossy, protectiveness, he had a soft spot.

"Please don't make me live with more death on my conscience. Please don't make me go to sleep every night knowing that because of my stupidity, my father has more marks on his soul. And before you say it, I know you'd gladly take them for me. But you don't have to because I don't want you to have them. I don't want that for my uncles, brother, or cousins. I want to crawl into bed next to Brady and do that free. So one more time, I'm asking you to give me that."

"Okay, baby girl," my dad croaked and I ran to him.

He rocked back, wrapped his arms around me, then shoved his face in my neck. Moments later, I felt his big body shake.

Yeah, my dad had a soft spot for his girls.

"I'm sorry, Dad. I swear I'll never do something like that again."

He nodded but didn't lift his head. I knew that wasn't the last of it. He'd give me a few weeks to get over what happened then he'd ream my ass. They all would.

But first, they'd let me heal.

They'd surround me in love.

Because that's what our family was about.

Love. Loyalty. Protection.

"You okay?" Brady asked.

It was hours later. Everyone had gone home and we were in bed. I was snuggled to Brady's side, his hand was on my hip, and I was worried.

"Are you and my dad okay?"

"What do you mean?"

"Don't play dumb. The two of you were giving each other a wide berth."

Brady's hand covered mine resting on his chest and he sighed.

"Your dad and I had words. He wasn't happy with me that I was stepping back and letting the police and the court system take care of what happened. And, baby, I understand why he was angry. Men like us don't like to stand down. I think whatever you said to him made him come around. Everything's gonna be fine."

"How do you know?"

"Because you're lying here next to me and I didn't have to fight your dad for the privilege."

"The privilege?"

God, could I love him any more?

"Yeah, baby. It's a privilege to sleep next to you. To know you trust me. To have you love me the way you do."

Yep. I could.

I could love him more and more and I hoped I never stopped finding new reasons to love him.

"Are you sleeping here?" I asked.

"Yeah."

"Will you be able to sleep?"

"Not sure. But you will. And you'll do it with me holding you close."

"I love you more than I did yesterday."

"Good."

"Thank you for coming for me."

"You never have to thank me for that."

I smiled against his chest and asked, "Who shot Bishop?"

"Luke."

"Seriously?"

"Yeah. Just because he lost most of his vision in his dominant eye doesn't mean he's not one hell of a good shot. He was nervous, I heard his voice trembling. But he took it, and his aim was true."

"I wasn't thinking about his ability. I was surprised you told me."

"I'll tell you anything you want to know."

That was news to me.

"You didn't tell me about the case you were working on with Liberty."

"You didn't ask."

Oh, well, he had a point. I hadn't asked. Not because I didn't care, I just figured he wouldn't tell me.

"Why was Luke nervous?"

"Because he's still not confident shooting right-handed and there were women and children around Bishop. If he missed, there was a strong possibility he would've hit one of them."

"But he did it. For me."

"Yeah, baby, he did."

"I hate I put him—"

"Stop." Brady gently shook me. "Stop calling yourself stupid. Stop saying you're sorry. You let your emotions get the best of you. Something we're all guilty of doing. You were angry, you acted on that anger, but you did it thinking you were safe, and unfortunately, you were not. I don't think I need to explain all the reasons why you're not ever gonna do that again because I know you learned something."

Oh, yeah, I learned something all right. But I was

annoyed he was talking to me like I was a petulant five-year-old and he had the authority to scold me.

"I did learn something. But just to point out, I'm not real hip on you being patronizing."

"It's not patronizing if I'm pointing out the truth."

So he had a point. But I wasn't ready to concede. So instead I suggested, "Maybe we should stop talking about it and go to sleep."

"Sounds good to me."

I closed my eyes and his body started shaking under me.

"Are you laughing?"

"Nope."

"It sure feels like you're laughing, Brady."

"Thought you wanted to go to sleep."

Annoying.

"I do, and I would if you'd stop laughing."

That made his body shake harder and the hand over mine pressed my palm deeper.

"Love you more than life, Hadley."

Okay, he could laugh at me all he wanted.

But I didn't tell him that.

Instead, I closed my eyes knowing I'd sleep safely in my man's arms.

38

"Finally." That was the first thing I heard when my eyes opened. Then a whispered, "Are you awake?"

"Yeah, baby, I'm awake. What do you mean, finally?"

"I've been waiting hours to do this."

I didn't have to ask what "this" was because she was up and straddling my hips before I could blink.

"You needed your sleep, so I didn't want to wake you," she lied.

I knew that wasn't why she hadn't attempted to wake me up but I smiled anyway.

"Sleep well?" I asked even though I knew the answer.

"Like a rock."

And she had. I was awake most of the night and only closed my eyes when the sun had come up.

"Now that you're finally awake, I want you."

My tee she'd worn to bed last night was up over her head and tossed aside. My eyes went to her full breasts and my body went solid.

"Hadley, baby—"

"I was afraid of this."

"Afraid of what?"

"Afraid you'd treat me like I'm breakable. Like we shouldn't be doing this because of what happened. So as I was lying next to you, with your arm tight around me even in your sleep protecting me, holding me close, I started thinking. And what I came up with is this. It is my privilege to sleep next to you. And since it's my honor, it's up to me to get us over this hump before it becomes a mountain. So that's what we're doing. I'm yours, Brady. Yours. And I'm not letting a bunch of creepy, cult perverts take this away from us."

My heart started pounding and once again I knew she had it right. I'd keep loving her more every day.

"Is that right?" My lips twitched and she smiled.

"That's right."

"Well, you seem to have me where you want me, so what's the holdup?"

Her smile became wicked. She leaned up and forward but stopped just shy of her mouth on mine. When her hand went between her legs and she freed my cock, I understood her smile. There was no holdup. Hadley knew what she wanted, and with born-and-bred determination, she set about getting it.

The tip of my cock notched inside her pussy, and in one, smooth downward glide, her wet heat enveloped my cock.

I groaned.

She sighed.

"Heaven."

"Need you to move, baby."

"Love you, Brady."

One hand went to cup her cheek, the other went to her hip and I repeated, "Need you to move."

"Whatever you want," she said on an upward glide and my hand on her hip moved and skimmed the crack of her ass.

"Wouldn't say that to a man with a hard cock and good imagination," I warned.

Then my jaw clenched as her pussy convulsed and she slammed back down hard.

"Are you planning on using that imagination

now or are you just teasin' me?"

"You want me to take you there?"

Hadley swiveled her hips with my cock planted deep. She didn't answer but she did moan.

"Answer me, baby. You want my cock in your ass?"

"I want everything."

Jesus Christ.

The woman had barely moved and I was gonna come.

"Then when I cuff you, I'm gonna take your ass. You still sure?"

"Oh, yeah."

Fucking hell.

"Lift up. I wanna watch you touch yourself."

No hesitation, she sat up and both of her hands cupped her tits as she bounced on my lap.

Fuck, yeah, heaven.

"As sweet of a view as that is, I want one between your legs."

Again, no hesitation. But she decided to give me a different kind of show and tipped her head back until the tips of her hair tickled my thighs. The slender column of her throat exposed, her beautiful tits on display, and her fingertips slowly skimmed her skin as they made their way lower.

Sexy as fuck.

"Gorgeous."

Hadley's hand dipped between us. Her fingers rubbed my shaft. I gave her a beat to play then warned, "Gonna flip you over if you don't stop playing."

She stopped playing and started working her clit. The second she started massaging, she went wild.

That wasn't heaven, it was mind-bending.

I laid back and enjoyed the ride. Tits bouncing, sexy-as-all-fuck mews turned into deep groans, and finally her pussy clutched my cock so tight I blew.

"Mouth," I grunted.

Hadley fell forward, gave me her weight, my arm went across her back, and I pinned her to me.

The come-down was long. Both of us enjoyed the kiss. It was slow and deep and wet.

Dare I say it, cleansing.

It was exactly what both of us needed.

I broke the kiss and smiled when Hadley's lips chased mine.

"More than life, Hadley."

Her eyes slowly opened. Languid, sated, satisfied.

But mostly full of love.

"More than life," she echoed.

I left Hadley in my office and went in search of Jasper.

I didn't have to look long when I caught him coming out of his office with a box.

"You got a minute?" I asked.

"Yeah. I was hoping you'd come in before I left."

Left?

Jasper turned back toward his office and I started to follow him in but stopped dead in the doorway.

"Come in, shut the door."

I didn't move. I just stared at the walls in his office, now devoid of pictures, plaques, and military memorabilia that less than twenty-four hours had pride of place.

"What's going on?"

"It's time," he answered.

"Time for what?"

"To tear down the shrine. Let go. Retire."

What the fuck?

"Retire?"

"Yeah, you know. Not wake up at the ass crack of dawn, drag my carcass into work. Enjoy my wife. Travel. Spend my money before I'm in a wheelchair."

Jasper Walker in a wheelchair? That day would never come.

"Why?"

"Brady, if I have to explain to you why I want to enjoy my wife—"

"Why now? You retired like...shit, I don't know, feels like five years ago. So why now are you packing up your office?"

Jasper leaned against his desk, crossed his ankles, and settled in. He also held my gaze.

"Yesterday, I fucked up, acted like a dick."

"Jasper, you don't—"

"I do, Brady, and you know I do. A man who's any sort of man admits when he's wrong and makes amends. I was out of line yesterday. My brothers pointed that out, but even before they got in my face about it, I knew I'd done wrong. And if I hadn't already figured it out, my daughter set me straight. You were right, it's about what Hadley wants even if it goes against what I want. And you were right to have your woman's back."

Jesus, that felt good. So good, I was struggling to keep my emotions locked down.

"'Preciate that. Now it's done, we move on. Why are you packing your office?"

"As you said, I retired. We were all staying

involved for Levi, to have his back while we found who sold Liberty out. That's done. Wick's on the mend. Liberty's good. Drake's gonna be living on a tightrope of worry while Liberty finishes her enlistment. Since she's made the decision not to re-enlist, that'll come to an end for him. But I was staying, putting off the traveling my wife wants to do so I could take your back."

"My back?"

"As you know, it was not lost on any of us my daughter was in love with you. All of us, especially me, saw when the change happened. She went from happily stringing you along, pushing your buttons to keep you close, to a full-court press. It took her less time than I thought it would to reel you in. And you didn't fight it...much. So, in the end, you didn't need me. Now, my girl's got her man. The two of you are working to make something solid even better. Which means it's time I leave."

The air in the room became so thick I was finding it hard to breathe. Jasper had stayed to have my back. Not Hadley's—mine. I didn't know what to do with that. All I knew was, it felt so fucking good I thought my skin would tear wide open.

"Coupla things, Brady," Jasper continued. "Switch over to my office, it's bigger and has a view of the range. Give Trey yours so he doesn't have to work out of the temporary trailer we set up. Jason's already lining up contractors to get bids on expanding the main building. We've already turned Triple Canopy over to all of you. Now I'm officially handing *you* over everything. Both personally and professionally. Build this company, so when the time comes you can pass *your* legacy down to my grand-children."

That burn hit my chest again and fear started to creep in.

Jasper read my reaction. "Heard what you said and I feel you about not strapping your family with something you find ugly. So listen closely to what I'm telling you, son. I'm handing you *everything*. All that is me, all that I have, all that I love. Four years ago, we claimed you. You are ours. But more, you're mine. You take my name and you marry my daughter. Not for her, for you. Take it and build a family. Give that to yourself."

Jasper stopped to clear his throat and pinned me with the same green eyes he'd passed down to his daughter. They looked better on Hadley. But right then, all I could think about was in an extreme act of vulnerability, Jasper wasn't holding anything back.

"I was lost when I met Emily. So lost, I never

wanted to be found. Never wanted a family. It's amazing what the love of a good woman can heal. I reckon you know already. But the last piece of this puzzle, the one you cannot know until the world is placed in your arms, is that while Emily freed me of my nightmares, it was Jason, Delaney, Quinn, Hadley, and Adalynn who made me strong. Made me a better man. Emily healed me, my children made me whole."

"I appreciate you sharing that," I said and found myself swallowing the lump in my throat.

"I know you do. But what I want to know is if you feel me."

"I feel you."

"Good. Now I know my brothers have made the offer as well, so I'm gonna throw this out there. No better men than my brothers. No one more loyal. But you take one of their names and not mine...just saying, it's gonna piss me off."

Even though my heart was thudding in my chest and drawing oxygen into my lungs was difficult, I still found it in me to laugh.

When I was done, Jasper was smiling at me.

"I hear that."

"Good. Now help me carry all this shit out to my

car. And while we're doing that, you can fill me in on how my daughter's doing."

"She's a Walker," I told him.

"Know that."

"No, Jasper, she's a Walker. In other words, Hadley's fine. All fine. Slept like a rock, not even a single twitch all night. This morning she woke up and in true Walker fashion, made it her mission to communicate just how fine she was. Not saying it won't fuck with her in the future, but for right now, she's doing what she always does—dealing with it head-on so it doesn't fester."

"No, Brady, she didn't sleep safe through the night because she's a Walker. She did that because she's yours."

Good goddamn, the power of his words slammed into me. A golden trail started to scorch through me.

Unfortunately, the goodness I was feeling was short-lived.

This was because I heard Hadley shout.

Jasper heard it, too, and was on my heels as I jogged down the hall and hit the reception area.

And when my eyes landed on the man I never wanted to see again, venom hit my stomach.

Then my world exploded.

39

I shouldn't have been doing what I was doing.

I knew it.

But this time, it was not anger consuming me, making me do something stupid. It was something different. Sure, anger played a part, but protecting the man I loved won out.

That was why when Lauren called back to Brady's office not knowing he wasn't in there, to tell him a Mr. Hewitt was there to see him, I jumped out of Brady's chair and flew down the hall.

Hell no.

Hell to the fucking *no* was Brady going to have to face the man who killed his beloved sister.

The bad part of this plan was Brady had

unequivocally made it clear I was never to be in his father's presence.

And I would've respected this if Brent Hewitt hadn't dragged his slimy ass to Georgia and dared to invade Brady's privacy.

There was no mistaking the man standing in the open reception area was Brady's father. I'd envisioned a pot-bellied, ugly, disheveled, dirty, smelly, old, haggard man. That was not who was standing in front of me. Either he spent his time in prison getting fit and healthy, or even as a sorry-assed, murdering drunk, he'd been physically attractive. It sucked, it really did, that a man as vile as Brent was as handsome as he was, and he'd passed his superior genes down to his son. There wasn't a streak of gray in his hair, his eyes were a nice shade of brown, meaning Brady got his gray ones from his bitch of a mother.

Brent noticed I'd entered the room and turned fully to me and smiled.

And that sucked a hundredfold because he had a nice smile.

Bastard.

"You've got some nerve," I hissed.

"Pardon?"

"You heard me. You got some nerve coming here."

"Ma'am, I think you have me mistaken. I'm Brent Hewitt—"

"I know *who* you are."

Brent flinched.

"Then you understand—"

"No, you asshole, I do not understand how after what you did you'd think Brady would want one thing to do with you."

"I paid for that," he snapped.

"Really? You did? You killed your daughter," I shouted. "There's no payment to wipe that debt clean."

And suddenly Brent Hewitt wasn't so good-looking. His face twisted in revulsion and he took a step in my direction.

"The next step you take will be your last, you move another inch toward my woman."

I heard the words, I knew it was Brady, but I didn't recognize the voice. It was low and deep and filled with a ferociousness I'd never heard and just yesterday he'd rescued me from a cult compound and witnessed a sick fuck in the middle of trying to cleanse me. So it was saying something I'd never heard this level of aggression coming from my man.

"Son—"

"He's not your son," I lashed out. "He's not anything to you."

"I don't know who you think you are." Brent's gaze came back to mine and I made sure I had his attention before I took a step closer to him.

"Babe—"

"I'm the woman you're gonna have to get through to get to Brady. And before you get too excited, I'll explain, it won't just be me. Not a single one of us will let you near him. You try, and hellfire will rain down on you like you cannot imagine. Brady's ours. He's mine. Which also makes me the woman who's gonna put you on your ass. You got two choices, turn your weak, low-life ass around and walk out or I'll physically remove you. And by me I mean every one of Brady's brothers will put you out. Then they'll teach you a lesson. There's not a man in this building who will take pity on a dirtbag who is such a piece of shit he killed his own daughter and in doing that stole the only good thing Brady had in his life. Choice is yours."

I stopped, took a breath, and stared at Brent Hewitt with more hate than I ever thought possible. The man responsible for all of Brady's pain. Strong, loyal, protective, beautiful Brady.

Brent's gaze went over my shoulder and his eyes widened.

"Maybe she didn't make herself clear. What she meant to say was, you don't look at my brother before you turn your ass around and leave. What she also meant was don't ever come back. Don't call Brady. Don't call here. Don't email. Don't write a letter. If Brady ever finds it in him to talk to you, he'll reach out. Until then, you pull another sneak attack, you won't be meeting my sister at the door. You'll be meeting me."

Maybe I hadn't mentioned how much I loved my brother. Jason had it going on. He was tall, broad, and packed a powerful punch. I knew this because I watched him work out with the heavy bag. I'd also watched him train Triple Canopy clients in hand-to-hand combat.

"I'm thinking he needs that lesson," my dad growled.

"I want a word with my son," Brent stupidly argued.

"*My* son."

That did not come from my father. Or I should say, not just from my father. Those two words were echoed by my uncles. All four men said them in unison, with equal ferocity, meaning equal protection.

I loved my family.

"Carter, Drake, Trey, Matt, Luke, Logan, get that motherfucker out of this building."

I had no idea everyone had come up behind me until they started skirting around me to get to Brent.

"I can leave on my own."

"Then get on that," Logan suggested sharply.

Brent turned and walked out. Carter, Drake, Trey, Matt, Luke, and Logan followed him through and formed a line in front of the door.

Protection.

I twirled around to see my dad and uncles flanking my man.

More protection.

"Are you okay?"

Brady's gaze went from the wall of windows that faced the parking lot and settled on me.

He didn't look angry, sad, hurt, mad—nothing.

Blank.

Shit. I'd seen that look.

For years, that was all I'd seen.

Once it was gone and his beautiful gray eyes had started to glitter I'd forgotten how badly it hurt to see nothingness.

"I'm sorry. I know you said you never wanted me to meet him. But, Brady—"

"Vicious," he strangely said.

"What?"

"Didn't know you were so vicious, baby." Some of the gleam started to come back and my body started to relax. "For a second, I was scared we were gonna have to stop you from clawing that fucker's eyes out."

"I was thinking about it."

"Know you were."

We were standing ten feet apart, my dad and uncles still had his side, Jason not far from them, when Brady announced, "More than breath."

"More than breath," I returned.

My anger had melted away, but I was overcome with so many other emotions I couldn't draw in enough oxygen therefore I was panting.

And Brady didn't give me time to recover before he stole my breath.

"Marry me, Hadley."

My body rocked so violently, I was shocked I kept my feet.

Then Brady prowled across the room repeating, "Marry me. You give me your name, I promise you I'll make you happy for the rest of your life."

Say what?

Give him *my* name?

I was speechless. So when he stopped in front of me, captured my face in his hands, and tipped it up so he was staring in my eyes, I still hadn't said a word.

"Loved you from the first minute I saw you. Spent years falling deeper, every minute I'm with you, deeper still. Bottomless. Endless. For the rest of my life, Hadley, I'm gonna keep falling and I'm taking you with me. Fall with me. Marry me, baby. Let me give you a family—"

"A family?" I croaked.

"You want kids, Hadley. And there's nothing on this earth I wouldn't give you. But I figure us making a family, will really be you giving me everything."

"Yes. I want—"

I didn't finish accepting Brady's proposal because his lips were on mine. And with a kiss that was far too indecent, we sealed our engagement.

I was going to be Mrs. Brady Walker.

And I loved that more than breath.

40

Adalynn

I tried. I really tried to calm my temper before I hit the reception area of Triple Canopy. But calm was history. Calm was so far in my rearview mirror it was a miracle I hadn't grown a second head.

Trey Durum was getting a piece of my mind.

No.

Trey Durum was going to get the hot side of my tongue when I reamed his butt out for blowing off another appointment.

Hard-headed man.

I was stomping down the hall when I heard my sister call my name.

I came to a stop in front of Brady's office door

and some of my irritation slid away when I saw Hadley and Brady together.

"How are you?" I asked, even though by the smile on my sister's face, it was unnecessary.

This was Hadley we were talking about. She was the one in the family who no matter what happened, just kept going. She was my twin, my identical twin, so when our mother's egg split she must've stolen all the keep-on-ticking genes.

We were the same but very different.

I was shy to her outgoing. Maybe it was because when we were kids she was larger-than-life and spoke up for both of us. We'd always been a unit.

I was not jealous she'd found Brady. I was over the moon happy for her. The same way she wasn't jealous when I found a job I loved and threw myself into it.

We were close, we supported each other, but we were happy to finally be two different people.

Hadley. Adalynn. Not "the twins."

"I'm fine, Addy. Ethan said the charges they already had and the more they uncover means the men who took me won't be out for a long time."

See? Keeps on ticking.

"Did Dad tell you he caught Mom on the phone

with Aunt Lily trying to corral her into going with her to burn down the cult compound?"

Brady sputtered a laugh before he choked it back and Hadley gave me big eyes.

"No, he didn't say. But I knew she was up to something. I just didn't think she'd do *that*. Obviously, Dad stopped them."

"Yeah. But Mom was seriously unhappy she'd been caught. Aunt Lily, too."

"Vicious," Brady oddly remarked then continued. "I see where you get it from."

Come again?

My mom was sweet as could be. And Hadley was outrageously protective. Even if she bitched about the men in our family being overbearing, she was no better.

"Whatever," my sister mumbled, then walked across the office and smiled huge. "Dad knows, so do the uncles, Jason, and the guys, but only because they were there or I swear you'd be the first to know."

"Know what?"

"Brady and I are getting married."

The look on my beautiful sister's face—which was weird to think because we looked exactly the same and I wasn't conceited or anything—could only be described as serene.

She'd loved Brady for years. I'd heard all about how much, though even if she'd never uttered a peep, I still would've known because she couldn't hide it.

And I loved Brady for her.

"Wow. My sister's getting married."

"Yeah."

Oh, yeah, Hadley was deliriously happy and that made me happy.

"I'm calling dibs on the bachelorette party," I told her, then added, "and if Quinn tries to horn in, I'm gagging her."

"Deal."

"Happy for you, Hads."

"Thanks."

I pulled my sister in for a squeeze and found Brady smiling at us.

"Welcome to the family, big brother."

Brady's face softened and it felt like a gift, him giving me that soft look that was only reserved for Hadley.

"Appreciate that, Addy."

With one last tight squeeze, I pulled away from Hadley.

"Dinner this week?"

"Absolutely."

"Text me what night."

I turned to leave when Hadley called me back.

"You looked pissed when you came in."

"Beyond."

"Oh, boy. Trey?" she correctly guessed but I still confirmed.

"Trey."

Hadley's face split into a huge shit-eating grin and I narrowed my eyes.

"Hads—"

"Just sayin'..."

I knew what she was just saying.

I heard her the first ten times she told me the only reason I got so pissed about Trey blowing off his PT sessions was because I had the hots for him. Which I absolutely did not.

Sure, the man was model-gorgeous.

But he was a *dawg*.

I didn't need that kind of hassle.

Besides, I was happily single.

Which translated into lonely.

But if I needed the company of a man, I knew I could find it.

Which translated into I was in a monogamous relationship with my vibrator.

"Whatever."

I left Brady's office. I didn't storm down the hall,

out the back door, up the steps of the temporary office trailer Trey shared with Matt. Unfortunately, my stop-and-chat with Hadley and Brady had dwindled some of my annoyance.

Fortunately, when I swung the door open and found Trey limping worse than normal to his desk, I found it.

Trey's head snapped in my direction and pain clear as day marred his face. But as usual, he masked his pain. It also took him a second to ascertain I was Adalynn, not Hadley. Something Brady never had to do. Something that, if I was being honest, even though it was stupid it hurt my feelings.

"What the fuck, Addy?"

"Yeah, what the fuck?"

Trey blinked, once, twice, three times, then he scowled.

"Watch your mouth."

"My mouth?"

"Yeah, Adalynn, your mouth."

As a general rule, I didn't curse much. Not because I grew up in a family where cursing was frowned upon. As a matter of fact, most people, male and female in my family, cussed like sailors. This didn't bother me. I couldn't say exactly why I rarely cussed when my sister the librarian made an art out of four-letter words when she was mad. I just didn't.

So I could see how my language might be shocking to Trey considering he'd probably never heard me say *fuck*, but really, who was he to try to correct me when I'd been repeating him?

"You missed your appointment," I accused.

"No. I canceled my appointment. I didn't miss anything."

"That's the fourth time, Trey."

"I'm aware, *Adalynn*."

"You need to—"

"Don't come into my office and tell me what I need," he snarled, and held my gaze captive. "I know what I need. You don't have the first damn—"

"I don't? I'm your physical therapist, remember? I've read your medical reports. I've been running your rehab. I think I know exactly what you need."

"Yeah, you've been running it for six fucking months and it's not working."

Damn, that hurt.

"Yes, it is."

"The fuck it is. I'm still not a hundred percent."

Caution. Caution. Caution.

Or maybe more like danger, with a capital D.

"We've talked about this. Your doctors have

talked to you about this. You're never gonna be back to what you were before—"

My words were cut off when Trey's arm swept out and the detritus covering his desk went flying.

"Fuck," he roared and stumbled when he turned to face me. "You don't think I see it? Every goddamned time I look in the mirror I don't see what was taken from me? I don't even need to feel the pain in my leg or look down at the scar. No, all I need to do is look at my face and I know I'll never be what I was."

He had to be kidding.

"You have got to be kidding me," I voiced my thoughts. "Egotistical much? You're seriously worried about what your face looks like? Good Lord, so what you have scars on your face? It doesn't stop you from being good-looking. And if you're so hung up on your looks, go get plastic surgery, you arrogant prick. The only thing I'm concerned about is getting back part of what you lost. Though that doesn't include your ability to pick up women."

Some of the fire left Trey's presence though it mostly still burned bright.

"Wasn't talking about my looks, Addy. I welcome the scars."

"What?"

Now I was confused. I thought he was complaining about looking in the mirror.

"I see it every day. I can hide that shit from everyone else. But I can't lie to myself, Adalynn. Can't deny it. Can't pretend it away. I know what I lost. I'm the one that has to live with it."

I still wasn't sure I understood what he was saying. Though I had a pretty good idea he was talking about no longer being in the military. He'd been a SEAL. He and Luke had been medically discharged after they'd been injured in an explosion.

I know what I lost.

Shit.

I didn't know what to say to that.

Or maybe I did.

"You know what your problem is, Trey? You need an attitude adjustment. You're focusing on the things you think you lost instead of what you didn't. You could've lost your leg, you could've lost your life, you could've lost one of the guys, but you didn't. And while you're focused on feeling sorry for yourself, you're missing the important stuff going on around you. You think you lost the Navy and your team. What you're forgetting is you're still surrounded by your team. They all left and followed you and Luke.

Besides a team, you've been given a family. One that will support you if you'd stop pushing them away."

"Is that right, Addy? You gonna support me while I'm limping around? You gonna help me up in the morning when my leg's stiff and I can't get out of bed? You gonna pop open my pain meds for me so I can self-medicate to numb the fucking pain?"

It was the self-medicating part that took the wind out of my sails. Concern crept in.

"Are you taking pain pills, Trey?"

"Fuck no."

"Then why'd you say that?"

"Because you don't think I don't know what happens to washed-up, has-beens like me?"

"I thought you were tougher than this," I told him. "Thought you were supposed to be some sort of badass, Captain America, Navy SEAL. But this? This is weak. This is you giving up. This is you having a goddamn pity party because you can't run twenty miles with five-hundred pounds on your back. Well, guess what, *you can't*. Welcome to your new life, Trey. Now fucking deal with it. You have an appointment tomorrow at five. You're not there, so help me God, I'll find you. And when I do, you'll wish you were back at BUD/s with some instructor in your face because I'll push you so hard you'll be crying."

With that, I turned and left.

I didn't look back.

Which meant I missed Trey do another triple blink before his beautiful full lips tipped up into a smile. And since I missed that, I also missed him shaking his head while muttering, "Goddamn, Adalynn Walker. Who knew?"

But he'd said it like he was impressed. Which would've gone a long way to untying the knots in my stomach as the guilt set in.

Adalynn and Trey are up next in Flawed.

Grab your copy here.

RILEY'S REBELS

If you are interested in joining Riley's Rebels newsletter sign up here:
https://www.subscribepage.com/RRsignup

—

ALSO BY RILEY EDWARDS

Riley Edwards

www.RileyEdwardsRomance.com

Romantic Suspense

Gemini Group

Nixon's Promise

Jameson's Salvation

Weston's Treasure

Alec's Dream

Chasin's Surrender

Holden's Resurrection

Red Team

Nightstalker

Protecting Olivia - Susan Stoker Universe

Redeeming Violet - Susan Stoker Universe

Recovering Ivy - Susan Stoker Universe

Rescuing Erin - Susan Stoker Universe

The Gold Team

The Collective

Unbroken

Trust

Standalone

Romancing Rayne - Susan Stoker Universe

ABOUT THE AUTHOR

Riley Edwards is a USA Today bestselling author, wife, and military mom. Riley was born and raised in Los Angeles but now resides on the east coast with her fantastic husband and children.

Riley writes heart-stopping romance with sexy alpha heroes and even stronger heroines. Riley's favorite genres to write are romantic suspense and military romance.

Don't forget to sign up for Riley's newsletter and never miss another release, sale, or exclusive bonus material. https://www.subscribepage.com/RRsignup

Facebook Fan Group

www.rileyedwardsromance.com

facebook.com/Novelist.Riley.Edwards

twitter.com/rileyedwardsrom

instagram.com/rileyedwardsromance

bookbub.com/authors/riley-edwards

amazon.com/author/rileyedwards

ACKNOWLEDGMENTS

To all of you – the readers: Thank you for picking up this book and giving me a few hours of your time. Whether this is the first book of mine you've read or you've been with me from the beginning, thank you for your support. It is because of you I have the coolest job in the world.

Made in the USA
Monee, IL
21 December 2022